Hating
Gladys

Hating Gladys

A NOVEL BY

Leona Gom

*to Rolf,
hoping to see you
in Bellingham,
Leona Gom*

SUMACH
PRESS

NATIONAL LIBRARY OF CANADA CATALOGUING IN PUBLICATION DATA

Gom, Leona, 1946 -
Hating Gladys: a novel/by Leona Gom.

ISBN 1-894549-19-8

I. Title.

PS8563.O83H28 2002   C813'.54   C2002-903610-0
PR9199.3.G6H38 2002

Edited by Charis Wahl
Copyedited by Emily Shultz
Cover photograph by Julian Chamberlayne,
www.gomagoma.com/americas/
Digital illustration by Liz Martin

*Sumach Press acknowledges the support of the Canada Council
for the Arts and the Ontario Arts Council
for our publishing program.*

ONTARIO ARTS COUNCIL
CONSEIL DES ARTS DE L'ONTARIO

Printed in Canada

Published by

SUMACH PRESS
1415 Bathurst Street, Suite 202
Toronto ON Canada M5R 3H8
sumachpress@on.aibn.com
www.sumachpress.com

for Aritha

Acknowledgements

Many thanks to Dale Evoy for his support and assistance, to a fondly remembered Earle Birney for first telling me this was a novel, to Rose MacPhail and Francis Kwik for their recollections and expertise, to Charis Wahl for her editorial advice, and to the staff of the White Rock Library for their help with research.

I am grateful as well to Monica M. Moore for her article "Nonverbal Courtship Patterns in Women: Rejection Signaling," published in *Semiotica*, and to Steven Pinker for his research in *Words and Rules*. The excerpt from "Kluane Lake" is originally from *Kindling*, published by Fiddlehead Press in 1972, and is currently in *The Collected Poems of Leona Gom*, published by Sono Nis Press in 1991.

Thanks also for their financial support to the Canada Council for the Arts and to the British Columbia Arts Council.

This novel is entirely a work of fiction.

. . . but at last we were gone

fled across borders

south and away

and now when we think of Kluane

we wonder what held us

repelled us;

we wonder who now

throws rocks in his rage

at your waves

and we turn our heads

suddenly northwards

and listen

excerpted from
"Kluane Lake, Yukon"
(for Erika, summer, 1965)

Later

It's so damned hot. The heat rises from the tracks like steam.

I feel like telling Rodney to come pick me up, but I can just hear the lecture. "I *told* you never to call me at work, Mom." Yeah, yeah. As though he'd ever listen to a word I said, anyway. *There cometh the wrath of God upon the children of disobedience.* Now where did *that* bit of wishful thinking get into my brain? Must have come from Olive. That woman did love her Bible.

The platform is getting more crowded. A herd of teenage girls gallops up, shrieking into the stale air. I give them a good glare, but they ignore me. A woman with a face like an old potato, right down to some white sprouts on her chin, jostles my arm, and I give her an even better glare, but she acts too tired to notice.

Across the tracks is a billboard-sized ad selling running shoes. Some bald, sweaty tennis player is whacking a ball. At the bottom it says, "Just do it." There was this TV program I saw about Japan, about how so many men were throwing themselves onto the subway tracks if they lost their jobs that the subway put up mirrors on the opposite wall so they'd have to take a look at themselves before jumping. It helped, apparently. Though the way some people look, I'd think seeing themselves in a mirror would make suicide a good choice.

Just do it. Boy, in this country we sure don't mollycoddle the depressed.

I can hear the slight rumble of a train coming. Finally. The people on the platform shuffle a little, rearrange themselves.

"So, Gladys. It *was* you, wasn't it?"

The voice is right in my ear, a terrifying whisper, and a hand is on my arm, pushing me, pulling me, I'm not sure. I whirl around, ready to beat back whoever is here to hurt me, whoever has come for revenge.

There are so many faces. Which is the one that spoke?

I step back, and I stumble. My ankle twists sideways, a jab of pain. A hand stretches out. To help me or push me? Should I reach for it? I start to fall, I'm falling.

Part I

1965

⚙

Gladys

Early May, 1965

Dear Rodney,
    No, I am NOT going to send you more pocket money.
You think it grows on trees up here? . . .

                  Mom

The second one came today. She didn't look like much.

I stood watching her out the office window that I'd told Basement Bobby to clean, but if he did it was already as dirty as before. Someday, they said, this whole damned highway would be paved and we wouldn't be wiping dust off everything every time a car, let alone a bus, came into the lot, but I didn't believe it. The Americans only built the highway because they were scared of a Japanese invasion, but since the end of the war nobody cared about it. Who was up here to care about, anyway, except a few Indians and Eskimos and idiots like us? The Yanks liked to brag how it took them less than nine months to lay down fifteen hundred miles of road, but so what? I'd have worked fast, too, to get out of here and back to civilization.

I shook my head at what-all Ben, the bus driver, was unloading for the new girl. What the hell did she need five suitcases for? And what was this? A typewriter case! Did the stupid girl think she was going to be a secretary here or something? Oh, boy. Two minutes and already I was getting a bad feeling about her.

She was just standing there surrounded by all her suitcases, looking around, so I figured I should get out there and tell her where to go before she began hauling all that stuff into the lodge. Five other passengers got off the bus and headed to the restaurant. They looked tired and stiff—this was their first real stop since Whitehorse. Given the way the roads were after the rains last week, the trip would have taken them a good three or four bumpy hours.

Five customers was a far cry from what the bus would be unloading in the summer months, July especially, when it was often full. Bad as a tour bus coming. Bad? I was starting to think like the staff. For them customers were work. For me they were money.

I left the office, which was only a reception area adjoining the three little rooms Charlie and I shared, and went out through the front door. Basement Bobby was shovelling gravel from the back of the old pick-up onto the parking area, doing as sloppy a job as he could. He'd filled in a few of the bigger potholes, but he'd made no effort to level the surface, and he'd left the biggest rocks right where the cars would hit them.

Well, I'd give him hell for it later. I thought about making him carry the girl's suitcases to her cabin, because I knew he'd hate that, but then he'd get out of finishing the gravel. He had a habit of disappearing after every chore if I wasn't right there to push his nose into the next one. Besides, the girl brought all this stuff. She should carry it.

"Hello," I said. "I'm Mrs. Pratt. You must be Elk."

"Elke," the girl said, adding an extra "ee" sound. Elk-ee. What kind of name was that?

She was, well, not fat, really, but she could have stood to lose a few pounds. She was only five foot three or so, and she had one of those plain faces where all the features look a little too small. Her hair was thick and dark and straight as string, cut just below her ears. Not flattering. Her complexion was good, though. I always noticed the complexions. Once we had a girl with acne and Charlie said it wasn't very appetizing. This one at least wouldn't put anyone off their food.

"Elk-EE," I said. "Well, welcome to the lodge. You'll be staying at the cabin, with the other waitress."

I pointed off toward the lake, where the cabin was. It was a good quarter mile from the lodge, but it wasn't me who'd built it there. And the other girls over the years had managed. It would have been better if they'd had an outhouse there so they wouldn't have had to keep coming up to the lodge, but no matter how many times I'd told Charlie to get one built, did he do it? No, of course not. So the girls kept coming up here and using the bathrooms that were supposed to be for the guests. Once one of the waitresses fell asleep in there. Nowadays every seedy motel room has its own bathroom, but this was a long time ago, in the sixties.

The girl was peering off to where I was pointing, but of course you couldn't see the cabin. A cold wind whipped around us from the north. It was May, but there was still snow on the ground. When we spoke we could see our breath.

"I'll get Faith to show you," I said. "Maybe she can help carry your stuff." I nudged the biggest suitcase with my foot. "I don't think you'll need all this."

She made some clumsy little sound that was probably supposed to be a laugh and said, "I wasn't sure. What I'd need."

"What's all in there, anyway? Clothes?"

"And some books. I brought some books to read."

Books. Oh, wonderful. An intellectual. I thought maybe she'd be a sensible type, since she wasn't from the university, like most of the summer girls. Her application letter said she was living on some farm in northern BC even though she'd finished high school the year before.

"You brought your own uniforms, didn't you? I said in my letter you had to bring your own uniforms."

She nodded. She looked like she thought I might bite her. Well, it was always better to have them scared than to have them think they could walk all over you.

"Okay, then," I said, "that's about all you need. And you get issued three aprons. See that they last you and that you keep them cleaned. You can start your shift tomorrow morning. Six o'clock. You go until three. Faith!"

The stupid kid was always popping up like an order of toast except when I needed her. I called again, and then I saw her gawking at me through the restaurant window. I gestured impatiently at her.

Faith was twelve, Olive's daughter. Who her father was nobody except Olive knew. Judging by the girl's dark skin, the father might have been one of the Indians from the reserve down the road, the reserve Basement Bobby came from. Olive was as religious as they come, always reading her damned Bible, so who knows where she'd got a kid from. Immaculate conception, maybe. As long as she cleaned the rooms and shut up about the deductions for the kid's room and board I couldn't have cared less.

"Faith. This is the new waitress. Take her down to the cabin."

"Sure," Faith said, grinning. One thing about Faith, she was always eager to please. Olive wouldn't let me use her to help out the waitresses when the tour buses came in, but I'd caught her using the kid to help her clean rooms and run the laundry and the mangle when things got hectic. *That* was okay, apparently.

The new girl gathered up some of her suitcases. There was no way she could carry all of them. "You can help her with those. If you want," I said to Faith. "That one there looks like a *type*writer. I don't think she'll have much use for a *type*writer out here, do you?"

"It's just ... to write letters and things," said Elk-EE lamely.

"You won't have much time for letters," I said. "Up here about all you get time for is work and sleep."

She got that scared look on her face again. Probably wondering what slave-labour camp she'd come to.

"Come on," Faith said. "Your cabin is the one Mom and I used to live in. Before we moved into the lodge. It's kinda neat. Right by the lake and everything."

Faith picked up the typewriter case and one of the suitcases. She was barely able to lift them, but she wouldn't put them down. She was a sturdy kid, built like a block of cement. She was wearing the pink, frilly new blouse with rickrack around the collar that had come in yesterday's Eaton's order. Already it looked too childish, too tight on her. You'd think Olive would have found better things to waste her money on.

I watched them head off, staggering under the weight of the suitcases. Elk-EE. We would be stuck with each other for four months. She'd better not let me down. In summer the Alaska Highway made up for its dead winters. In summer the Highway had no patience for lazy people.

Basement Bobby had stopped shovelling the gravel and was staring after the girls. He was wearing the jeans with the knee torn out that Charlie had given him and a green sweater so brittle with dried-out sweat and dirt it could stand up on its own like a piece of cardboard. When the tourists came I'd told him to stay out of sight—the thing he did best. If he'd cleaned himself up he wouldn't have been bad-looking. Kind of swarthy, of course, the way the Indians are, but his features were okay, nice eyes when he wasn't using them to glare and scowl, and a regular-shaped long-lipped mouth some girls might have found sexy if he'd let one get close enough. He communicated mostly by snarls and grunts and curses not quite under his breath. Last summer he'd had a front tooth knocked out in a fight in Whitehorse, and maybe that was why he barely opened his mouth now when he talked.

Olive said once he reminded her of Heathcliff. "In an old novel by Emily Brontë," she'd explained, trying to show off her book-of-the-month-club education.

"I *know* who Heathcliff is," I'd snapped. As though she was the only one who'd ever read *Jane Eyre*. As though Basement Bobby could have been a hero in some novel.

"Hurry up and finish that parking lot," I said to him now. "You should have been done two hours ago."

"Yeah, yeah."

He jammed the shovel back into the pile on the truck, hoisted up a load and sprayed it out in an arc in my direction. A couple of pebbles bounced right onto my feet. The little bugger.

Okay, not so little any more. He was eighteen now. It was hard not to still think of him as the snot-nosed kid that more or less came with the lodge when we bought it from old George ten years ago.

Basement Bobby's mother lived with God-only-knew how many other of her kids and family in a trapper's shack in the bush, where her brothers ran a trapline into what later got turned into Kluane National Park. Basement Bobby's father was the white man who drove the grader for the south section of the highway. He often had to stay at the lodge overnight, and Basement Bobby's mother must have told the boy to hang around there, too. So he seemed to think he belonged at the lodge. George, who was too soft-hearted for his own good, finally tossed a mattress into the basement by the furnace for the boy. That's where that Basement-Bobby name came from, I suppose. That and the fact that the father's name was Bobby, too, and somewhere along the way people began calling the father Upstairs Bobby. Well, nobody gets asked permission for the nicknames they get.

When we bought the lodge I wanted the kid out of there, period, but Charlie said he could stay if he did enough work for his room and board. That was a laugh. He rarely worked enough to earn a glass of milk, but here he still was, after ten years, old enough to have some Basement Bobbies of his own by now. Maybe he did. When we shut the lodge down over winter and went back to Vancouver I didn't know where he went and I didn't much care.

"See that you smooth that gravel out, too. It's not doing much good if it's not filling in the potholes." I pointed at the rut he was standing beside. "Like there. That's got to get levelled. You hear me?"

"Yeah, yeah." His frown was pinching in his face so much it looked like his eyebrows were going to collide. He climbed up into the box of the truck and began scraping together the remaining gravel. There were only a few shovelsful left. "I'm not an idiot," he mumbled.

"You're an idiot if you think I didn't see you leering at the girls instead of working."

Well, that got to him. I could see him flush. Whether it was with anger or with embarrassment I didn't know, but either one was fine by me.

When I turned to go back inside I almost stepped on Basement Bobby's damned dog, some mongrel thing that looked too much like a coyote to be a coincidence. "Here Boy" was as close to a name as it had. If it had been up to me, Here Boy would have gone to dog heaven the first day it bared its teeth at a tourist, but Charlie said it was good to have a dog around the place. For protection, he said. From what, I'd have liked to know. From me, maybe.

I went inside. Logan Lodge, said the sign carved into the big log above the door. The tourists assumed the lodge was named for Mount Logan, the highest peak in Canada and second highest in North America. You could see it from here, off to the south sixty miles or so. I didn't tell them old George Logan had named the place after himself.

I stopped in the lobby to pick up the juice glass I'd left on the registration counter, and my hair brushed the nostril of the huge old moosehead mounted on the wall. I hated the ugly thing, the way the tourists always remarked on it, the way Charlie would, if he didn't think I could hear him, tell them he'd shot it. When I was around he'd tell them George's version of the truth, which was that George had killed it trying to break into the lodge. I'd have chopped the damned thing down by now, no matter what Charlie wanted, if it hadn't been for Olive saying she'd gotten fond of it over the years, even if it was a pain in the ass to dust.

To my left I could see Olive now, scrubbing the walls in the hallway that ran between the two rows of rooms, twelve on each side, with the one-bedroom suite at the end. She had only two rooms to clean today, but in another month the place would be too busy for her to handle alone. Another maid was coming in June, somebody from the same northern BC town as the new waitress. I assumed they knew each other. Meanwhile, I had Olive cleaning everything I could think of. She wasn't somebody to avoid work, but I hated to see people sitting around doing nothing when I was paying them. Besides, to me the place always looked dirty. It was sixteen years old and built on the cheap, cracks everywhere for the damned dust to seep in.

I knew I should get back to the pile of purchase orders I'd been fighting with all morning, but I went into the restaurant instead.

Since we'd added on the dining room three years ago, with lots of windows facing the lake, I must admit it wasn't a bad set-up, with thirty-five tables in all. Once a couple from Whitehorse stayed overnight only because, they said, they liked to sit in the restaurant and look out at the lake. Well, sure, the lake *would* seem pretty, to people with the time to sit and look at it. The lodge was built at its southeast tip, on a slight rise about two hundred feet from the shore, just where the highway started to loop around but far enough back from the road to avoid the worst of its noise and dust. The view had impressed me, too, the first time I saw it. Maybe that was why I let Charlie talk me into buying the place. It was almost all my money, of course. So now we had it, and did he do any of the work? No, he'd sit on his ass like the tourists and look out at the lake.

And that was where he was now, at a table by the window with a cup of coffee, doing nothing, even though I'd asked him a thousand times to fix the cracked furnace pipe and change the filters. We'd been married for fifteen years, and sometimes I'd think that if I had any choice I'd pack up and just walk away—from him, from this stupid lodge, from that stupid lake out there that glittered like acres of diamonds but that up close looked like a field of cheap glass.

Kendy came out of the kitchen carrying a hamburger deluxe for one of the bus passengers. My eyes flicked from her to Charlie. I could just feel how the sight of her was revving up his motor, his mouth opening and his big fat tongue idling against his teeth.

Kendy was, I had to admit, someone your eyes were drawn to. She was nineteen, here after her first year at UBC, and she was tall and slim, with a perfect figure and thick, wavy, red-gold hair that always seemed to be catching the sun. She had that white, slightly freckled, weak-looking skin redheads often have, but her features showed no misgivings about anything: large pale-blue eyes, a ruler-straight nose just on the passable side of big, and a plump mouth whose smile had probably already sucked in some sweet tips. It wasn't a face I'd have called cute. It was more like what cute could grow up into.

She'd been here a week. A part of me had wished she'd be all looks and no talent, but even though she'd never waitressed before she was already doing as well as any of the girls we'd had. Her third day at lunch the bus had had a dozen people, and there were two tables of tourists, plus Al the outfitter with two of his people, and she handled them all, no getting flustered, no mixed-up orders.

So even though a part of me wanted her to screw up, to make up for how she looked, for how she made Charlie ogle her, I knew she was good for business, and that was all that mattered.

I went into the kitchen, my eyes moving up automatically to the crack in the kitchen ceiling from the big earthquake near Valdez last year. That crack was something else Charlie was supposed to see about getting fixed and didn't. We were damn lucky the whole roof didn't collapse over winter.

I set my glass in the sink, nodding at Laura, the cook, who alternated shifts with her sister, Lena. They were the least-talkative people I've ever met. I needed a crowbar to pry a word out of them. I didn't like either of them much, but they'd come up from Yellowknife the last few summers, and they'd been okay, more or less, though Lena was lazy about keeping up with the baking, so we'd sometimes run out of desserts. When I'd lecture her about it she'd just tighten her lips and nod. I had this urge to smack her sometimes, the way she wouldn't answer me when I talked to her.

"Taciturn," Olive called the sisters, showing off her vocabulary. She was learning a new word every month from *Reader's Digest*. When the season was at its height and we'd run out of rooms, I'd make the sisters move in with Olive and her kid. It was a tight squeeze, but at least I didn't imagine they'd be sitting around gabbing. Maud, the relief worker for the cooks and waitresses and maids, stayed in a camper she had rigged up on her old Chevy pickup. She was too cheap to rent a room from us, but that was just as well since we'd be sending people away by July, and if there was anything I hated it was to see money turn its back and drive off to Destruction Bay or Whitehorse.

Kendy came into the kitchen, writing an order on her pad and then handing it to Laura, who slapped another burger on the grill.

"Your roommate just arrived, Kendy," I said.

Kendy. Another stupid name. Elk-EE and Kend-EE. Of course, Kendy wasn't this one's real name, and I shouldn't have given in and begun using it, but it was too late now to change. Her real name was Loretta Kennedy, but she didn't like her first name, she said, so at university she got people to call her Kendy. With President

Kennedy just killed it was sort of a tribute, she said. Tribute, my ass. It was just showing off.

My name is Gladys, and I don't like it a whole lot, either, but that doesn't mean I can make up some fancy new name. When I was ten or so, a teacher said, "People must sometimes call you 'Glad-ee,' do they?" and I said, not meaning anything particular by it, "I don't have much to be glad about." Well, the teacher thought this was so cute that she told my mother. Who whacked me on the back of the head and said, "You trying to be smart? Making fun of your mother for the teachers?"

Kendy looked me right in the eye, the way not many of the staff are able to do, and said, chirpily, "Really? She's here? That's great."

"I told her to start tomorrow morning. So you can take the evening shift for the next two weeks."

"Okey-dokey."

Okey-dokey. Like she didn't know how to speak English.

"Bring me a coffee," I said.

The pot was right there, and I could have poured myself a cup, but that was what we paid the waitresses for. Right when we first bought the lodge I drew the line: I didn't do waitressing and I didn't clean rooms. Period. There was enough other work for me around here without doing stuff I had hired people for. Even when we got real busy I stuck to that bargain with myself.

I went over to Charlie's table and sat down. He gave a grunt of acknowledgement and pulled the *True Detective* magazine down onto his lap. As though that would have kept me from knowing he'd been reading it. I hated those damned magazines. He had subscriptions to three or four of them, *True Crime, Real Police Stories*, all garbage as far as I was concerned. Pictures on the cover of some woman lying in a pool of blood with her legs spread. A few times I'd gotten hold of the renewal notices and thrown them away, but he always managed to keep the subscriptions coming.

"The new girl here?" he asked.

I used to like his voice. It used to have a smooth, easy sound to it, but now it was raspy and coarse from the cigarettes. Kind of like the rest of him. I fell head over heels for him, I admit to that, because he was as handsome as they come. That thick, jet-black hair, those eyes tilted just a bit down at the outside corners, that mouth with the lopsided smile and the snaggletooth I used to think for some reason was sexy. Now he just looked gone to seed, everything about him grey and droopy and baggy. Even his teeth looked old and yellow, like newspaper left out in the sun. He was forty, five years older than me, but he looked sixty. When my father first met him he said he had "those lazy good looks." Well, the "lazy" part of him was all that was left.

Did I still love him? I don't know. We were just stuck with each other, that's all. Two yoked plough horses, one of them stepping along enjoying the view and the other one with her head down doing all the pulling. Still, I must have had some feelings left for him that weren't sour, that weren't about disappointment.

"Yeah, she's here," I said. "Came with enough luggage to stay for a couple of years."

"What's her name again? Elk?"

"Elk-EE. She made a point of pronouncing the 'e's."

"Huh. That's no kind of name. Well, what's she like?"

I shrugged. "Nothing special. Guess we'll see tomorrow if she knows how to work. There's that right-off-the-farm feel to her."

"Not another looker, then, eh?"

Kendy was coming over with my coffee. She'd taken her sweet time. She had that hair up in two ponytails at the sides of her head, and Charlie looked as if he wanted to take hold of them like the handles of a jug and take a big, long drink.

She set down the coffee, and the little pitcher of cream. I checked to make sure it was whole cream, not the stuff we watered down for the customers.

"So your partner's come, I hear," Charlie said to her.

She gave her ponytails a perky little flick. Made me want to bring back the hairnet rule. "My partner," she said, giving Charlie a grin that was, goddamn it, I didn't imagine it, flirty.

"The other waitress," Charlie said, as though there could have been any doubt.

"Yeah. It might be nice to share the cabin with someone."

"The other maid has to stay there, too," I said. From the look on her face I could tell she'd forgotten. "And if Maud gets tired of her camper she stays in the cabin, too," I added, not because Maud would ever prefer the cabin to her camper.

"There are only two beds," Kendy said, the smirk gone from her voice.

"We can throw in a few mattresses."

"Maud won't want to give up the camper," Charlie said. "She likes her privacy too much." I could have kicked his ass.

Laura dinged her bell in the kitchen, so Kendy pranced off. Ben, the bus driver, got up, stretched, lit a cigarette and watched Kendy bring the order out. There wasn't a man in the room who wasn't looking at her.

"So you told her to start tomorrow morning?" Charlie asked. "The new girl. The deer."

The deer. I had to laugh.

"Yeah. I don't suppose you want to be the one to get up and show her the ropes."

"I don't suppose I do."

One of the bus passengers was coming to the till to pay, so I went and took his money, even though it was up to the waitresses to do that. But I never could get comfortable with letting them into the till. If they were going to cheat me that's when they'd do it, even though at the end of the day they had to tally the bills and balance with the cash. If there was a difference, I'd told them, it would be coming off their cheques at the end of the summer. Maybe they were counting on my forgetting that, but I wouldn't. So I shouldn't have worried, but I did. There were all kinds of schemes they could have used to swindle us. It was the days before credit cards, everything either cash or traveller's cheques, both easy to pocket. Then they'd just have had to sneak the bill off the spike. I'd always kept a sharp eye on the trash cans, looking for bills.

Faith came skipping into the restaurant. Skipping.

"So you get the new girl settled?" I asked her.

"Yup." She took a package of gum from the display stand and, acting important, handed me a nickel. She looked exactly like her mother, a miniature version, like I'd see if I looked at Olive through the wrong end of binoculars.

"You get a look at what was in all them suitcases?"

"Books. Serious ones. Mathematics and stuff. She said she was going to university in the fall and wanted to study beforehand."

I snorted. "I thought we'd found one that wasn't into all this university stuff."

"*I'm* going to go when I'm old enough. Mom says I can, if my grades are good enough."

"She does, does she?" I gave the girl a hard little smile. "And where does she think she's getting the money to send you? It's expensive, university. It's not for kids whose mothers are maids and who live up in the Yukon and get their schooling through correspondence."

Maybe I shouldn't have tried to squelch her like that. But it was true, wasn't it? University wasn't for our sort of people. Anyway, it was hard to squelch Faith. Guess she had to live up to her name. It was like stepping on a patch of moss. You take your foot off, and sproing.

"Well, I want to go," she said doggedly.

"You *want* to. Well, wouldn't it be nice if that's all that had to be considered."

She peeled a stick of gum, folded it into her mouth, chewed at it noisily.

"Besides," I went on, "some boy'll sweet-talk you into making a baby, and goodbye to all your fancy dreams."

"It won't happen to me."

"Huh. It happens to all women. Even your mother." Even me, I didn't add.

"What about Lena and Laura? It didn't happen to them."

I laughed. "So you want to wind up like them? Dried-up old maids?"

Faith chewed at her gum like it was dough that needed a good punching. "Maybe," she said, but she didn't sound so certain now.

"Well, go bother your mother for a while. I've got work to do."

"I don't bother her. I help. I can do the high-up cleaning. She doesn't like to go up on the ladder."

"You just be careful. I don't want to be scraping your brains off a nice clean floor."

She skipped off. Well, she was about at the end of her skipping days. That eager-to-please wasn't going to last for more than another year. And then the hormones would kick in, and she'd be a snotty teenager. Like Rodney. My son. Used to be he couldn't wait to join us up here as soon as school was out, but this year he refused to come. He would miss his *friends,* he said. Friends. What kind of friends could he have at fifteen? But we gave in, said he could stay in Vancouver with Charlie's parents.

To tell the truth, I didn't mind as much as I pretended. He was just a nuisance around here, always underfoot, hanging on to me when I had more important things to do. Still, it hurt when he was the one to say, go away, I got other people I want to be with.

Well, at least those people weren't Basement Bobby. Last summer Rodney spent most days following him around. Talk about a bad influence. Once Basement Bobby showed him how to build a campfire down by the lake, the way the Indians do it, I suppose— that would impress a kid. If I hadn't seen the smoke and gone tearing over there, they might have burned down the whole Kluane forest. And the lodge with it.

Mind you, there were times I'd have liked to do the same thing myself. To the lodge, I mean. The bush I didn't care much about one way or the other.

Gladys
Late May, 1965

Dear Rodney,
    Yes, yes, I remembered to give your old wristwatch to
Basement Bobby. He's not wearing it. Knowing him,
he probably threw it away. . . .

                                        Mom

I couldn't believe what I saw. She had all these coffee cups, five or six of them, lined up on her left arm, and then when she set the two in her right hand onto the table the others skidded down her left arm.

The man closest to her, a big lumberjack-sized man with a reddish moustache, leapt up and shoved his chair back, but even so I think he got splashed. The woman beside him pushed her chair back quickly, too, and grabbed her purse from the floor. It had gotten a nice little shower, that's for sure. She grabbed her napkin and dabbed at it. The other man at the table began helping the stupid girl pick up the cups and saucers from the floor. Amazingly, none of them had broken. The two women mopped away at the coffee on the table with serviettes they dug out in wads from the dispenser.

Charlie was saying something to me but I was already striding across the room. Everyone in the restaurant, and that was about twenty people, was gawking.

I jerked the chairs out from the table beside the one she'd messed up, and said to the people, trying to sound nice, "Here. Take this table. I'm so sorry for the inconvenience." I took the serviettes from the two women. "Leave it, leave it. She'll clean it up." They smiled and murmured something I didn't bother to hear.

I got them settled, and then I went over to Elk-EE, who was still crouched on the floor. I grabbed her arm and dragged her up.

"Go into the kitchen and get the mop," I hissed.

She nodded. For one funny moment I thought: what's wrong with her eyes? They seemed to be growing blisters. Then I realized her mouth was quivering. Good Lord, she was going to cry. She scuttled away into the kitchen. The customers went back to eating or reading the menus. The show was over.

"Sorry about this," I said again to the two couples, stretching a smile onto my face. "She shouldn't have been trying to carry that many cups."

"Accidents will happen," said the woman whose purse had taken the bath. She'd wiped it clean by now. Lucky for her it was some cheap plastic thing. "No harm done."

"She has to rush, I guess," said the man beside her. "Looks like she's the only waitress for the whole place."

He was making it sound like my fault. I bit my tongue to keep from saying something I'd regret. Though it wouldn't have mattered. I could tell from their accents they were Americans, southerners at that, and they were hardly likely to come this way again.

"I'll see you get your coffees right away," I said.

Elk-EE had come out of the kitchen with not just the mop but the wheeled bucket, and she was swirling the mop around on the floor. There wasn't much left to sop up. The serviettes, sitting in a sodden brown heap on the table, had gotten most of it. The women had emptied the whole damn dispenser.

I said right in Elk-EE's ear, "Get that bucket out of here." I don't have a voice made for whispering. She winced. "And get those people their coffees. One in each hand. You think you can do that? Handle two cups at a time?"

She nodded, looking down at the mop as she pushed it into the wringer part of the bucket.

I said, right into her ear again, "You think you're rushed now? Wait until July, when the tour buses are in. How long is it going to take for you to learn? When you're not coming out of the kitchen carrying just one damned fork you come out carrying more than you can manage."

"I'm sorry."

There was more I wanted to say, but she might have started bawling in front of the customers so I knew I had to swallow it. Besides, I'd said a lot of it to her before.

She was a lousy waitress, that was the bottom line. I knew it. She knew it. Everybody who'd eaten here the last month knew it.

"Just ... try and do better," I said.

Lena dinged the bell in the kitchen, sharply, three times. Something was sitting there getting cold. I sighed, walked back to my table and sat down.

"Every day she does something," I said to Charlie.

He just picked at the cover of his magazine. A policeman on the cover was holding up a blood-soaked brassiere. "She's a little better than she was at first," he said.

I snorted. "She's still taking the orders to the wrong tables. Yesterday she got one so botched up Lena had to completely redo it. And I watched a table ask her twice for their cutlery and finally go get some from another table. And if I hadn't galloped up to the till and caught a couple as they were leaving I bet she'd have let them walk out. Plus she can't keep up with the dirty dishes. She ran out of dinner plates. Dinner plates! If Lena hadn't helped her wash some I don't know what she'd have done."

"Yeah, well, the dishes are hard to keep up with...."

"Lord almighty, Charlie. It's only *May*."

"You want to fire her? We could try to find another one."

"Who would we get this late in the season? Some other loser. God help us. We're stuck with this one."

"The deer," Charlie said.

"The deer."

"At least Kendy's working out. She was a pretty quick learner. And the pressure doesn't seem to bother her."

I hated to agree with him about Kendy, but he was right. "Maybe that's part of the problem with this one. She sees Kendy carry cups like that and she thinks she can do it, too."

We sat there watching the deer. My little pep talk must have helped because I didn't see her make any more mistakes. Though she cut the pieces of pie too big. If the pieces went with the meal she was supposed to cut them half the size of the ones ordered separately. Maybe she was doing it on purpose, some little snotty way of getting back at me.

Charlie pointed at her chest as she walked by. I was going to slap his hand down when he said, "She's gonna lose something," and I could see he was right. A button on her uniform was working itself loose, drooping on its wilted threads like some daisy with its petals blown off.

"Hey," I said to her, nodding at it. "Get that sewn on properly. You look like a refugee."

She looked down at herself. Her cheeks reddened. "Oh. Yes. Sure," she mumbled.

"You brought a needle and thread, I assume. With all that luggage you probably brought a sewing machine."

Charlie laughed. "A sewing machine."

"See you get it fixed for your next shift. Before it falls off into somebody's coffee."

Charlie kept staring at her chest as though he couldn't wait for that to happen. I gave him a glare that finally made him drop his eyes.

When the girl turned to walk away I had a good look at the rear-end of her uniform. At least she'd gotten the blood spot out. *That* had been something. Charlie had come snickering up to me and said he knew she was on the rag and to ask him how he knew. One look at her and I didn't have to ask. I yanked her into the kitchen and asked her what the hell she was advertising. Lena gave her one of the kitchen bib aprons so the silly girl could wear hers around her backside until she had time to run to the cabin and change. Her second uniform wasn't clean, but it was better than one with a goddamned bloodstain in the back.

"I'm sorry, I'm sorry," she'd kept bleating. "I just got so busy—"

"For God's sake," I'd snapped. "Don't you know how to look after yourself? *Charlie* saw that. *Men* saw that."

Boy, oh, boy, I'd thought. What next?

Some tourists were coming in now and hesitating around the reception counter, and Charlie leapt up and trotted over to them. That was the only work he'd do without being nagged, check in the overnight guests. He liked to be Mr. Big Shot, Mr. Lodge Owner, Mr. Yukon, Mr. Moose-hunter. Once I heard him say a grizzly had come right into the lobby. What a pile of bearshit. We might have seen a grizzly once in a while down at the lake, but they never came near the lodge.

The tourists were leaving. If they thought they'd find something cheaper down the road, they were in for a nasty surprise.

Charlie came sauntering back to our table, and he made a point of brushing up against Elk-EE as she stood clearing a table near the door. She had big breasts. He liked big breasts. Mine, he told me once, were too skinny.

The girl knew his bumping into her like that hadn't been an accident. I could see her glance at me. What the hell did she think *I* was going to do? If Charlie had listened to anything I said none of us would even have been here in this godforsaken place. But the glance was more than I got from Charlie. He didn't care if I saw. Besides, it was Kendy he would really have liked to have rubbed up against, even if her breasts weren't any bigger than mine. But Kendy was out of his league. This one, though, he must have thought, the plain one, the deer, well, she'd think he was doing her a favour. He made me sick.

She managed to get a pile of dishes up in front of her, so Charlie had to move aside to let her get to the kitchen. He headed back to our table, stopping at the jukebox to waste a dime on Johnny Cash. He loved Johnny Cash. Sometimes I thought if I heard "Ring of Fire" one more time I'd turn Charlie's brainless head into a burning ring of fire.

"No luck?" I asked.

He pretended that I'd only been talking about the tourists. "They just wanted directions."

"What directions? There's only one road. They were on it."

Charlie shrugged. "They wanted to get to Destruction Bay."

"You should have told them you didn't know where it was."

I was watching a mosquito fill itself up on his elbow, and finally he must have felt something, too, because he whacked the thing so hard blood squirted down his arm. "Jesus," I said. "You didn't have to hit him that hard."

"It's a her, not a him," Charlie said, wiping his hand on his pants. "Only the hers bite."

"I know that. Only the hers do any of the work. The hims get the credit." I stood up. "So, you fixed that front step yet or do we wait until somebody puts a foot right through it?"

"Yeah, yeah."

"Maybe you'd rather do the paperwork and *I'll* fix the damned step." That made his squirm. We both hated paperwork, but at least I knew how to do it. "I have to get the accounts up to date and figure out those new tax forms before the end of the month. Plus try to get Lena to explain to me why we ran out of milk and soap two weeks in a row after I damn near doubled the order."

Charlie nodded, as though he had any idea what I was talking about. He lit a cigarette and sat drumming his fingers on the table while Johnny Cash yowled on about the flames rising higher.

The Americans the deer had spilled coffee on were getting up to pay. She was in the kitchen, not keeping an eye on the till the way she was supposed to. I took their bill and the money. U.S. dollars. Amazing how many of them were indignant when we gave them Canadian change. It wasn't my fault they were so stupid. I'd told the girls that if the customers argued they should give them a lower exchange rate than what we posted. If they were so slow that they didn't know they were in another country they'd be too slow to do the math.

"And could you give this to the waitress?" The man who'd had the worst of the coffee spill handed me two dollars. Two U.S. dollars.

"That's a lot," I said. I doubted if even Kendy'd had a tip that big. "You didn't exactly get great service."

"She did her best," the man said. "My wife used to be a waitress and she said she could never manage a place this big on her own."

Tell your wife to mind her own bloody business, I didn't say. I gave them all a sweet Canadian smile and drawled, "Well, y'all have a good trip now, hear?"

The man smiled back uncertainly, not sure if I was making fun of him. Another glue-brained American. I gave him a lower-than-posted exchange on his money. He didn't notice. When they were gone I pocketed the two dollars.

I felt a little guilty about that later. About keeping the tip. But nobody deserves a reward for screwing up.

⚛

Olive was mad at me. She thought we should have hired another maid by now, but the new girl wasn't coming until the end of June and that was that. We'd never needed a second maid until the end of June the other years.

"Maybe you're just getting fat and lazy." But I had to say that with a smile, even though I wasn't totally joking, because Olive took offence easily, and her bad mood was like a thunderstorm rumbling up and down the halls, slamming the doors and rattling the windows. When she ran the washing machines and the mangle downstairs, even they would sound mad and louder than usual.

Olive was a solid chunk of a woman, with her hair, gone prematurely and completely grey, anchored behind her ears with two big bobby pins. She wasn't much older than me, but her face had a scowly and droopy look that was getting worse. I remember looking at her once and thinking she and gravity did not have a friendly relationship. She had a habit of shoving out her bottom lip when she worked, and it had started to stay that way.

Like Basement Bobby, Olive had more or less come with the lodge, and I admitted to myself that, the first years, anyway, she knew more about how the place ran than I did. If Olive ever left she'd be damned hard to replace. So I guess you could say I had some respect for her. More than I did for anyone else whose salary I paid, anyway.

"I'm not lazy," she snapped. "Things are busier than they used to be. Last night over half the rooms were full. And they were all checkouts, no stay-overs, so they need the full treatment."

She was wolfing down her lunch, hamburger steak and canned corn for the second day in a row. I could always tell by a glance at the menu if it was Laura in the kitchen. She had the imagination of a burned-out skillet.

Olive ate with her whole hand clenched around her fork, the way you'd hold a shovel. Her wrists were as big around as a coffee mug. She pointed at the clock attached to the top of the jukebox. "Three-thirty. I'm not half finished, and I haven't started the laundry."

"Then I guess you'd better get at it," I said.

She gave me a black look and pushed her plate back. "It isn't Christian," she said.

Not the Christian stuff again. "What isn't?"

"Overworking people."

I snorted. "Nobody's overworked around here. Besides, doesn't the Devil find work for idle hands?"

"The Devil doesn't own the lodge."

I wasn't sure how to take that, so I just said, "That's right," like she'd said exactly what I'd wanted her to.

"God wants us to think about more than money. He cares about our souls. He has compassion."

"If you say so."

"It's not me that says so. It's in the Bible. 'Jesus wept.'"

"Okay, 'Jesus wept.' Not 'Jesus slept.' He kept busy."

"Don't mock," Olive said.

"I'm not mocking. I'm just saying. The Bible tells us to work, not laze around."

"There's a time to work and a time to rest."

"Well, summer in the Yukon is the time to work. You can rest in winter."

Olive shook her head. It tickled me that that was the only answer she could come up with.

"God doesn't like shirkers," I said. I was pushing it. "God expects us to work."

"I'm not a shirker, Gladys."

Gladys. Not Mrs. Pratt. Olive called me Gladys only when she was really serious. It always gave me a little start. Nobody else would have tried it twice, but from Olive, well, it was funny how I sort of liked it. Maybe because she was smart enough not to do it very often.

"Look." I made myself smile. "If we get over three-quarters full I'll pay Maud a few extra hours to help with the laundry."

She mulled that over for a minute, taking a gulp of coffee that emptied her cup. "Okay."

I got the annoyed feeling I'd given her more than she'd expected. She got to her feet. "By the way," she said. "My daughter's not stupid."

"What?"

"Telling Faith she was too stupid to go to university. You had no right to do that."

"What are you on about? I didn't tell Faith she was stupid."

"You said she wasn't smart enough or rich enough to go to university."

"Oh, for Pete's sake." I should have known Olive had been mad about more than work. "I didn't say she wasn't smart. As for rich, well, you got money stashed away I don't know about?"

Her bottom lip pushed out even further than usual. "Whether she goes or not isn't up to you. Or me."

God's decision, probably. I sighed. "Okay, okay."

I should have said outright I was sorry, but they were words I always did choke on. When people would say "I'm sorry," I couldn't help sneering a little. Apologizing made them seem weak.

When she'd gone I sat chewing at the last of my hamburger steak and flipping through the government pamphlet about qualifying for an agricultural write-off. Last year Mike, who ran the service station down the highway, asked if he could plant some oats on an acre we weren't using in exchange for handyman work he'd done for us, so we said sure. Well, I never saw such a tall crop, almost over my head. Those long summer days made up for the short season, I suppose, plus the land had been unbroken, the soil not all used up. This year he was planting wheat.

It seemed to me there should've been some way to get a tax deduction out of this, but I couldn't make any sense out of the damned pamphlet. How were ordinary dumb farmers supposed to understand it? By the sound of it Mike would've had to have paid me in cash. I sighed. I'd have to leave well enough alone. Probably the work Mike did was worth more to me than either rent from one measly acre or a tax deduction—or the aggravation of nagging Charlie and Basement Bobby endlessly to do the same chores.

Kendy came past with the coffee pot and smiled and asked if I wanted a refill, so I nodded and she poured me one. I watched her walk away, sliding the bill onto a customer's table just as he was finishing his piece of pie. Couldn't she drop at least one plate, give at least one customer the wrong change, forget at least once to bring out the water glasses?

The Department of Transport crew, mostly young guys hired for the summer to paint the bridges and do road maintenance, were in for their afternoon coffee break and they were trying to get her to sit down with them. She laughed and said she had work to do, but she made it seem that if only she had the time she'd like nothing better than to have sex with every one of them right then.

Basement Bobby was sitting in the corner closest to the door stuffing a piece a cake into his mouth, and he was glowering at all of them. I wondered what he must think of them, those young university types, his own age now, who breezed in for the summer and got cushy union jobs and breezed out again in the fall to their real lives in the city. I actually—surprise, surprise—felt a little pity for him. Even though he was eating a piece of cake that he knew damned well he wasn't supposed to have unless we had leftovers at the end of the day.

And it was just as I was thinking that, feeling sorry for the useless clot, that his father walked in.

It was the first time this year I'd seen Upstairs Bobby. I didn't know whether he wasn't working our stretch of the road any more or whether he'd just decided not come around, but, anyway, here he was.

I'd always had a soft spot for him. Even though he slept with the Indian women. Well, one at least. The tourist man in Whitehorse said we weren't supposed to say "squaw" any more. "Half-breed," either. Yeah, sure. I knew they weren't nice words. Basement Bobby, and Faith, too, probably, were both half-breeds, but I'd never called them that to their faces. And not just because Basement Bobby might have brained me with his shovel and Faith's mother might have called the God police.

Anyway, here was Upstairs Bobby, looking better than ever. With his thick, curly hair and big, round, heavy-lidded eyes with not a wrinkle around them he looked far too young to have an eighteen-year-old son. Basement Bobby must have come from his first sperm with serious ambitions.

He saw me and came striding over, taking off his dusty cowboy hat and scooting it onto the table. There was a nice natural smell to him, like wet pine needles.

"Hey. Gladys. How's it going?" And he chucked me under the chin. Like I was a little kid.

I batted his hand away. "Not bad."

"Sounds like it might be a good year for business. At least that's the buzz up the highway. Lots of Americans coming this year, they say."

"It's been okay so far."

Kendy had seen him come in and was heading over, opening her order book. "Nice-looking waitress," Upstairs Bobby said, looking her up and down. "Almost as cute as her boss."

I could feel myself blushing. We both knew I wasn't as cute as Kendy. I wasn't cute, period. I was tall and thin and big-boned, with a face my own mother had called horsey, and I was a few rungs up the ladder from young. But still. It made me feel good, knowing a man as handsome as he was would bother to say that to me.

When Charlie was around he wouldn't say that flirty kind of stuff, but he would listen when I talked. He acted like I wasn't just some stupid woman he wouldn't pay attention to if there was a man to talk with.

"You're not as tough as you pretend to be," he'd said to me

once. Well, *that* was about as true as I was cute, but I'd appreciated him saying it. Because I didn't start out tough. I grew that way from the slops life dished up for me. "Oh, yeah," I'd answered him back then. "A regular whore with a heart of gold." That shocked him a little, my language, and I wished I hadn't said it. Being tough wasn't the same in his mind as being vulgar, I guess.

"Coffee and a doughnut," he said now to Kendy, who didn't bother to write it down. The deer would have and still gotten it wrong.

"That's what you always have," I said. "Coffee and a doughnut."

"That's me. Predictable."

"You staying the night?"

"Nope. Going to try make Whitehorse."

"Looks like rain to the east," I said.

"Yeah, well. Keeps it interesting."

Kendy brought his coffee and doughnut.

"Thanks," he said, giving her that little sideways grin that always lifted his right eyebrow, too.

"You're welcome." Kendy seemed to give him back the same smile, her eyebrow raising a little. When she looked at me her smile didn't change. That must have taken an effort.

She began clearing a table close to us. When she leaned over, her uniform pulled up at the back halfway up her thigh. Upstairs Bobby was the only one in the place not watching her. That must have taken an effort, too.

He poked at the tax brochure on the table. "What's this? Agriculture? You planning on going into farming?"

I laughed. "I was just wondering if we could qualify somehow for a tax write-off from Mike's acre of wheat on our land."

"I wouldn't get into anything new with them, if I were you. You don't want to get audited."

I didn't tell him we had been, once, five years ago. That was sure a trip to hell. Charlie sitting there whining, "I don't know, she does all the books," and the auditor finally assessing us for an extra two thousand. Two *thousand!* The bastards. Just because I didn't keep every goddamned receipt.

"I suppose you're right," I said. I scrunched the pamphlet up and dropped it in the ashtray.

"So, Charlie around today?"

"He's got the boat out on the lake."

"Fishing! Lucky dog. So you get to stay here and run things."

"That's about it," I said grimly.

I'd been keeping one eye on Basement Bobby. He'd seen his father come in, and he kept staring at us. I never did figure those two out. Upstairs Bobby never denied the boy was his son, but the few times I'd seen them together they'd acted almost like strangers.

Basement Bobby got up. I thought he was going to slink out, as he usually did after he'd eaten something he knew he wasn't supposed to, but he started shuffling over to our table. Upstairs Bobby saw where I was looking so he glanced over that way, too.

"Hey there, kid," he said. His voice sounded uncomfortable, but not a whole lot.

"You gonna stop by to see Mom?"

Upstairs Bobby ran his fingers along the brim of his hat, keeping his eyes on it. "Not this time. Gotta make Whitehorse tonight."

There was an awkward silence, and then Basement Bobby said, in that annoying hard-to-hear mutter, "I guess she'd like to see you."

"Yeah, well. Next time, maybe."

Basement Bobby just stood there staring down at his feet. If I hadn't known he was too dim-witted I'd have sworn he was deliberately doing what would embarrass Upstairs Bobby most. The DOT crew was looking over at us, grinning. They probably knew the story.

"Well, I'd better get going," Upstairs Bobby said, sounding a little too hearty. He took a last swallow of coffee, grimacing a little, surely not because it was still hot, then anchored his hat on his head and stood up.

Basement Bobby didn't move, just kept looking down at his feet. He had that whipped-dog look people can get and that drove me crazy, that made me want to slap it right out of them.

"You know you weren't supposed to eat that cake," I said.

He glanced up at me, a look flaring in his eyes that he must have wanted me to be scared of. Well, if looks could kill I'd have ordered my coffin long before I met the likes of him.

"Take it out of my next paycheque," he growled.

Paycheque. Downright witty.

"Here." Upstairs Bobby was digging out his wallet, and then he held out two ten-dollar bills.

I expected Basement Bobby to snatch the money and bolt, the way he used to when anybody handed him candy. But he stood looking at the bills for a few minutes, and then, not hurrying, he plucked first one, then the other, with crisp little jerks, out of his father's hand and stuffed them into his jeans pocket. It must have been hard for him not to say anything. Or maybe not. I had no idea how his brain worked.

When Kendy saw Upstairs Bobby standing up she wrote something on her pad and brought it over to him. "Your bill, sir," she said.

"Don't charge him," I said, annoyed I hadn't headed her off.

"Okay," she said, eyeing Upstairs Bobby with that little side-ways smile again, as though she'd been practising it. She had a thin red scarf braided into her hair today. I had to admit it looked pretty nice. I'd had a good look to see how she'd done it, but my hair wasn't long enough to braid, anyway. Plus if I did try something like that Charlie would just laugh and say, what you tarting your-self up for?

"No, no," Upstairs Bobby said, pulling another bill out of his wallet and leaving it on the table. "You can't be giving out freebies to bums like me."

"You're no bum." So then it sounded like I didn't know he was kidding. Having Kendy standing there with her smirky smile made it worse. "The DOT table wants more coffee," I snapped. "Stop dawdling around here."

Upstairs Bobby laughed. "Her bark is worse than her bite," he said to Kendy.

I was mad enough to have given them both a good bite right

then. Kendy flounced off, the sun angling in through the west window glittering in that hair.

Basement Bobby had taken advantage of our distraction to shuffle himself off outside. I'd wanted to tell him, for the hundredth time, to clean up that nest he slept in. It was a damned fire hazard, so close to the furnace. One of these days he'd go down there and find all his smelly old stuff gone, and I would tell him, well, it must have just burned up.

"You're a classic, Gladys," Upstairs Bobby said, giving me a wink. "See you next time."

A classic. I smiled about that, later. Even though I was never quite sure how he meant it. Maybe it was only the wink I was thinking of.

Elke

Early June, 1965

Dear Mom and Dad,
    Hello again. Everything is still going fine with me.
The Yukon is so beautiful—I'm pressing a buttercup
for you inside this letter. . . .

                                                          Elke

Faith was shaking me awake.

"Tour bus! You've got to come."

I pulled myself back from a very long way away. "What time is it?" I murmured, squinting an eye open.

"Eleven." She was hopping from one foot to the other, as though she were standing barefoot on ice. "Eleven in the morning," she added, which was not an unnecessary bit of information.

Of course, it didn't really matter if it was morning or night; either way, I knew I had to get up and get into my uniform, fast, and run down to the lodge. That it wasn't my shift was irrelevant. Even today, if someone shook me awake and said, "Tour bus," it would send a spike of adrenalin and fear through me.

Faith had already left the cabin, her duty done, by the time I was reaching for my uniform. It made it easier that I had begun sleeping in my bra and panties. It was partly for the warmth; partly because I never knew who all, exactly, had keys to the rusty lock on the door; and partly for times like this, when I had to lurch up and go help Kendy get through the next harrowing hour and a half. If I hadn't gone, I couldn't have expected her to come and help me. Kendy had said once that the tour bus was the earthquake, the tourists were the tsunami, and we were the poor fools trapped on the beach.

I was wide awake now. Six hours of sleep wasn't too bad. I'd had to stay late at the lodge after my shift because the till didn't balance and I had to wash the floors, but it was my own fault I'd stayed up even later reading, then writing letters. I couldn't use my typewriter because it would have woken Kendy, but at least by now my fingers didn't cramp and stiffen from the cold as they had in May, when it still could go below freezing at night. There was no heat in the cabin, except for the little bit produced by the two coal oil lamps, one at Kendy's side of the cabin and one at mine.

The cabin was old, built of logs that had lost much of their chinking, and it was tiny, barely twelve feet square. A small window with panes divided into quarters was inset on each side of the door, which was made of a rough, unsanded lumber that gave us slivers if we weren't careful. A closet holding a small desk and chair took up the wall opposite the door, and our beds took up most of the rest of the room. In front of the beds were thin, water-stained, blue curtains on rods that ran the length of the cabin. If we drew the curtains we could have a bit of privacy, but we rarely bothered. Considering how cramped we were, Kendy and I got along surprising well, but maybe that was because we were rarely in the cabin at the same time, at least when we were both awake.

I headed for the lodge at a lope that wouldn't tire me but that was faster than walking. The trail angled slightly uphill, so I had to be careful not to let myself get out of breath and sweaty.

The first month I'd been here I don't think I travelled that quarter mile more than a couple of times without crying. It seemed as though I had well and truly gone to hell, and that the Pratts were in charge of it.

Was I *that* bad a waitress? Sometimes I got orders mixed up, and I had difficulty handling pressure, and I certainly wasn't as good as Kendy. But was I was worse than average? The Pratts certainly made me think so. All I knew was that I was doing the best I could.

The last few weeks, well, it wasn't that they were treating me better, but I'd become more inured to them. I'd grit my teeth and keep saying to myself, "You're not stupid," and I tried to be more like Kendy, who'd say, "This job isn't our real lives, right? It's a means to an end."

So lately, when I didn't have to hurry, I would actually enjoy the walk along the lake. The morning air always had a fresh, clean smell, as though overnight someone scrubbed it with an astringent. The landscape wasn't that different from what I was used to on the farm near Fort St. John where my parents had homesteaded and where I'd lived all my life. But here I had a sense of discovering it on my own, and in a more natural state, before the farmers moved in and cut down the old poplars and spruce and lodgepole pine, before they plowed under the surprising varieties of wild grasses and mosses and the red fireweed and wild vetch. Sometimes I would stop to watch the white trumpeter swans that had started coming to this corner of the lake, maybe because Lena had been feeding them there with kitchen scraps. I'd seen two deer once, too, at the lake, taking turns drinking and keeping watch. And a red fox, who froze in the middle of a patch of yellow saxifrage and bush willow and stared at me until I waved my arms to remind us both that even though there were few farmers here there were many men with rifles.

The tour bus was as big as they got. It was parked in the front lot beside three cars, whose owners, having a leisurely lunch, would have looked up in alarm as thirty or forty people suddenly flooded in and killed any chance they might have had to get one more refill of either a coffee or a smile from Kendy; now they'd get nothing else but their bill slapped onto the table as she flew past.

"Hello, Here Boy," I said to the beaten-up coyote-looking dog that seemed to belong to Basement Bobby and that hung around the front door. He looked up at me with his mournful eyes and managed a small limp movement of his tail.

Inside, I stopped to remove the hat someone had hung on one of the moose antlers. Having his moosehead used as a hat rack annoyed Mr. Pratt, as though it meant people didn't have the proper respect. The moosehead was huge and just about the saddest thing I'd ever seen. It was mounted too low, for one thing, so that tall people risked having an eye put out by the horns, and it was in too tight a space, so that the Pratts brushed up against it every time they went behind the check-in counter. The bottom left side of the head had been rubbed completely bare.

I set the hat on the counter, took a deep breath, and went into the restaurant. It was the predictable chaos.

"Thank God you've come," Kendy cried, racing past with two ketchup bottles in her right hand and four orders balanced on her turned-up left wrist and fingers. "I haven't done any of the people by the windows," she shouted back.

I hurried through the small drugstore and candy-bar area in front of the till, picked up an order pad, and headed to the windows. There were five tables, all impatient to order.

"Can I substitute chips for the mashed potatoes if I get the hamburger steak?" asked a teenage girl at the second table.

"I suppose so," I said.

"And can I substitute peas for the corn?" asked her brother. "I don't like corn."

"I'm not sure," I said, wishing I had said no to the girl.

"Could you go check?" asked the mother, smiling disarmingly. "He really does hate corn."

I sped into the kitchen, where Laura had packed every inch of the grill with hamburgers or veal cutlets and was slicing up tomatoes at the speed of light. When I asked her about the peas she looked at me as though I were insane, and said, "No! No peas! Green beans, he can have green beans," and she dashed over to the deep fryer and dumped out a load of French fries, even though it was usually up to the waitresses to do that.

I galloped back out to the table. "You can have green beans," I told the boy. "Is that okay?"

He pouted, turning his fork in a circle, making me wait. "That'll be fine," his mother said.

"Miss! Miss! Miss!"

I smiled, promised I'd be there in a minute, just one more minute. Someone had put money in the jukebox, but it didn't sound like music, just more disorienting noise. I handed my orders to Laura, who read them back to me so fast I wasn't sure whether she'd gotten them right or not, and then I began dishing up the orders of fries and ladling up the soups and slapping the bread and butter onto plates and getting another pot of coffee ready and running out to the till where someone was waiting to pay.

"We're almost out of cutlery," Kendy cried, running in and dumping a load of dirty dishes into the overloaded sink. "Spoons! We need spoons!"

"And big plates!" Laura added, shouting over the sizzle of the steaks.

I raced out, shedding coffee cups, breads and butters, incomplete smiles. Then back to the kitchen to wash up dishes. Practically nothing was left on the shelves. There weren't enough dishes in the lodge to handle a full-capacity crowd. When it was busy we had to do the washing-up at the same rate as the dishes came in.

Ding, ding, ding, went Laura's bell. "Order up! Order up! Elke—two of yours."

I blotted my hands on my apron. They stank so strongly of bleach from the dishwater that it made my eyes teary. I grabbed the orders, almost falling on the floor slick with spills. Kendy came in carrying a load of plates with about a dozen spoons on the top one. "Spoons!" she said. "Except for these every damned one is being used."

When I took my orders out, I could see Mrs. Pratt taking money at the till. And then she went and sat back down at her table with her husband. Sat there and watched. Watched as we snatched spoons from customers who had barely finished. Watched as a child dumped its meal onto the floor and we didn't have time to clean it up. Watched as dirty dishes piled up on tables, Laura twice coming out to hunt down plates so she could rinse them and slap on the next hamburger steak. Watched as fingers plucked at us as we rushed by, arms laden. "Miss! Miss! Miss! Could I have some mustard? This is the second time I've asked for a glass of water. Does dessert go with this? My tea is cold. We need another menu. Do you have buns instead of sliced bread? This fork is dirty. I specifically asked for no onions. Do you sell Nivea Cream up at the counter? These pancakes taste like bacon grease. I think there's a mistake on my bill. Do you sell stamps? The bus is leaving,

leaving, leaving, and I still haven't gotten my order, order, order."

After, we collapsed. Laura lit a cigarette and let herself fall with a sigh onto a chair. Kendy, who wasn't supposed to sit down unless she was on her half-hour meal break, put her arms on the till and leaned her head on them, probably thinking about the tables piled high with dishes to clear and wash. I pulled off my apron, soaked with a spilled glass of orange juice, and thought that if I went back to the cabin right then I might squeeze in another hour's sleep before my shift began at three.

Mrs. Pratt beckoned me to her table. I went over, put on my most ingratiating smile.

A smile was something with which Mrs. Pratt's thin and narrow features seemed little acquainted. Her face was wrinkling in an odd way, as though its habitual frown were collapsing it into a central point somewhere around the bridge of her nose. Her green eyes would have been pretty except that they seemed hard, mineral, like the pieces of jade we sold at the front counter. A large brown mole grew on her right cheek; Kendy had nicknamed her "Warthog" because of it, and when we were talking about her and were afraid of someone overhearing we'd refer to her as W.H. I had heard the Pratts call me "the deer" behind my back, so I didn't feel guilty about "Warthog." A zoo, that's what we were, where we were.

"Sit down."

I sat down at the end of the table, as far from Mr. Pratt as I could get, pressing my knees together. I'd felt his cold hands on my legs before, though I didn't think he'd try it with his wife there.

Mrs. Pratt leaned toward me, clasping her hands together on the table and leaning on her elbows. She must actually be intending to thank me, I thought, for coming in to help.

"Those people who wanted you to substitute something in their order. You make a whole special trip into the kitchen to ask Laura. You waste all that time. You should know whether she can do it or not. You're supposed to know. You think this was busy? Wait until July. This is how it is every day in July."

"I'll try to remember," I said, standing up.

I hated her. Truly and deeply I hated her.

I turned quickly away, afraid she would read too much on my face, telling myself it was for Kendy, not the Pratts, that I'd come in, anyway.

Kendy had said that we would have to be paid overtime for the extra hours, but even though I trusted Kendy to know more than I did about nearly everything, I was dubious. Maybe she knew more about the law, I thought, but I knew more about people like the Pratts. She'd also shrugged at my concerns about the Pratts not paying us until the end of the summer. "You'd just lose it," Mrs. Pratt had explained. "There's no bank you can put it in. So we keep it for you. Any things you need you can buy with your tip money." Kendy had already said that was okay with her, so it had to be okay for me, too. I told myself I was foolish to worry if Kendy didn't. Her father was a chartered accountant, and though I didn't know quite what that was it sounded like a profession that knew about money. Besides, how could I contradict Kendy? It wasn't just that she was smart and beautiful and from the city, but that she seemed so sure of what she deserved and that she would get it.

I went out through the kitchen so I could tell her I was going back to the cabin. The kitchen looked disembowelled, shreds of food everywhere. My shoes stuck to the floor. The smell of bleach as I got near the sink where she was scrubbing a pot was overwhelming.

"Wasn't that a nightmare?" I said.

"The worst." Kendy looked up, face flushed, brushing a strand of hair from her cheek with the back of a soapy hand. "Thanks for coming in. I'd have died if you hadn't. Be lying on the floor under the trampled lettuce. What did W.H. want?"

I glanced toward the cold room, a big walk-in refrigerator at the rear of the kitchen, where Laura must have been, taking inventory.

"To complain that I was too slow handling one of the orders."

"Jesus." Kendy ground the steel-wool pad harder at the bottom of the pot.

"I never do anything good enough for her. They don't give *you* as hard a time." I sounded jealous. I was.

Kendy snorted. "You should have been here when I dropped the bowl of soup. I thought she would rupture something racing over to give me shit."

I laughed. The thought of Kendy getting shit made me feel better, though we both knew I was the favoured recipient.

I walked slowly back to the cabin, enjoying the feel on my face of a warm westerly breeze that jostled the old pine trees on the south side of the path. The days had been getting warmer quickly—it would soon be the longest day of the year, and up here that meant about twenty straight hours of daylight. Last night I had almost been able to read all night without lighting the lamp.

I had been gazing out at the lake, the small ripples the wind was making in it, and when I turned back to the path I almost fell over Here Boy, who was standing in front of me with his head down, looking not exactly threatening but not friendly, either.

"What are you doing here?" I asked him, gently, my voice low, the way I'd learned to do with the farm animals.

He raised his head a little and cocked it to the side, by way of answering my question, it seemed, because Basement Bobby was sitting there just a few feet away from me in a little depression formed by two exposed roots of a pine tree. An empty beer bottle was lying beside him; another was propped upright. He had a length of white wood in his hand, and he wasn't so much whittling it with his knife as just slicing off long, thin strips, which lay in curls around his feet. My mother would do that, to make shavings and kindling, but I didn't think Basement Bobby was doing it for any useful reason except to work off whatever he was feeling. There was always a strange kind of smell to him, not smoky, but burning somehow, as though it were the odour of fire itself. When I remember it now I think of it as the smell of pure rage.

"Hi," I said. My voice sounded the way it had with the dog.

He grunted, not looking up at me.

"There was a tour bus in," I tried.

"Why should I care?"

Of course I wish now that I hadn't winced and been hurt by his rough words, hadn't been afraid to talk to him more, hadn't been afraid that I would hear only more Pratt meanness. But I wasn't Kendy, who could have laughed and answered back or not answered back and not had it affect her either way. I was Elke. The deer. I didn't understand that his muttering hostilities had nothing to do with me, and that my own humiliations and resentments were pale creatures next to to his.

I can't remember what I said, something clumsy and apologetic, probably, so that I could slink away. Here Boy began to follow me; I could hear his feet padding behind me, and it frightened me until I saw him move up alongside, and then we walked along together for a while. I would have liked to have talked to him, but I didn't want Basement Bobby to hear and think I was trying to steal his dog. After a while, when the cabin was in sight, he dropped back, and when I turned to look he was trotting back up the path. I wasn't sure what the nature of his escort had been, but I felt a twinge of sadness seeing him go.

Maybe it was just homesickness for my own dog back on the farm. My father had said he'd look after her. I tried not to imagine what that might mean. My father was furious with me for leaving. "If you'd pay me what you pay a hired man I might stay," I'd said stubbornly, and he, just as stubbornly, yelled that it would be a cold day in hell before he paid his own daughter to drive a tractor or shovel a few loads of grain. I'd pleaded endlessly with him to let me go to university, and it had gotten me exactly nowhere. I'd lost a whole year, and I knew if I lost another he'd have won; I'd never escape the farm. I'd marry Pete or Lothar or George and start the same life my mother had. That mightn't, of course, have been the devastating fate I'd imagined, but for an eighteen-year-old whose passion had always been books it was a black hole for a future.

My job at Logan Lodge, as I saw it, was all that stood between me and going back to the farm in September. Even if my mother could sneak me a few dollars to help with tuition, and even if I were still eligible for the small provincial scholarship I'd won, I knew that financially I was basically on my own.

I managed to get an hour's sleep before my shift started. Kendy looked as tired as I'd ever seen her when she pulled her order pad from her apron waistband and dropped it onto the front counter.

"I just couldn't get all the dishes finished, Elke," she said. "I'm sorry. Even though—" she glanced behind her and lowered her voice "—Laura helped me." We both knew the cooks weren't supposed to do dishes. Any extra time they had was supposed to go into baking and inventory and menu planning.

"That's okay. The place looks just about empty. I should be able to get them done before the supper rush."

"Let's just hope there isn't another tour bus."

I shuddered. "Don't even think it."

"Some letters for you," she said, gesturing at the nook under the counter where the freight-truck driver stuck the mail for the staff.

I grabbed them eagerly. One from my mother, one from Alice, who would be coming up here in less than a month. I slid them into my pocket, something to look forward to after my shift, a small reward. There was no phone service along the highway, so letters were our only contact with the outside. Or just "Outside," as they called it here, dropping the article. Outside. A separate, distant country.

Lena had already taken over from Laura, and she jumped back from the sink when I came into the kitchen. She'd been washing dishes. I knew that thanking her in anything but a perfunctory way would have made her uncomfortable; and maybe she wasn't doing it for me or for Kendy particularly, anyway, but for the lodge, for that part of its machinery that had most urgently to be oiled and tended and whose malfunction made all the work harder. Like her sister, she was a small, round-faced woman, probably in her mid-forties; if you looked closely you could see her face networked with very faint wrinkles, as though she'd run into a spiderweb. Her hair was cut so short it could have been done with a razor. She had unusually muscular upper arms, which I assumed came from lifting heavy vats and pots and boxes.

I took the bill out to one of the four occupied tables, then took the money and cleaned the table, dropping Kendy's tip in my left pocket so I wouldn't forget to give it to her. The Pratts were still sitting where they were this morning. She was eating a piece of cherry pie, and he was reading one of his magazines, wetting his finger slowly and deliberately every time he turned a page. I tried not to look their way, but it was almost harder if I didn't, the back of my neck prickling, the way it's described in books when a character senses danger creeping up.

The other tables had just started their meals, so I went back to the kitchen and got at the dishes.

"I should be able to finish them now," I said to Lena. "It's pretty empty out there."

"Yuh," she said. She poured what was left of the green beans from the steamer into a bowl. They would have been overcooked into virtual sauce by now, but she would have to find some way to use them.

Mrs. Pratt was not one to waste food. Anything that didn't smash to a pulp when it slid off the plate as we sped out of the kitchen was to be wiped or rinsed off and returned to the plate. Buns and butter that seemed untouched went out to the next customer; butter that *was* touched got scraped into a bowl and saved for cooking. I was also supposed to toss larger pieces of uneaten steak into the bucket beside the sink, "for the dog," Laura had said vaguely, but I had my doubts that Here Boy ever saw any of it. What really happened to the contents of the bucket wasn't information I was trusted with.

And I didn't exactly want to know. It was bad enough to see the kind of meat the cooks had to save for "well-done" orders: old to the point of stinky, tough, full of nerve and connective tissue. The Pratts, who ate their meat almost raw, believed that anyone who ordered theirs well-done wouldn't know what was edible and what wasn't.

The jukebox came on. Johnny Cash. I was so sick of Johnny Cash. I hoped the DOT crew would come in later. They were the only ones who'd play the few rock tunes. "Satisfaction" by the Rolling Stones was my favourite, its hungry beat making me feel a little insane with desire for the future.

The DOT guys were, except for the foreman, about my age. At least two of them, I'd learned from Kendy, were UBC students, and just hearing "UBC" made me tingle with excitement. The University of British Columbia. Vancouver. That's where *I'm* going to go, I'd wanted to tell them, as I stood there, invisible, while they scanned their menus. Sat-is-FAC-shun, I'd think, feeling my body hum along with Mick and yearning for something wild.

Scrape, scrape, scrub, scrub, rinse, rinse. Sweat was running down between my breasts, gathering around my waist. My back was aching. I shifted from one foot to the other to relieve the pressure. The smell of bleach was making me dizzy.

And suddenly Mrs. Pratt was boiling into the kitchen, words sizzling out of her so fast I felt a sting of spittle on my cheek as she grabbed my arm and spun me around.

"What's the matter with you? Are you blind? Are you deaf? Didn't you see those people come in? They sat there and sat there and then they got up and left! You hear what I said? They got up and left! What's the matter with you?"

She flung my arm down to my side as though it suddenly disgusted her. My wrist banged on the sink.

"Look at her, Lena. She hides in here and customers walk out."

"I'm sorry." I could hardly form the words.

"Sorry! You're always sorry! What use is sorry? You keep *watch* out there! That's your job."

The tears were starting to come, but I blinked them back. *This job isn't your real life. This job isn't your real life.*

By the time she'd raged out of the kitchen I had swallowed back my tears, but I was still shaking. My wrist stung from where it had hit the sink. It's not fair, I wanted to cry, it's not fair! And why had she just sat there, watching, when it would have been so simple to stick her head into the kitchen and tell me there were new customers?

"Go on out," Lena said. "Don't worry about the dishes."

I tried to rub the pain out of my wrist and then made myself pick up the coffee pot and go out into the restaurant. It wasn't easy. Mrs. Pratt was standing at the entrance to the hotel part of the lodge, saying something to Olive, whose eyes flicked to me, then went quickly away.

I refilled two coffees, smiled at the diners, answered a question about the lake from the Germans who were staying at the lodge. I could have spoken to them in German, in which I was still reasonably fluent and which had impressed a group last week enough for them to leave me a generous tip, but I could barely muster the courage now to speak in English.

When I brought out the napkin packages and began going around to the tables to fill the dispensers, Mr. Pratt sauntered over to me. Ash from his cigarette dropped on the floor; he didn't pay any attention. He came close to me, close. I could smell his breath—cigarettes and coffee. I didn't look at him. I grabbed a wad of serviettes, headed for a table closer to the Germans.

He followed me around to my side of the table, putting his back to the customers. He pulled the serviettes out of my hand and pressed them into the dispenser, then turned it over and handed it to me. The backs of his hands were heavily sown with large, dark freckles.

"You better watch out," he said in a low voice. "The way you keep screwing up. Gladys isn't going to put up with it forever."

I nodded, keeping my eyes on the napkins I was pressing into the other side of the dispenser.

"I keep sticking up for you with her. You should know that. That I keep sticking up for you."

I nodded again. I knew he was expecting me to thank him, but I couldn't force the words past my throat.

As I leaned over to set the dispenser up against the wall, he reached up, quickly, clamped his hand onto my breast and squeezed. I dropped the dispenser, jerked back, stumbling over a chair. He stepped away, too, throwing a look at the door, where Mrs. Pratt still stood talking to Olive. Then he took a long drag on his cigarette and tapped it into one of the clean ashtrays I'd brought out to the tables half an hour ago.

"Oops," he said. A smile wiped itself across his face, showing me his dingy teeth. "Guess I just made more work for you." He turned and strolled back to his table, nodding at the Germans.

This job isn't your real life.

It was well after one in the morning before I finished the cleaning and balanced the till. Lena handed me a glass of milk as I put on my coat. She and Laura were great believers in the soothing nature of a glass of milk, and I rarely left the evening shift without one, especially if it might go sour overnight.

"Have another one," Lena said. She must have thought I was in special need tonight.

"It'll just make me pee," I protested, but I drank it down, a good girl, grateful for everything Lena knew and didn't say.

I used the flashlight on my way to the cabin, even though it was still light outside, that strange, arrested, mauve dusk that would only thin and then lighten into dawn. From the way I was holding the flashlight, clenched hard in my fist, I knew I was imagining it as something else, as a weapon. I clicked it off when I saw the glow from the lamp in the window. But I still tried to be quiet when I opened the door because I was pretty sure Kendy wouldn't be awake.

She lay sprawled across her bed, eyes covered with sleep, dressed only in jeans and a bra, as though she'd started to get undressed and simply passed out. The room was still a little cloudy with the heavy, sweet smell I was coming to appreciate.

I picked up the wrinkled stub in the roach clip on the floor and put it in the ashtray with the two others. Then I pulled the blanket up over Kendy, set her alarm for 5:15, and sat down on my own bed and opened my letters.

Elke

Late June, 1965

Dear Mom and Dad,
    Everything is still going well. Thanks for the parcel!
I needed the shampoo and toothpaste, and I'm
already using the new typewriter ribbon. . . .

Elke

When I walked into the kitchen that morning to start my shift, Lena was standing completely motionless, staring into the deep fryer. Her hands were raised, palms out, the classic posture of someone transfixed with shock.

I suppose it was because I came from a farm and had seen my mother in such a state that I knew immediately what had happened. When I looked inside the deep fryer I saw the dead mouse floating in the cooking oil.

Lena lowered her hands and backed away. I'd never seen her look so helpless. "Oh, God," she whispered. "Laura forgot to put the cover on last night."

"What should we do?"

"I just filled up with new oil yesterday. Five gallons. It's supposed to last for over a week. I used up the last pail. The freight truck won't be in for three more days."

"Could we just substitute mashed for fries? There's not much besides potatoes that use the deep fryer, is there?"

Lena kept staring at the fryer. When she answered she was still whispering. "Mrs. Pratt told us to set traps and I said we had but we hadn't. We just ... couldn't do it."

"My mom's the same way. Nothing scares her, except mice."

"I *can't* throw all that oil away. Gladys will kill me."

I could see her, a tornado in the kitchen, shrieking at all of us for being stupid and careless. Just the thought of the storm made me take hold of the counter.

"Okay," I said. "The mouse fell in sometime last night—"

"What if it was earlier? What if it's been in there for, for days?" Lena was looking sick.

"But if you changed the oil yesterday it couldn't have been in there very long. I put a basket of fries in just before I went off and I'm sure it wasn't there then." I wasn't sure at all, actually, but neither of us wanted to hear that. "Okay, look. The oil can get heated really hot, right, to boiling point, so what if you turn it up as high as it goes for a while? It should kill any germs."

Not waiting for her answer, I found a thick paper bag, took the big slotted spoon hanging by the grill, and scooped the grease-sodden mouse into it. Lena just stood staring, a little whimper escaping from her as the spoon cleared the rim of the fryer.

"Oh, God," she said. "Can we get away with it?"

The grease was soaking through the paper bag, so I found another, this one with a waxy coating, and put the first bag into it. I squeezed out the air, folded over the top and dropped both bags into the big garbage container under the sinks. It was a tiny package, really. In a few hours it would be covered with new kitchen debris.

"Sure we can," I told Lena. "We just did."

She went over to the deep fryer and peered inside, as though she didn't believe the mouse was gone, and then she reached over to the propane tank that powered the fryer, grill and stove and turned the fryer temperature dial up as high as it would go.

I washed my hands, retied my apron, and put on the coffee.

When the Pratts, looking surly and hungover, came in at nine for their breakfast, I felt a certain smugness, as though for the first time I had put something over on them. All I'd done, I suppose, was keep the machine running, and since they owned the machine they were the ones I was helping most.

I took the coffee pot past their table. "Would you like a refill?" I asked.

Mr. Pratt grunted, shoved his coffee mug a fraction of an inch closer to me. I filled it. I imagined the dead mouse going, plop, into his cup. The Warthog ignored me, frowning moodily out at the lake glittering with sunlight.

One of the tourists that Al, the outfitter, was taking out to pan for gold today had put a dime in the jukebox and was trying to decide what to pick.

"You choose one," he said as I walked by.

"Sure." I'd have picked A-14 automatically, but I was cocky enough to think that today I *had* gotten satisfaction, so I chose "Hard Day's Night," partly because the Pratts hated the Beatles.

When I went back to the kitchen Lena looked up from slicing carrots on the cutting table and gave me a little collusive grin. It might have been the first time I ever saw her smile.

"Don't tell anybody, okay?" she said. "Not even Kendy."

"Okay," I said, although telling Kendy would have been the best part.

It was Kendy's day off, and she had gone for a drive with one of the DOT crew, Sean, the one we both thought was the cutest; so when my shift was over it was Maud who would relieve me. She was tall and slim, with unevenly cropped, thick, dark hair and a face with a weathered, crinkly eyed look that made her seem older than the thirty Faith said she was. Of all the people at the lodge it was Maud I might have wanted to get to know better, but, although she was friendly enough, in an abstracted kind of way, she was also relentlessly private, and even Kendy couldn't once charm her out of her trailer on the rare occasions we were all off shift at the same time. Faith told me Maud had been to just about every country in the world and that she worked here in the summer just to get enough money to travel. It sounded like an exciting life, although not as exciting as moving to Vancouver and going to university. I was counting the days.

I spent the afternoon walking around the northeastern part of the lake, keeping an eye out for grizzlies. When the berries ripened I knew the grizzlies would come out into the open and closer to the lake, but I hoped it was too early in the year for that. Grizzlies in Arizona, I'd read, ate only moths for all of August, but I didn't expect them to do that here. I knew a lot about bears. They were the only wild animals I was afraid of.

I picked some new and tender fireweed shoots to chew on and then sat down and tried to do some reading from one of the university books I'd brought along, a psychology text, but my eyes kept drifting up and over the quiet, blue lake, to the snow-capped St. Elias Mountains to the south. Mount Logan was there, the highest peak in Canada, a mountain *massif* that didn't just shoot up into the sky but that had several peaks and stretched over three hundred square miles from west to east. At least that's what a geologist staying at the lodge had told Kendy. On the closer slopes some of the white specks I saw were probably Dall sheep. The ewes would have had their spring lambs by now.

If I hadn't known it was there I could have looked right across at the lodge and not seen it. I pretended the light reflecting from the windows was from a pond, from glittery rocks, from something natural.

I tried to imagine what it had been like here during the last ice age, when the Yukon, along with Alaska and eastern Siberia, was the subcontinent of Beringia, untouched by the glaciers that covered the rest of Canada. The grassy tundra had been rich with plant and animal life. Bears, much larger than the grizzlies I was nervous about, and woolly mammoths, which had probably come across from Asia on the Bering Land Bridge when the sea levels dropped, lived here for thousands of years. Were there people? Yes, of course, there must have been, the ancestors of Basement Bobby, but the history book I'd read mustn't have found them worth mentioning.

It was getting late, and the damp ground was making me cold and stiff. I got up, stretched, took in as deep a breath of the clean air as my lungs could hold. As I headed back to the south side of the lake I picked a small bouquet of yellow poppies, although I knew I shouldn't because they were scarce, and stuck them into a moist chunk of moss. In the cabin I pressed the moss into Kendy's ashtray, where the arrangement looked surprisingly pretty.

It was early evening, and I had just started typing a letter to one of my half-dozen penpals, when I heard a sound at the door.

I'd been expecting Kendy so hadn't turned the nailed-on piece of wood that held the door shut.

But it wasn't Kendy. It was Charlie Pratt.

I jumped to my feet. Maybe he was just here to tell me a tour bus had come in, I told myself. Don't panic don't panic don't panic.

"Hey, there, Elk-EE," he said, saying my name the sneery way his wife did. "What ya doin'? Want a little company?"

"No, thanks."

"I thought you might be lonely. I thought you might be missing all your *boy*friends."

"I'm not lonely. I was busy. Writing a letter."

"A *letter!* A *letter!*" He laughed, as though "letter" were the funniest word he'd ever heard.

The door was still open behind him. I began edging toward it, but he saw what I was doing and kicked it shut. I grabbed for the handle, but he got a hand on my arm and pulled me away.

I stumbled, and, perhaps to stop me from falling, perhaps just taking advantage of the opportunity, he grabbed at my blouse. The top button ripped loose, pinged across the room, and the next two buttons twisted open. I wasn't wearing a bra. I pulled desperately at the blouse to cover myself, but he wouldn't let it go. His other hand grabbed my right breast, squeezed, hard. I screamed.

"Shh," he said. "Jesus, you got big titties."

I managed to twist away from him, hearing my blouse tear at the shoulder seam, but I was off-balance and could only fall back against the rounded metal headboard, then onto the bed. He stood there looking down at me, his whole face a leer. My right hand clenched the two sides of my blouse together so tightly my fingernails bit into my palm as though there were no fabric in between.

It had all happened so fast. Only now was the darker fear catching up with me, the cold, horrible fear of what he might really have come here to do. He smelled of beer, but he didn't seem drunk, at least not drunk enough for me to overpower him. My heart sounded like thunder in my ears.

"Come on. You want me. The way you been looking at me."

I pulled away as far as I could from him on the bed, pressing my back against the wall and pulling my knees up to my chest.

"Please go away, Mr. Pratt."

"Don't be scared. I brought you something. Something to show you. Something you'll like."

He zipped open his pants, shoved them down. I don't think he had on any underwear. All I saw was his erection, the first uncovered one I had ever seen on a man. It seemed huge, utterly out of proportion to the rest of him.

He turned a little to the side so that I would have to look at him in profile.

"You want that, don't you?"

"No, please. Please leave. I won't tell anyone. Please."

"Come on. Don't be shy."

He gave a hard, excited, little giggle. I expected him at any moment to lunge at me, to fling his huge penis on top of me and then somehow, impossibly, try to shove it inside of me, and my whole body was clenching against him, getting ready to fight as desperately as it knew how. But he just stood there, grinning, looking down at himself and then back at me.

"Nice, isn't it?" he said.

What I would have answered, and what he would have done then, I don't know, because suddenly the door opened and Kendy was there. Her face was flushed, and she was breathing hard.

"What's going on?" she demanded. "I heard a scream."

Charlie Pratt whirled around. I could see Kendy's eyes drop, heard her gasp.

"Just showing your roommate something nice." His voice had lost its self-confident sneer, but he made no attempt to reach down and pull up his pants. I realized he was sucking his stomach in a little, tilting his pelvis up. He wanted Kendy to look at him, the same way he'd wanted me to look at him. I pressed a hand to my throat to stop the sound that was building there, something loud and hysterical.

"You all right, Elke?" Kendy asked, her voice sounding flat and practical. She was wearing high heels and lipstick and eye shadow, and she had her hair coiled on top of her head. She looked dazzling, and five feet taller than Charlie Pratt.

I had to clear my throat before I could answer. "Yes. I'm just glad you're home."

"So am I." She looked Charlie Pratt right in the eye. "You leave Elke alone. You hear me?"

"Who's going to make me?" He sounded tougher again, not exactly confident but less intimidated.

Kendy stood for several moments appraising him. His erection hadn't subsided. I was afraid to move, to speak, as though anything I did might interfere with Kendy's power to negotiate.

"Tell you what," she said. "You leave Elke alone, and I'll give that thing—" she gestured at his penis "—a treat it will never forget."

The man actually licked his lips. "What?"

"If I do it, you'll leave Elke alone."

"Sure, all right. If you do what?"

"You'll see."

Kendy slid her jacket off. Her black sheath was cut so low in front it barely covered her nipples. She knelt down in front of him, put her hands on his hips, and slowly, very slowly, slid his penis into her mouth.

I'd never even imagined such a thing. I truly thought she must be intending to bite it off, which didn't seem undeserved. I sat on my bed, clutching the edges of my blouse together, barely breathing, and watched as Kendy worked her mouth around Charlie Pratt's penis. In and out. Slow. Faster. His body seemed to be going into spasm. He groaned, grabbed Kendy's hair, groaned louder. I deduced that if she had been biting his penis off his groans would have been more shrill, and that, though I'd never seen a man have an orgasm, Charlie Pratt must be having one.

Kendy stood up, went to the door, and spat out what was in her mouth. I heard it go splat against the rocks outside. Charlie Pratt collapsed gently against the wall beside the door, as though someone had knocked him on the head. His penis subsided into something small and shrivelled and wet, barely visible in its nest of hair. He reached down, pulled his pants up over it.

Kendy held the door open.

"You liked that, Charlie?"

He nodded, not looking at her.

"If you touch Elke again, I'll tell Gladys. Look at me, Charlie. You know I'm not afraid of Gladys."

Charlie looked up at her, squinting, as though she were too bright a light, and nodded. His jowly face had an empty, sleepy look to it.

When he had gone, Kendy poured herself a cup of mouthwash from the bottle we kept on the desk, rinsed her mouth with it, and spat it outside.

She turned, grinned at me. "That," she said, "was a blow job."

"God, Kendy." I started to cry, feeble sobs of relief and confusion.

"Hey." She came over, sat on the bed, patted my knee. "It's okay. Are you all right?"

I nodded. The sobs seemed to be shaking me, every part of my body trembling. "If you hadn't come home just then ..."

"But I did. Sean just dropped me off. Luckily."

"I don't know what Mr. Pratt would have done—"

"Mr. Pratt. Jesus, Kendy. You think he deserves to be called Mr. Pratt? When he's not even in the damned room? Call him Charlie. Call him Asshole. Call him anything but *Mister* Pratt."

At any other time the annoyance in her voice might have upset me even more. Now, oddly, it calmed me down. Maybe I was thinking that after what Kendy had done for me she could, forever after, talk to me in whatever tone she wanted.

"Charlie," I said. "He might have, you know, raped me."

"Maybe. Though I think he might just have wanted to stand there and be admired."

"What you did to him ..."

Kendy got up, went over to her side of the room, started to take the bobby pins out of her hair. I was hoping she'd finish my sentence, but she didn't.

"I mean, how could you make yourself do that? He's so, so repulsive."

She shrugged, sat down heavily on her bed. I could tell now she had been drinking—the odour in the room was no longer of beer but of something stronger, rum perhaps.

"What did it cost me? Five minutes of my time and a mouth full of scum to spit out. And what did I get? A man who's going to be dreaming about this for the rest of his pathetic life. That's what men are like, Elke. They want us to think they're strong and in charge, but sex is what it's all about with them. We have it, they want it. So we can get them to do anything. For the rest of the summer I can snap my fingers and Charlie will jump. Hoping that maybe, just maybe, I'll do it for him again."

"But you won't, will you?"

She laughed. "Fat chance."

"But what if he tells someone, brags about it?"

"Who'd believe him? High-and-mighty Kendy sucking off *Charlie?* They'd think he was even more pathetic, making something like that up. And you think he'd risk having the Warthog find out? Meanwhile, he knows I can tell her any time I want. Every time I look at her mean little face I can think of her husband's cock in my mouth and how he's going to think sex with her now isn't worth shit."

I thought for a moment of the mouse in the deep fryer, how I'd thought, too, that I knew something the Warthog didn't and how that secret gave me a bit of power over her. Of course, a mouse in her deep fryer was hardly in the same class as—

"That ... thing you did to him—"

"The blow job."

"I've never heard of that before. It's ... I mean, where did you learn to do that?"

She laughed, shook her hair out. A couple of bobby pins dropped to the floor. "My mother showed me."

"Your *mother?*"

"My mother is, well, very practical. She gave me this book, I think it was in Swedish, and it showed how to do it. She said it was a useful thing to know for when a man was pressuring you for sex. It would make him happy, and you didn't have to worry about getting pregnant. The trick is learning to control your gag reflex."

I imagined Charlie Pratt's enormous penis in my throat, and I had a hard time controlling my own gag reflex.

"Well," I said. "I can see how it would be a useful ... skill." I tried not to sound straight-off-the-farm. "Did you, I mean, have you done it a lot? Given blow jobs?"

"Some." She unzipped her dress, shimmied out of it. "This was the second of the day, actually."

"*Sean?* You did it to *Sean?*"

She pulled her robe on, thumped back down on the bed, began brushing out her hair. "Maybe that's why I thought about giving Charlie one. The one with Sean didn't, I don't know, it didn't go well. He didn't come. Maybe I thought I needed more practice."

The idea of that, of Charlie being used for practice, made me giggle, and then I was laughing, loudly, shrilly, and then Kendy began to laugh, too, and I thought I had never laughed so much at anything in my life and that I should remember this moment, that maybe life didn't give us a lot of them.

❀

I kept an eye on Charlie, whom I could never again think of as Mr. Pratt, for the next few days, but he was ignoring me so studiously that I could see Mrs. Pratt frowning, glancing at me suspiciously. When I walked by all he would do is lick his finger, a little more deliberately than usual, perhaps, to turn a page in his magazine. When Kendy was in the room, he would look up at her with his desires so plain on his face the Warthog must have noticed; but of course that was what he had been doing before, too, so she wouldn't have observed anything particularly different. Kendy would catch my eye and wink. It was working out the way she'd said it would.

Still, when my shift ended in the afternoons, I would ask Faith to walk me back to the cabin. She was more than happy to do so. I remembered what it was like to be her age, to be paid attention by someone a little older, and I felt guilty for wanting her company mostly just to make sure Charlie kept away. But she was a cheerful and likable girl, and I enjoyed our walks, the things she told me about her life, her determination so like my own to go to university—that sparkling future we believed would save us from the lives of our mothers, whom, with the casual brashness of youth, we patronized and pitied.

"Mrs. Pratt says I'll never get to go," Faith said once. "She told me it's only for rich people."

"Well, *I'm* sure not rich. And *I'm* going to go," I said firmly. "There are scholarships and student loans—"

She nodded, a little impatiently. "She said I'd probably get involved with some boy, and get pregnant, and that would be the end of everything." I could tell this had been troubling her more than the question of money.

"You'll just have to make sure you never let any boy get that important to you." That had been my solution, I suppose. I thought of Kendy, and smiled, thinking maybe she should be the one to have this conversation with Faith.

When I went on night shift I could hardly expect Faith to walk me home at one or two in the morning, so I asked Lena or Laura, whichever one was on duty, to watch me until I was out of sight. Since the cabin was downhill from the lodge, I jogged there quickly, and they could see me until I was practically at my door. Neither of them asked why I was suddenly nervous about a walk I had made alone before, but they must have known.

Sometimes Here Boy would appear from among the trees, giving me a fright, and I wondered if Basement Bobby was there, too. The thought of him lurking there didn't scare me as much as the thought of Charlie did, but, still, it made me uneasy. Inside the cabin, I made sure to turn to horizontal the bar of wood that served as a lock. I had even pounded in the nail holding it to the jamb a little deeper, and Kendy complained she now needed both hands to move it.

⚇

It was the last week of June when Alice arrived.

I'd been looking forward a lot to having her come and start work as the second maid. She was someone from home, from a farm only ten miles from ours, and we'd become quite good friends in high school, despite my father's suspicions of her Ukrainian background. "They're Russians," he would say. "You can't trust the Russians." It was Alice, actually, who'd sent me the ad for this job from the paper in Calgary, where she'd moved after graduation to go to secretarial college.

Eager as I was to see her again, I was worried about how the three of us would manage in the tiny cabin, where accommodation for her consisted just of another thin and stained mattress Basement Bobby threw on the floor.

What I hadn't expected was that Alice and Kendy would almost immediately and instinctively loathe each other.

"She *snores*," Kendy said indignantly.

"She can't help that." I didn't add that I'd heard Kendy come up with a few good snorts herself.

"And she's used my cosmetics. I know I didn't leave my mascara on the desk like that."

"That's no proof she used it. It's so cramped in here it's a wonder not more things get misplaced."

And when Alice came back from her shift, collapsing, exhausted, onto her mattress, she'd say things like, "How can you stand the way Kendy gets her hair over everything when she brushes it?" and "Why does she have to drape her wet panties over the chair? Yuck."

And I would say something placating, dismayed at the way things had started out between them and at the tension in the cabin. But perhaps I was also a little flattered, to be the one they both still liked and confided in, the peacemaker. It never occurred to me that I might have been at least a partial cause of the friction between them, that each might have been jealous of my friendship with the other.

Alice had been there less than a week when she came into the restaurant during my lunch break and sat down dourly opposite me, looking as though she had something particularly grim to tell me. I knew that, aside from her problems with Kendy, she had been finding the workload gruelling and Mrs. Pratt oppressive, so I sighed, prepared myself to be sympathetic. Alice was small but efficient-looking, with short, permed hair she had dyed ash blond and the kind of face with upturned features that people would call perky, but there was nothing upturned-looking about her today.

"I've made up my mind," she said.

I put down my fork. "About what?"

"I'm leaving."

"What?" My voice had been too loud. I looked quickly across the room, afraid the Pratts had heard. "You can't. You came all this way! You can't just go home."

"I'm not going home. Remember I told you about sitting beside this guy on the bus until Whitehorse, and how he owned this bar in Dawson City? And how he said he's always looking for barmaids, and that the tips are fantastic, and that if I wanted to come up there he'd practically guarantee me work? So I'm going."

"*Practically* guarantee! He's probably forgotten he even talked to you. Oh, Alice. Dawson City is so much farther north."

She pointed her perky nose toward the Pratts. "I can't stand working for that Mrs. Hitler. She comes and stands in the door-ways watching me make the beds and no matter how fast I move she says hurry up, it's not fast enough. If I moved any bloody faster I'd go up in smoke. Then there's grim old Olive, spouting the Bible at me whenever she opens her mouth."

"There's me," I said plaintively. "I'd miss you like crazy."

"No, you won't. You've got Kendy."

"Kendy isn't the same as you. You're, well, you're from *home*. I *know* you."

Alice picked up my spoon and scooped up a glob of my mashed potatoes. I had more or less lost my appetite for French fries. She tongued the lump around in her mouth for a while before swallowing, and then she said, "Well, I can't stand it here any more. That's all there is to it."

"It's such a long way. Dawson City is three times as far from Whitehorse as this is. And on poorer roads. I'll worry about you."

"Yeah, I wish we could phone," she said. "I got so used to having a phone in Calgary."

"They're supposed to be getting service up here in a year or two."

"Well, I'm not going to wait around until then."

"I wish you wouldn't go," I said, looking at her helplessly.

But after I'd had time to get used to the idea of her leaving I wasn't as upset as I expected to be. You won't miss me, she'd said; you've got Kendy. And, yes, I thought guiltily, there was considerable truth to that. If it had been Kendy leaving I'd have been devastated. But then Kendy had more or less saved my life, I told myself. Alice wouldn't have been much better at handling Charlie than I was.

What I didn't care about at all was that Alice would be walking away from the lodge at the beginning of July, at the start of its busiest two months. But Mrs. Pratt would care.

Gladys

Early July, 1965

Dear Betsons,
    I am NOT paying the full invoice. I ordered TWO
DOZEN new bath towels, and you sent only twenty-three. . . .
                                              Mrs. Gladys Pratt

I couldn't believe my ears.

"What are you talking about?" I snapped. "It's the start of the busy season."

"Well, I'm sorry, but I've made up my mind," Alice said.

"You can't just up and quit on me. I took a chance on you, I hired you without an interview, I gave you a good job. You can't just walk out."

"I'm not just walking out. I'm giving you a week's notice."

"And where am I supposed to find another girl on a week's notice at the start of the busy season?" I could hear my voice starting to sound shrill, not even angry any more as much as desperate. But it was anger I felt, all right, bright, blazing anger.

"I'm sorry, but that's how it is. I've made up my mind. I'm going up to Dawson City."

Oh, of course, it would be Dawson City. The rumours about how rich the girls could get up there working in the bars made them believe it was another gold rush. "You think it's so wonderful there? I had a girl went to Dawson City and came crying back to me begging for her job back." That wasn't true, but I didn't care. The two waitresses I did have who went up there I never heard from again.

Alice shrugged. *Damn* her. I'd never seen one as cool as she was. She just stood there as though we were discussing how hot the water in the laundry had to be.

"I'll take my chances," she said. "So anyway, I'm gone in a week. You can have my pay ready."

"*Pay?* You think you deserve *pay* for making this mess? For a few lousy days getting in Olive's road more than helping? You owe *me,* for training you, for room and board! A kick in the ass, that's the pay you deserve."

She considered that for a bit, and I thought I had her. But then she said, "Well, in that case I guess I'd be a fool to work for another week. I'll just go this afternoon."

I wanted to kill her. I wanted to put my hands around her goddamned little neck and squeeze. If we hadn't been standing in the lobby with a load of tourists walking out the door I don't know what I might have done.

"You little bitch," I hissed. "I got friends in Dawson City. And I'm going to tell them you walked out on me in the busy season. They'll fix you. They'll see nobody there hires you."

That shook her a little, finally. I should have said that right to start with. But she was too stubborn to back down now.

"We'll see," she said.

And she turned and marched out of the lodge, heading for the cabin, where I supposed she would pack her stuff and wait for the afternoon bus to Whitehorse.

I went into the restaurant, dropped into the chair opposite Charlie. Of all things, he'd brought his new electric razor out to the table and taken it apart and was poking around trying to fix it. As though he had any clue. It must have looked really appetizing to the customers.

"What's wrong?" Charlie asked.

"The new maid. Alice. She's just quit."

"What? Jesus. Olive won't like that."

"Of *course* Olive won't like that. She's been whining for the last month for us to get the second maid, and now here she is, and she up and quits." It had been a relief to get Olive off my back. She'd liked the new girl, even though she was a bit too "secular," whatever that meant.

"So what happened? Why's she going?" Charlie asked. "You do something to her?"

"It's *my* fault, is it?" Lucky for him it wasn't a straight razor sitting there between us. "*My* fault?"

"Well, I didn't say that...."

"She smelled better money up in Dawson City, *that's* what happened. She's leaving this afternoon."

Charlie shook his head. "Well, gee. What are you going to do?"

Why was it, what are *you* going to do? Not, what are *we* going to do? Or, heaven forbid, what was Charlie Pratt going to do? He was the one who wanted this goddamned lodge, but whenever something went wrong I was the one who had to fix it.

"Olive can't manage on her own. She didn't think I noticed, but she's been taking shortcuts, especially with the laundry—just refolding the towels, changing only the bottom sheets, sometimes not even that. But I'll be damned if I start turning customers away when we've got empty rooms."

"You want to take an ad out again in the papers?"

I laughed sarcastically. "Oh, *that'll* help. There'll be lots of girls looking to be maids with the summer half over. You know how many applied last time." There'd been one. Alice.

Charlie began prodding at his razor again. I could see bits of hair from his beard on the table. "Well, if Olive can't handle it, what'll you do?"

I sighed. "I suppose I'll have to ask Charlotte."

Charlotte was either a half-sister or cousin to Basement Bobby, and she had worked for us once before when we got in a fix. I'd hated having her. Not because she was Indian, and not because she was lazy—she knew how to work, I had to give her that. The reason I hated having her was because she demanded to be paid at the end of every day, and not minimum wage like the rest of the staff got, but double, because she knew we had no choice but to use her. It got so that I couldn't stand the sight of her, of that hard stare at the end of every day, that look of a rock you'd use to break a rock. She'd stand there with her hand out and wait for me to open the till and count out her money. Never once did she say thank you, just got on her beat-up bicycle and pedalled back to her mother's shack. I knew she'd expected to work until the end of August, so it had given me a particular satisfaction to fire her with one week left to go, even though Olive made a fuss and I knew I'd probably be renting rooms with at least one dirty sheet until September.

"Charlotte," Charlie said. He couldn't hide a quick little smirk. I'd seen him sidle up to her in the hallway, nudge his hip against hers. He made me sick. But he was all bluff, showing off. I was sure he didn't have the guts to do anything more with the girls, not even Charlotte, even though he might have thought that an Indian would be desperate enough to have him, Mr. Wonderful White Man.

"Yeah. Charlotte," I said sourly. "Unless you got any better ideas."

He looked around the room, as though he was seriously hunting for a better idea. "Maybe Alice will come back."

"I don't think so." I knew damned well there were always jobs in Dawson City in the summer. And of course I'd been lying about getting her name dragged through the mud there. I didn't know one person in Dawson City.

"Well, let's hope she doesn't give the other girls ideas about leaving."

A chill went up my back. I hadn't even thought about that. My God. She and the deer were friends. Their families had farms down the road from each other or something. Of course they'd have talked all this over. Maybe Alice, the more resourceful one, was going up first to check things out and set up a job for the deer.

What if she quit, too? We'd never get another waitress up here on such short notice. There wasn't even another greedy Charlotte in the bush somewhere I could ask. Even with two waitresses and Maud we were stretched awfully thin, especially when a bus came in and the off-shift waitress had taken off somewhere, like Kendy was doing more and more with that DOT boy. And in the restaurant there weren't many shortcuts you could take. You couldn't get away with not washing the dishes the way you could get away with not washing the towels and the sheets.

If I hadn't been so upset about what could happen if the deer quit it might have struck me as funny, in a grim kind of way, that here I was, panicking about her quitting, when not more than a month ago I was thinking I should just fire her and get it over with. She'd improved since then, I had to admit that, but even if she hadn't she'd still have been something, she'd have been arms and legs, to carry food out of the kitchen and the dirty plates back.

She was on shift now, cleaning up a table by the window. A kid had smeared ketchup on the glass, and she was reaching over and wiping it off. I glanced at Charlie. I expected him to be ogling her, the way her uniform was pulling tighter across her chest, but he was back to tinkering with his razor. He'd lost interest in her lately, it seemed. Maybe she'd told him off, though I doubted she had the spunk.

On her way back to the kitchen a couple stopped her and I could hear them asking her what the dessert was. She actually remembered that it was lemon custard or apple crisp today and didn't have to go running around looking for the menu like she used to. The woman didn't want anything, but the man ordered the lemon custard. So I knew the deer would be heading into the cold room.

I waited until she went into the kitchen and then I followed her. Laura glanced up at me from where she was washing the rhubarb in the sink, and I nodded at her, but I didn't stop. I followed Elk-EE into the cold room.

She was spooning up the custard into the dessert bowl, still making it too full no matter how many times I'd told her to go easy on the custards, but that wasn't what I cared about now. I closed the door behind me. It made a hard click, startling her. She turned around quickly, almost dropping the bowl.

I wasn't mad. I was very calm, very clear-headed. But when I marched towards her I acted mad. No, I acted furious, out-of-control ferocious. Enraged, that was the word. I acted enraged.

I jerked the bowl out of her hand and slammed it down onto the metal rack beside me. I grabbed her arm and shoved her, maybe harder than I intended, than I needed to, against the racks behind her. The containers of milk and cream and pop there bounced and would have fallen over if they hadn't jostled against each other. Something Laura had in a bowl on the bottom shelf skittered over about a foot. But Elk-EE was looking at me the way I wanted her to. As though she thought I would kill her if she blinked at me the wrong way.

"So your friend Alice quit," I hissed. I got right up close to her face. She was cringing away, against the metal racks, turning her head a little to the side. "Now you listen to me. You even *think* of quitting you'll be sorry you were ever born. You hear me? I know people up and down the highway, up in Dawson City, down in Vancouver where you want to go. I *know* people. You understand what I'm saying? And if you even *think* about quitting on me at the start of the busy season, after I spent all this time training you up from nothing, well, it's not just me you'll be answering to. You understand what I'm saying? I've got friends. And some of them aren't very nice. You think I'm kidding? You think I'm making this up? I'm not kidding. I'm not making this up. You leave and you'll never be more sorry for anything in your whole life."

She was sinking a little to the floor. I grabbed her arm, jerked her up. "You understand me, Elk-EE?"

She swallowed, nodded. "I won't quit."

I pushed my face even closer to hers. "See that you don't," I said.

And I turned and opened the door and went out.

By the time I got through the kitchen I was almost laughing. No, I thought, she wasn't going to quit. Gladys Pratt was powerful. Gladys Pratt was God.

⚜

Okay, I had scared her good, I thought, but even by the next day I was wondering how long it would last. I kept watching her, but there was no way of telling what she was thinking.

It was just by accident that I noticed the letter to her parents in the tray under the till that the freight driver picked up on Tuesdays. I'd never paid much attention to what was being sent out—usually it was just postcards from the tourists. But I couldn't get that letter sitting there out of my mind. She'd have told her parents about what happened in the cold room. She'd have told them about Alice leaving. She'd have told them if she was planning to go, too.

I waited until she was busy with the dishes and then I pocketed the letter. My heart was beating fast, as though I'd committed some big crime. But if she was intending to leave it was my right to know.

I went into the kitchen and picked up the kettle and threw a tea bag into a cup.

"I'm taking this to my room for a while," I said to Laura. "You can boil water on the stove if you need to."

She nodded, didn't answer, though this wasn't anything I'd ever done before. The few times I had tea I used the loose leaves, not the bags, because sometimes Olive would read the tea leaves for me after.

I went out into the lobby. Somebody had hung a dishtowel, of all things, on one of the horns of the moosehead. I was just starting to get mad at whichever of the staff was trying to get Charlie riled up when I remembered I'd hung the towel there after I'd wiped something off the counter. Well, on a different day that might have given me a little laugh.

I opened the door to the office, which was really just the reception area, glancing at the names in the register for today. Only four. Well, it was early. Most of the overnighters staggered in at five or six, some as late as midnight if they'd overestimated the roads west of Whitehorse.

I unlocked the door to the three little rooms that Charlie and I shared behind the office. One was just a bathroom, one was a bedroom so small we had to shuffle sideways around the bed, and the other was what I suppose would be called the living room. I hated to call it that. It had no windows, it smelled musty, and the furniture was mostly what old George Logan had left behind. He'd built the bookshelf and the little tables himself, and the man was no carpenter.

I'd wanted to buy a new sofa, at least, but Charlie said it was a waste of money shipping it from Whitehorse and that over winter it would just be a temptation for someone to steal or for the mice to get into. Maybe he was right. Besides, I didn't want anything I'd regret leaving behind in September. Above the bookcase was a huge, gilt-framed photograph, its colours all faded to dull pinks, of Kluane Lake. It had come with the place, too. Beside it I'd tacked up a glossy page from a calendar, of Vancouver. Just to remind me. That this wasn't all there was.

I'd never let anyone but Olive come in here, and then just to clean. But maybe I should have invited the whole works in sometime just to show them I didn't live in any big palace back here.

I sat down on the creaky sofa whose stuffing was coming out in about five places and plugged in the kettle. I took out the deer's letter. *Mr. and Mrs. Horst Schneider, Box 22, Fort St. John, BC.* Horst. Boy, they liked stupid names in that family. When the kettle boiled, I steamed the flap open, pulled out the letter. It was exciting, like pulling the gold pan out of the water and looking for something valuable among the grey pebbles. The letter was two pages, neatly typed. I'd have been annoyed if Rodney ever wrote me a typed letter. It was too impersonal. Though it made it easy to read.

Dear Mom and Dad,
Hello again from the Yukon. I hope you are both well
and that no more of the pigs have died. Do ask Matthew's
advice about that—

There was a bunch more stuff about the damned pigs, about the crops and not enough rain, about stupid people I couldn't have cared less about. My eyes flipped down the page, turned it over. Blah, blah, blah. At last, in a paragraph halfway down the page the girl began talking about herself.

All goes well here. I'm fine, and working very hard,
as usual, but I suppose, as Dad would say, hard work
never killed anybody. There are more tour buses coming
now, one every third day or so, it seems to me, and, as I've

told you, it gets awfully frantic then. I always think,
we can't do it, we can't run fast enough, but somehow we
do. Alice—

Finally. Alice.

—has quit! I was looking forward to having her here so
of course I'm disappointed, but in some ways it's nice for
Kendy and me to have the cabin to ourselves again. It's
just too small for three people. I wonder where Alice is
now. She was heading for Dawson City, where she'd
heard there were good jobs. I hope I hear from her soon.
It was nice having somebody from home here.

   Ich habe nicht viel mehr zu sagen, aber ich muss doch
etwas auf Deutsch für meinem Vater schreiben—

What the hell was that? The whole last two paragraphs were in
some foreign language. German, maybe. I saw the word "Alice"
mentioned again, but I couldn't make head or tails of the rest of it.

What was she *saying?* Why had she suddenly started to use
another language, right in the middle of talking about Alice? Did
the stupid girl think I was reading her mail? Was this like some
kind of code? What she'd said about Alice in the English part
sounded harmless enough, not as though she was thinking of
following her, but it also sounded sort of, well, too cheerful. Not
natural. Was she really saying what she thought about working
here?

I mulled that over. Maybe everything really was "fine" with
her. Maybe she was one of those spoiled brats whose parents had
never expected anything but laziness from her, so after the shock
wore off she appreciated doing an honest day's work. Maybe she
appreciated somebody finally being strict with her. Hadn't Daddy
told her hard work never killed anybody? It sounded like maybe
she was admitting he was right.

Well, it was sure a temptation to believe that's how it was. But
if I let myself think it was the only explanation I'd be a fool. More

than likely she just wasn't telling her parents what she was really thinking. I sure in the hell never wrote my parents what I was really thinking. Not that they would have cared, one way or the other. Of course I knew I couldn't judge other families by my own. The deer probably came from one of those lovey-dovey ones where the kids never had to lie to their parents. But maybe she just didn't want them to worry and wouldn't say anything about Dawson City until it was a done deal. So she mightn't have told them even in that foreign part if she was planning to join Alice. What *was* she saying there? I tried again to figure some of it out, but it was gibberish.

I should never have opened the letter. It just made me more suspicious and unsure than ever.

I felt like wadding the whole thing up and throwing it away. But I made myself fold it up again, put it in the envelope and glue the flap back down.

I was supposed to be having a cup of tea. I shoved the tea bag into the cup and sloshed in the water. I should have brought the water to a boil again, because the tea tasted like piss.

⊪

Last night a big thunderstorm knocked out the power for most of the morning. We'd only been on Yukon Electric for two years, and it was supposed to make everything oh so wonderful, but I'd just about rather have had the old generator back. When the overnight guests came wandering into the restaurant this morning we couldn't even give them a cup of coffee. At least the power came back on before I had to start worrying about the stuff in the freezer.

I'd heard some rattling on the roof at night, so I went outside to see if the wind had done any damage up there. Sure enough. It had torn some shingles right off and sailed them up the driveway. Most of them could be reused, I thought, so I gathered them up and then walked around the building to see if I could find any more.

I didn't find any shingles, but I did find Basement Bobby and Charlotte and Kendy leaning against the west side of the lodge having a smoke. They gave me a start, and that annoyed me, but I couldn't bawl them out since there was no law against them leaning against the building, and none of them were supposed to be on shift right then. Well, Basement Bobby was always supposed to be on shift, but his way of seeing it was that he was always off shift.

I'd given *them* a start. Kendy, who was scrunched down with her back braced against the wall, almost fell over she tried to stand up so fast. Here Boy was lying at her feet, and he lumbered up and away from her, or maybe it was away from me. I'd given him more than one kick for hanging around the front door where the tourists could see him.

Charlotte passed Kendy the cigarette she was smoking, a skinny, wrinkled-up roll-your-own. You'd have thought Kendy could buy her own cigarettes, tailor-made ones.

Kendy gave me a lazy smile, and then she held the cigarette out to me. "Want a puff?" she asked.

"No thanks." What did she think, I couldn't get a decent smoke of my own if I wanted one?

"Okay."

She took a pull from it, passed it over to Basement Bobby who, to my surprise, took it and had a puff, too. If it had been me offering him a cigarette like that he'd have sneered and spit on it, more than likely. But Kendy—oh, she'd turned her charm on him, like she had on everybody. She was wearing a tight beige turtleneck sweater and jeans that started low on her hips, and her hair was loose and sort of tousled in the wind, and her eyes were that pale blue darkening to navy around the edges like she'd outlined them somehow.

For one odd moment I could feel what men must have felt looking at her. A kind of desire, I suppose. It passed.

I was still carrying the shingles, and I held them out to Basement Bobby. "The wind ripped these off the roof. If it rains we'll have leaks. Get the ladder and get up there and see where they came from and get them hammered back in."

I hadn't made my voice mean or hard, but he just stood there, looking at me.

"You hear me?" I snapped. "I'm talking about *now*. You do this *now*." I set the shingles down at my feet, dusted off my hands.

Over the years I'd gotten good at staring right into someone's eyes until they looked away. He tried, but he was no match for me. He looked off towards the lake and mumbled, "Yeah, yeah."

That was as much of a commitment as I'd get from him. I smiled a little to myself because I knew it had cost him something to give in to me in front of the two girls.

Charlotte said something to him. It took me a moment to realize it must have been in some Indian language. Maybe if I hadn't just gotten so aggravated at the way the deer's letter shut me out the same way, it wouldn't have made me so mad.

"You speak English at the lodge! Talk whatever gibberish you want when you're at home, but on my property and working for me you speak English, understand? I don't want the tourists to hear that jabber."

Charlotte's face got tight, and I could see the muscles bunching in her neck where she had the long and nasty scar someone told me she'd gotten from a boyfriend with a knife. She was short and square, pushing thirty, I guessed, with a large but mannish chest. Her features had the same stubborn squareness as her body and seemed to specialize in looking blank and flat and hard to read. But it wasn't hard to read her now. She felt like belting me one. But I didn't care. I was her boss, and that money she was only too glad to take out of my hand every night bought me some rights.

"Yes, *ma'am*," she said.

Kendy giggled. We all of us turned to look at her, but she was watching an eagle circling the top of a pine tree down by the lake.

I knew the only time Basement Bobby would start any work was when I wasn't watching, so I turned and strode off. I listened for anything they might say behind my back, but there was only silence.

It wasn't until I was turning the corner, heading back to the front of the lodge, that I heard Kendy say, "I want a fight."

I stopped dead in my tracks. Then I heard the flick flick of a lighter, and I realized she must have said, "I want a light."

Huh. People didn't have to use a foreign language to stop me from understanding them. They could just speak English.

I want a fight. That was a good one.

Gladys
Late July, 1965

Dear Betsons,
    I don't care WHAT your records show. I'm telling you
your order was short and I'm not paying for something
I didn't get. . . .

                    Mrs. Gladys Pratt

It always surprised me how people expected they could just write and reserve a room without any hint of a down payment. Of the half-dozen reservation letters I answered this morning not a one included money.

I said we'd hold rooms for them until three. Not often were we full up by three. Only a couple of times did I take the bird in the hand and then have the reserved people show up. I guess I didn't blame them for being mad, but what did they expect, without a deposit? It's no contract if the commitment is only on one side. And sometimes people just didn't show up. Nowadays hotels would laugh in your face if you expected to reserve without paying for the whole night in advance.

When I'd finished with the reservations I spent the rest of the morning paying bills. If anyone thought we were getting rich here they should see the bills. I hated paying them, watching the money trickle out to the suppliers, who I knew inflated their prices because we had no choice but to use them. Well, I cut ten percent off the dairy bill because that ice cream had melted somewhere along the line, even if it was frozen when it got here. It wasn't like I had to throw it out, but I'd be damned if I'd pay full price for poor quality. I always seemed to be in a fight with somebody over the perishables.

The payment for the propane could wait another two weeks, I decided, even though Sam's invoice had "second notice" stamped on it. He didn't need to get paid until just before our next shipment was due. He drove the truck himself sometimes, and he hadn't been too happy with me the last time he'd come, but he was a businessman, he knew how things worked.

Besides, the chequing account was down to only a few dollars. I'd underestimated the bills. I'd have to make a trip to Whitehorse in a few days to shuffle some money into it from savings. Just the thought of that long, boring, dusty drive made me groan. And there was nothing to look forward to in Whitehorse. It was named for the rapids on the Yukon River that were supposed to look like the manes of white horses, but if you ask me Whitehorse was more like a horse's ass. It was full of drunks and the people who made money off them.

I put the chequebook away, put my hands into the small of my back and had a good stretch to pull away the soreness. I sure hoped I hadn't inherited my mother's bad back. She was just in her sixties, but she'd walk hunched over like she was a hundred. It didn't improve her mood any, either. She'd whacked me a good one with her cane a couple of times, and it took what she'd have called "strength of character" for me not to whack her back. I nearly did the last time, though, when she laid the stick across the back of my thighs for no reason except that I was late picking Rodney up. I threw that cane across the room so hard it put a dent in her old wood cabinet.

"Do that one more time, old woman, and it'll be you flying across that room, you hear me?" I was yelling.

She cowered back a little from me. I was surprised to see that. It had always been me who did the cowering. I should have thrown her damned stick across the room years ago. But it scared me, too, to think how, just like that, someone's power could be over.

Was I as bad a mother as my mother? Couldn't be. Rodney'd gotten spankings when he needed them, so he'd learn, but I held back whenever I could with that slapping on the side of the head she'd do, sometimes just for the fun of it, it seemed, and calling me an idiot. It was worse after my dad left, and she was taking it out on me. I looked like him, she said. Rodney at least had a dad who didn't leave, but Charlie was about as much help as the dog was. Raising kids was up to the woman, he'd say. Anything he didn't want to do was up to the woman.

Well, Rodney was fifteen, and whatever I'd done wrong or right with him it was too late to change, so no use brooding or whining about the past.

As I left the office, Olive, carrying a big load of towels she could barely see over, almost ran me down. She was sweating—I could smell her. I didn't dare to comment, because I knew she was working hard. There hadn't been a night for weeks that we weren't full up.

"Gladys," she said. "Take these to Room Seven, would you. I've got to run down and put another load of laundry in."

And she shoved the towels at me and pulled her arms out from under them so that I had to grab them or let them fall.

If it had been anyone but Olive those towels would have been on the floor. She was gone before I could get a word out.

I took the towels down to Room Seven and dumped them on the bed, which looked like she'd just made it up. Two closed suitcases were sitting at the foot, so I gathered she was just a step ahead, or behind, the guests Charlie had checked in half an hour ago and who were probably waiting in the restaurant. Room Seven was one of the rooms with a sink, so I could have hung the towels up on the rack beside the basin, but I didn't want Olive to think she could take any more advantage of me. No waitressing, no chambermaiding: that had been my bargain with myself and I had stuck to it.

Olive was already trotting back up the hallway. Her uniform had big blotches of sweat under the arms and around the waistband, and her hair had pulled away from its bobby pins and stood up in tough little sprigs around her head. There was a smudge of something yellow on her chin. She was a sight.

"Where's Charlotte?" I asked.

"Doing Room Ten."

"You're supposed to be working together. It's more efficient."

Olive sighed. "No," she said tersely. "It's not."

She picked up the broom. I took a step to the side, but she was sweeping so fast that the bristles still flicked across my shoes.

"If you're not going to help, get out of the way," Olive said.

"What?"

She stopped dead and looked up at me. I told myself she was as shocked as I was by what she'd said, but looking back on it I don't think she was. She'd simply said what was on her mind.

We just stood staring at each other. And then, God knows why, I began laughing. Not my usual sarcastic laugh that could freeze people in their tracks, but a laugh I'd almost forgotten I had, from thinking something was genuinely funny. And then slowly Olive cracked a smile, too, something her face wasn't known for, and then she started laughing, too, and we stood there like two idiots, cackling away.

Charlotte came running from across the hall to see what had happened and then stood gaping at us. For a minute it was like she was the boss, catching us acting up.

"Get back to work," I told her.

Saying that sobered me up quick. I felt I'd behaved in a dangerous way, let both of them see something they could use against me, somehow. Charlotte clomped back to Room Ten. Lucky she had the curiosity of a dishrag. Olive shut right up, too, and concentrated harder than she had to on her sweeping, turning her back to me when she bent over and flicked her little pile into the dustpan.

Later I thought of all the smart things I could have said to her. Like how Jesus would've been disappointed in her attitude, like how weren't good Christians supposed to be humble, like how weren't the meek supposed to inherit the earth? But at the time I couldn't think of one damned thing to say. So I just turned and headed off to the restaurant.

If you're not going to help, get out of the way. The *nerve* of her. I shook my head at the moosehead.

At least I hadn't hung up the towels for her.

I sat down at my usual table, where Charlie was doing a crossword puzzle in one of his stupid magazines. I could tell just by a glance it was a simple one, but Charlie had filled in only four or five words. Once upon a time he'd have asked me to help him.

Once upon a time I would have. Once upon a time I could have told him what had just happened with me and Olive. He wouldn't have understood, but he would have been someone to share it with. Someone besides the moosehead.

Out the window I could see a young couple and two kids in bathing suits down at the sandy part of the lakeshore. They were jumping around and chasing each other, and I could almost hear their screaming whenever they got a toe in the water. Like it was scalding them. More likely they were Americans and it was too cold for them. They were probably staying overnight at the lodge. Just what Olive needed: people bringing in sand as well as dirt.

It was Lena cooking and Kendy waitressing today. Maybe I was imagining it, but Kendy seemed to be making more mistakes than she used to. Not that she was as bad as the deer, though the deer had improved, but Kendy was dropping things and forgetting orders. I'd had to tell her a couple of times lately to smarten up. Maybe she was just hungover or not getting enough sleep. I knew she was hanging around with the DOT crew, running off to Whitehorse whenever she got a chance.

The freight truck came in, and I went to the front to pick up the mail. I flipped through the pile, dropping the letters for the staff in their box.

Except for the last one. It was addressed to Elke Schneider, and the return address was Alice Douglas, c/o General Delivery, Dawson City.

It took me just a few seconds to decide to slip it into the pocket of my sweater. If anyone had been watching they'd have just assumed it was a letter for me. Still, my heart was beating fast. I was sure Alice and the deer had exchanged letters by now, but I'd never been able to get my hands on one before. It would have been better to get hold of one the deer wrote, but she wasn't leaving her letters in the tray anymore, just keeping them until the driver arrived and then handing them right to him. She must have been suspicious. Or guilty about what she was writing. Or both.

But it was the end of July, and she was still here. Surely if she'd been planning to go she'd have gone by now. Still, I wasn't taking anything for granted. My little pep talk in the cold room had scared her, but it could be wearing off. Good thing she'd agreed to let me hold her pay until the end of August.

I went into the kitchen, picked up the kettle and a cup and a tea bag, and told Lena I'd bring the kettle back in half an hour. Charlie was looking at me oddly as I left the restaurant, but he didn't say anything or follow me, just went back to his puzzle-for-morons and his drooly looks at Kendy. It was like she was a movie he'd paid to watch, and no matter how boring it got he'd stay to the end.

In my so-called living room, I sat down on the lumpy couch and steamed open the letter.

It was handwritten, kind of sloppy and loopy with big round letters like a kid would write, and just one page, front and back.

Dear Elke,

Hi! Great to get your letter and hear you're still surviving the lodge and the old bitch. I can't believe what she did to you in the cold room! She's bloody nuts. I'm still pissed off that she didn't pay me for all that work I did for her, but, well, what can I do? I just tell myself it's worth it to be outta there.

Things are great here! The tips are just fantastic. I'm working my ass off, but everybody is into more or less constant drinking and partying, so the barmaids get $20 bills stuffed down their blouses all the time. Yeah, it's sleazy, but if you can stand it you make a lot of money. Joe is great to work for, a really casual guy not much older than me and he's always laughing and joking and buying the barmaids little presents. Like the complete opposite of your old witch and her creep husband.

Speaking of the creep husband, is he keeping his hands off you? God, it still makes me sick to think of him coming into the cabin like that and grabbing you and waving his willy around. I know Kendy and I didn't hit it off, but I guess you're lucky she's there. And her sucking his dick!

Oh, puke. I can't imagine anybody doing that. Especially not Kendy!! Especially not with that creep!! But I guess it worked, eh? Hope he's still leaving you alone.

I heard from Mom a few days ago, and she said Brian's had his appendix out. Poor kid. I remember when I had mine out—

There was more, another two paragraphs, but I let the letter drop to the floor, leaned back against the couch. I felt cold, cold all over. My heart seemed to be taking big gulps, as though it needed more air.

Whatever I might have expected to read here, this was worse. *Grabbing you. Waving his willy around. Her sucking his dick.*

Could Charlie have gone into the cabin and tried to ... tried to force himself on that stupid girl?

And could Kendy—Kendy, of all people—have done that, *that*, that whorish thing? The thought of it was beyond disgusting. I shuddered, put a hand to my mouth. I felt dizzy, nauseous.

I stumbled into the bedroom, lay down, waiting for the sickness in my gut to pass. It did, slowly.

I'd been so sure Charlie wouldn't dare do anything more than that rubbing up against the girls, that he was all just show. But he'd gone to the cabin and tried to— And then Kendy had—

No, it was too much. I could just maybe believe some of it, even that Charlie could have gone there, and ... showed himself, but not that Kendy, Miss High-and-Mighty Kendy, would suck anybody's cock, let alone Charlie's.

The deer had made it all up. Eveything. To give Alice a good laugh. They'd all had a good laugh, at Charlie's expense. At my expense.

The old witch and her creep husband, Alice had called us. Maybe that was what the deer and Kendy called us, too. I didn't expect them to like us. I didn't want them to. But I had a right to some respect. God *damn* them.

I sat up, put my hand on the rickety night table to steady myself and felt my palm squish into a tissue there. I knew right away what it was. I'd caught Charlie before, jerking himself off into a Kleenex and then being too damned lazy even to throw it away. It wasn't as though we never had sex. We did. Not as often as we used to, of course, but sometimes. Enough for him, I'd have thought. Maybe he only did it with me because it was the one time he'd see me weak, hear me say what a big man he was. He needed to be told what a big man he was.

I lifted the tissue up by a corner and took it into the bathroom and flushed it.

Had he been thinking of Kendy while he went at himself like some retard? Probably. But did he have a reason beyond just fantasies?

I took a deep breath, let it out slowly. Then I picked up our old clock from the dinky shelf beside the sink and wound it. Even when it was as tight as it would go, my fingers kept pressing the key so hard it's a wonder it didn't snap off. My fingers hurt when I set the clock down. Tick, it said. Tick, tick, tick: listen to your life, Gladys Pratt.

I wanted to believe the deer had made the whole thing up, but I never did find it easy to lie to myself. Charlie had been in the cabin. I wasn't going to get away with thinking everything in that story had come from somebody's imagination.

The water pressure was so low the Kleenex hadn't gone down. Before I flushed the toilet again I tore up Alice's letter and envelope into a hundred little pieces and dropped them in the bowl, too. I watched them all go swirling down with Charlie's Kleenex. The bits of the letter left floating on the top I picked out and dropped into the garbage.

I remembered to take the kettle with me when I went back to the restaurant, and I slammed it down on the kitchen counter so hard the glasses on the shelf above it jingled. If Kendy had been in the kitchen at that moment I might have slammed it on her head and made her jingle, too.

I went up to our table, where Charlie was still struggling with his feeble puzzle. What was I doing with this useless man, I asked myself. What the hell was I doing?

"I want to see you in Reception," I snapped. "Right now."

I strode out, not looking to see if he was coming. He knew that voice. He'd come.

By the time I got back to our rooms I was regretting having torn the letter up. It might have been good to shove it at him and watch his face while he read it. On the other hand, it might be better for him not to know how or how much I'd found out.

"Sit down," I said, giving him a little shove onto the couch. I stood.

"What's going on?" he whined. "You mad about something?"

"Tell me what happened when you went to the girls' cabin."

Well, that made him sit up straight. He licked his lips, squinted up at me. "What d'you mean?"

"Don't lie to me, Charlie. I know what happened. I know everything. I just want your version."

"What're you talking about? I didn't do nothing to those girls."

He'd managed some real indignation there. I almost told him I was impressed. "You showed the deer your fat, lumpy dick, for starters."

He could tell there wasn't much hope. He looked at his hands, rubbed them up and down his thighs. "I didn't do anything to her," he mumbled.

"And Kendy. What happened with her? You better tell me, Charlie, or I'm going to rip your lying head right off your shoulders."

I was mad enough that I felt I could do it. I bet Charlie thought I could, too. I was stronger than he was. Always had been.

"Okay." And he got a stupid little smile on his face. I didn't expect that, the smile. "Kendy came in and she, I didn't ask her to or anything. She saw my, my cock, how big it was, and she wanted it. She wanted to put it in her mouth. I didn't make her do it. I didn't ask her to. She wanted to."

Everything in Alice's letter was true. I could feel myself staggering even though I wasn't moving.

"That's what happened. She came home, and she saw my cock, and she wanted it, and she put it in her mouth."

I turned away. I couldn't stand to have him see how much he'd gotten to me. "It was just that once," I said, not making it a question.

"Yeah. I felt bad about it afterwards. I wouldn't let her do it again."

I could hear somebody come into the lodge and stop at the front desk, so I opened the door and glanced out. Two young guys were standing there, wanting to check in.

"Customers," I said to Charlie.

He hopped up, went out. Sauntered. Like he had nothing to be ashamed of.

I slammed the door shut, making the picture on the wall jump. Nothing made any sense. Kendy doing that to Charlie. Could she really think he was that great? Was she that man-hungry that she had to go after Charlie? She could have had any man. Why did she want Charlie? The little bitch. If we hadn't had another month of busy season she'd have been out on the highway in five minutes. That goddamned little bitch.

⌘

It was hard to be in the restaurant for a while after that, especially when Kendy was on shift. Just the sight of her upset me, and it didn't seem to help if I could yell at her for getting an order wrong or breaking a glass. She just got this vacant look on her face and kept on doing whatever she was doing, and the yelling gave me no damn satisfaction at all.

Jealousy. It wasn't an emotion I'd ever had much acquaintance with, but I knew it for what it was: stupid jealousy, and over a man like Charlie.

So I stayed out of the restaurant unless there was a tour bus in and I had to do the till. There was a bus every few days now. The deer still got dithery under pressure, and Kendy wasn't around as much to pitch in. She always seemed to be out with one of the DOT boys and God knows who else. But I was almost glad now when she couldn't come in to help. It meant she was off with some man who wasn't Charlie. I hoped he liked seeing her go off with other men. One of those Wally Byam airstream trailer caravans had come in and set up camp at the lake for two weeks, and the doctor travelling with them had started sniffing at Kendy and I saw her drive off with him once. Well, sure. I knew what she was giving men now. She could have set herself up in business.

It was the last Thursday of July. I remember it because it was a day that started bad and kept getting worse. First of all, a tour bus from the southern States showed up at lunch, when we were already busy, and the stupid deer had extra trouble with them because their English was so hard to understand.

"Pardon? Pardon?" I kept hearing her say, while her orders piled up on the pick-up window, Laura's bell going ding ding ding ding, and the other customers gestured impatiently for her attention, and the row of cups got shorter and shorter while the unwashed dishes piled up.

I sent Faith running to get Kendy, but when she came puffing back I wasn't surprised when she said Kendy wasn't in the cabin. I told her to go get Maud, who fortunately was on housekeeping and could be pulled off in an emergency.

With Maud on, things speeded up a bit, but the deer had gotten so behind that there was a jam-up in the kitchen. Gridlock, they'd call it today. And some of the tour bus people were sending their orders back because they were cold. I could have told them something about keeping the bird in the hand.

It was a real mess.

Faith was standing there staring at everything the way she did, like she needed to memorize it for a test, so I took a chance and said, "Faith. I'll give you a dollar if you get in there and do that pile of dishes." I made myself add, "I'd appreciate it."

She pursed her lips. "My mom doesn't want me to work in the restaurant."

"We won't tell her. It'll just be between us. A whole dollar, Faith." I pulled one out of the till, laid it on the counter, smoothed it down. "In advance. That's a deal you'll never get again in your life."

She reached up, pulled at the bill under my fingers. I let it slide away, but keeping a little pressure on it, so she could tell this was serious, this was a lot of money.

She slid the bill into her jeans pocket and trotted off into the kitchen. I took the little stool from the cold room for her to stand on and got her started, making sure she used enough bleach.

Laura was too busy to give us anything more than a surprised glance. As I left the kitchen I said to her, "Olive doesn't find out about this."

She nodded, slapping her spatula down on the porkchops on the grill like that bit of pressure would make them cook faster. Maybe it did.

Of course, ten minutes later, who stomped into the restaurant to get a coffee but Olive. She was already mad because I'd taken Maud off housekeeping with her for an hour. She took one look at Faith up to her elbows in dishwater and she raced in there and yanked her away, kicking the stool out practically from under her feet.

I was at the till, trying to sell a jade necklace to a young Negro couple, so Olive knew better than to tell me what she was really thinking. But she did manage to squeeze out through her clenched teeth as she pulled Faith past me, "You *know* she's not supposed to."

I gave her a wide-eyed innocent look, for the benefit of the customers, and said, "Oh, well, we were so busy, Olive."

Faith gave me a mournful look as she was dragged away, her hands still dripping. She knew that she was going to have to return most of that dollar.

The Negro couple was staring at something behind me. When I turned around I saw Basement Bobby, wearing his huge, greasy bib overalls, taking a package of cigarettes from the display shelf. He was allowed three packs a week. To the couple, though, it must have seemed, with his shifty look and his grubby clothes, like he was stealing.

I grabbed his arm. I could hear the woman at the till gasp.

"You get in there at those dishes," I told him.

"Ah, Jeez," he said.

"I got no time for any of your lip. You can see how busy we are."

"It's women's work," he muttered.

"Pardon?" I said loudly. If there was one thing he hated it was being made a spectacle of in front of strangers.

He said something too low for me to hear, a curse, probably, and tried to jerk his arm away, but I had too good a hold on it. I steered him into the kitchen.

"Get busy."

I stood blocking his way out. Of course he could hightail it through the kitchen out the back door, but I didn't think he would. He knew that if he showed his face and the waitresses weren't keeping up with the dishes he could get hauled in. It happened a few times every summer. But he was always a last resort, because he'd be in a foul temper and left things sticking to the plates on purpose. And he'd always manage to break something. One thing each time. For spite.

Too bad it was the deer's shift. He'd probably have been only too glad to help out Kendy.

I turned back to the couple, gave them a tight smile, let them think whatever the hell they wanted. The man bought the jade necklace. Maybe he was scared that if he didn't he'd get strong-armed into washing dishes.

With Basement Bobby helping, the orders started moving again, even though it took longer than usual and the bus driver kept looking at his watch. Well, too bad if we'd put him behind schedule. It wasn't like he could take his business across the street.

As soon as the bus passengers began to file out, Basement Bobby took off, too. Well, he'd been better than nothing. The deer could get the rest of the dishes done.

I sent Maud back to her maid duties. I could imagine Olive would tell her the things she hadn't dared say to me.

The old witch and her creep husband. Maybe that's what Olive thought of us, too.

I remembered the way we'd laughed together a few days ago. Her cheekiness had been such a surprise that neither of us could take it seriously, I guess that's what happened, but this was different. This wasn't something to laugh about. This was Gladys breaking Rule Number One about precious Faith.

I took the twenties from their tray in the till and made sure there were no ones mixed in with them, and then I checked the bundle of ones for stray twenties. Why the hell the government didn't make them different colours was beyond me. Though they weren't as bad as the US money—that had sure been designed by a colourblind moron.

Arranging the bills was something that usually relaxed me, cheered me up a little, I don't know why. Maybe I just liked looking at them, touching them, knowing the money was mine and real, cash, not numbers in a chequebook. The first two years I used to take any chance I could to go through the till, organizing the bills, making them lie all face up or all face down. I liked the smell of them, too, that musty, inky smell. I cut back on doing that, though, thinking what a story someone could make of it, greedy Gladys in love with her money. Well, that someone would never have grown up dirt poor. Besides, I wasn't in love with it. I just knew what it could do. It didn't let you down the way people could.

But the bills didn't cheer me up today. Today it would have taken more than money.

Elk-EE the deer came out of the kitchen, her face looking like she'd been roasting herself over an open flame and her hair half pulled out of its elastic band. The hem on her uniform was coming down at the back. She went to the side counter, where maybe she thought I couldn't see her, and leaned back against the wall. I stuck my head around the corner and said, "You're still on shift, girl. I can see ten tables from here that need to be cleaned."

"All right," she said. "I was just a little tired."

"Tired! What have you got to be tired for? Too much partying last night?"

"No, I mean, the bus and everything—"

"I hope you appreciate I had to pull Maud off housekeeping to help you. And me, I had to do all the till work."

"Yeah, I know."

I'd expected her to thank me. *Yeah, I know* wasn't thanks. But if I hadn't been in such a sour mood I might almost have been amused that she was trying to grow a backbone.

"Well, get at those tables," I snapped, turning back to the till. I was startled to see Olive standing in front of it. Olive wasn't the sort of person who was good at sneaking up on anyone.

She held out a dollar bill to me.

"I didn't know you'd paid her," she said. "It's not so bad, then, I guess."

It's not so bad, then? I'd been expecting to get a lecture.

"She can keep some of it," I said. "She did some of the work."

But Olive just slapped the bill down beside the till. "Paid or not, I don't want you using her."

"It doesn't do any harm," I said, knowing I should shut up while the shutting up was good.

"She's just a kid. She's entitled to have her childhood."

"She's not such a kid any more. If she does some work here I could write her a reference someday."

"She's not going to need that."

"You never know."

"The point is—" and she gave me a look so hard and stiff you'd have thought she'd been using the spray starch from the laundry on it "—that you know how I feel, Mrs. Pratt. You don't use Faith. Period."

"Okay, okay."

I watched her trudge off. Lord, but that woman was stubborn.

⚬

When Kendy came on shift it took only about two minutes until Charlie pranced into the restaurant and on over to our usual table, giving me a wall-eyed look he must have thought was daring me to say something. I started going through the receipts on the spike at the front counter like I was looking for one in particular. When he asked Kendy to bring him a cup of tea, not coffee as usual, I wondered if he might be trying to remind me of the kettle I'd taken to our rooms. Maybe he was telling me he knew what I'd done with Alice's letter, although I didn't know how he could have.

No matter how much I was staring down at the receipts, I couldn't make myself not be aware of Charlie, the way he was watching Kendy. She flounced around like she always did, flirting with every man in the place. She was wearing a bright red lipstick that made her mouth look big and pouty. As though she'd like to suck at something.

I'd go for a walk, I decided abruptly. I wasn't a nature lover, but I suddenly felt like I had to get outside, away from Charlie and Kendy and this whole ugly, hot, greasy-smelling place.

I was just heading for the front door when who should come in but Upstairs Bobby. He was wearing cowboy boots and a cowboy shirt with blue fringes and a bolo tie, and he gave me a big grin and said, "Hey! Gladys! How's my girl?"

I suppose I made up my mind right then.

"I'm good," I said, giving him my best smile. I took his arm, which I could see surprised him because I'd never done anything like that before. "Come back to my rooms with me. I got a bottle of champagne there I've been looking to open."

He glanced over at Charlie, who couldn't have missed what was happening but who kept dunking his tea bag into the pot with so much concentration he looked like some hoity-toity Englishman.

"Well," Upstairs Bobby said. "That sounds nice."

I wheeled him around before he had a chance to think about it and steered him through the lobby into the office—"Whoa!" he said, as his right ear barely made it past the moosehead—and then into my livingroom.

"Sit down," I said, "Bob." I made a point of never calling him Upstairs Bobby to his face. Sometimes the lodge staff did and I knew it embarrassed him. "I'll get the champagne."

It was in a box under the bed in a jumble of other dusty stuff. I'd brought it along from Vancouver, something expensive that I knew we couldn't get in Whitehorse, and I'd been saving it for when we closed up the lodge. It was what old George Logan told us he'd always done, cracked open a bottle of champagne when the season was over, and I'd kind of liked that idea so I did it every year, too. Well, this bottle wasn't going to make it to September.

I started prying up the cork.

"Charlie joining us?" Upstairs Bobby asked, trying to sound casual.

"Nope."

The cork shot across the room, making us both exclaim and laugh. I thought that was a good sign. I poured us each some champagne into the water glasses I'd brought from the bathroom and sat down on the sofa beside him.

"What's the special occasion?" He took his glass, held it up as though he had to make a toast.

"Nothing. You're here, maybe that's special." I put my hand on his arm.

I'd been too blunt. I could see him flush, look down at his fancy cowboy boots. I pulled my hand quickly away. I'd forgotten all those little dances men and women had to have with each other. I'd been forward. Men didn't like forward women.

He set his glass down on the side table, on top of one of Charlie's magazines.

"Gladys," he said.

I heard in his voice, in that one word, everything he was going to say next. I took a big gulp of champagne, knowing that in a minute it would all be spoiled, that I'd want to pour the rest down the toilet.

He stood up. "I'm awfully flattered," he said. "I really am. And I like you, you know I do. But, well, you're a married woman."

I could feel my face burning, just burning. "I'm sorry," I said stiffly. "I thought you might want to …"

He was shuffling his feet, awkward, like a real cowboy doing his aw-shucks in front of a real lady.

"Maybe you can save the champagne," he said, gently. "Have a glass with Charlie."

Stick a knife in me, why don't you, I wanted to say. But I just sat there like a lump and nodded.

"Come on," he said. "Give me a smile."

I looked up at him, tried to smile but it wouldn't work.

"You go with squaws," I said. "But I'm not good enough for you."

Right away I wished I hadn't said that.

"Oh, hey."

But it was only the truth.

"I'm sorry, Gladys. It's my fault, the way I act. I didn't realize you—"

"Forget it. Let's just forget it."

"Sure. No harm done, eh? We're still friends. I don't like you any less."

"Okay." I wished he would go, just go.

"It's that you're married. You know? Charlie is my friend, too. If you weren't married, well, hey, things would be different...."

I got up, busied myself with straightening the couch cushions that always slid up on each other after people had been sitting on them. I picked up the glasses and bottle, tidying the table, keeping my back to Upstairs Bobby. When I looked around he was at the door, opening it.

"Oh. By the way," he said. He reached into his top shirt pocket and took out a ten-dollar bill, folded it in half, and set it in the big ashtray stand by the door. For one sick moment I thought he was paying me, like he would a prostitute, but then he said, "Would you give this to the kid? I should go find him and talk to him, but, well, it's so awkward, you know? We got nothing to say to each other."

I nodded, turned back to fiddling with the table, and then I heard the door closing, slowly, behind him.

I pocketed the bill and took the glasses and the bottle of champagne to the bathroom and, as I'd known I would do the minute he said "Gladys" in that sad, apologetic way, I poured it all down the toilet. It bubbled and fizzled in the water, like some kind of acid. I watched until the bubbles were all gone, and then I wrapped the bottle up in some old newspaper and put it in the garbage. If Charlie asked about it in September I'd say I must have forgotten to bring it.

I'd been heading outside, for a walk, before I'd run into Upstairs Bobby. I should have kept going, walked right on by him. So I made myself do it now, go outside, pretend this whole stupid thing had never happened.

I stopped at the front door, took a deep breath. Upstairs Bobby's truck was there, so I knew he must still be inside, probably sitting with Charlie. What if he told Charlie what I'd done? What if they were having a good laugh about it right now?

I walked away as fast as I could from that thought.

As I came around the front bumper of the last car in the lot—a Volkswagen that must have really loved these roads, every inch of it mud and dust except for the little scoops the wipers made—I stepped right on the tail of that damned dog. He yelped, jumped up. He'd been lying there by the front tire, wanting to get himself run over.

"Damn you," I shouted. "Damn you! Damn you!" I aimed a kick at him, and just like that he turned on me and chomped down on my pants leg.

I was furious. If I'd had a stick of wood in my hand I'd have beaten his head in right there. I would have. I shook my leg as hard as I could. I heard the cloth rip, but he let go, and gave me one last snarl before he galloped off, his tail low. I picked up some stones from the gravel and threw them after him.

"Damn you! Damn you! Damn you!"

"Don't do that."

I jumped back, startled, banging against the headlight of the car. Basement Bobby sneaking up on me like that made me even more furious.

"Look at what he's done!" I waved my torn pant leg at him. "That goddamned shit dog. What if he did that to a customer? He's dead, you hear me? Dead! If you don't get a rifle and put a bullet in his head I will!"

Basement Bobby looked down at his feet and said nothing. But I could feel his whole body hating me. I didn't care.

"You hear me? That dog is *dead!*"

He walked away.

"Come back here. I got something for you."

He kept walking.

"Your father was here. He left this for you." I dug the bill out of my pocket and held it out to him.

He stopped, turned around but didn't move towards me, making me stand there and wait, like some damned fool. I crumpled the bill up, threw it at him. "There," I said. "I'm not your delivery boy just because your old man can't stand to see you."

We stood there glaring at each other, the crumpled bill on the ground between us. I should have just kept the damned thing. Would he leave it there and walk away? I wondered what I'd have done in his place. Money or pride. Finally he reached down and picked the bill up and slouched off toward the lodge.

I let myself slump back against the car, knowing I was going to get myself covered in dirt, but my pants were already ruined, anyway.

I felt like just crying. Crying. Me.

I swallowed it back, walked away, toward the lake. I sat down at the base of a poplar tree and looked at the water. There were geese in it, swimming around, bobbing their heads down sometimes looking for something.

If you weren't married, things would be different. That was something, at least.

Elke
Early August, 1965

Dear Registrar:
   I'm hoping it is possible for me to delay my tuition
payment for another month. . . .
                              (Miss) Elke Schneider

I was on morning shift, buttering an order of toast, when I smelled it, not the usual greasy stink from the grill, but something lighter, more like wooodsmoke.

"You smell something?" I asked Lena.

She was making up next week's menu and she said absently, "Smell what?"

"That!" I pointed at the grey curling up out of the furnace vent.

Lena leapt to her feet. "God," she said. "I've never seen that before. The furnace shouldn't even be cutting in this time of year. I better go tell the Pratts."

She ran out of the kitchen. I put the toast on a plate and stood holding it, uncertainly, not knowing if I should take it out to the customer or stay here and keep an eye on the smoke.

I saw the Pratts run past the kitchen, heading outside. I'd never seen either of them move so fast. I assumed they were going around to the door at the side of the lodge that led to the basement. I'd never been down there, but I knew it was where the furnace was and where the extra supplies were kept and where Basement Bobby slept.

The smoke was getting heavier, not wisps any more but grey puffs, making the kitchen hazy. I soaked a couple of dishtowels in the sink and laid them over the vent, although I didn't suppose they would do much good. Lena came back, looking frightened.

"It's getting worse," I said. "Should we tell the customers to leave?" It was mid-morning, the slowest time of the day, and there were only half a dozen people in the place.

"We better not. If it's nothing serious Gladys would be really mad."

I went out into the restaurant, checking the vents. A little smoke was trickling from the one closest to the kitchen, but the others seemed clear.

Charlie came racing through the front door, panting. His face seemed dark, and I realized it was covered with soot.

"Water!" he shouted. "Tell Lena to bring water!"

I ran back to the kitchen. "Run some water! They need water down there!"

Lena scrabbled for one of the slop pails under the sink, dumped it out and began to run water into it. The pressure was so low it would take forever to fill.

I grabbed the other bucket, emptied it into the sink. "I'll run down to the lake," I said.

"Good idea."

"And I'm telling the customers."

She looked nervous about that, but she nodded.

I went out into the middle of the restaurant, holding my bucket. "I think there's a fire in the basement," I said loudly. "You should probably all go outside."

I felt foolish, telling people that, when they could see no sign of fire, but they murmured to each other and then stood up quickly and headed for the door. One man took his plate with him and kept eating as he walked out.

I ran towards the lake, the bucket banging against my hip. I almost fell as my foot skidded off a stone, sending a quick sting of pain into my ankle, and I slowed down a little, remembering how hard it was to keep a sure footing on the rocky shore. When I reached the lake, I realized it was too shallow for me to scoop up a pailful and that I would have to wade in to a deeper spot. I kicked off my loafers, grateful I'd sneaked in today without wearing nylons, and stepped into the water. It was surprisingly warm. I waded in a few feet, until the water was up to my calves, and scooped up a full bucket.

As I ran clumsily back up the slope, trying not to spill the water, I saw the smoke billowing from the side door of the lodge and Olive coming towards me carrying a metal wastebasket she must have brought from one of the rooms. Without a word, we exchanged containers and ran back the way we had come.

When I came back with the filled wastebasket, I shouted at Olive, "How bad is it?"

"I don't know. It started in the furnace room, that's all I know." She handed me the pail from the kitchen.

I filled it, turned back to the lodge. A man from the restaurant had come down to the water's edge carrying a pot that must have held barely two quarts, and he handed it to me and reached for my pail.

"Here," he said, in an authoritative voice. "Fill this."

His container hardly seemed worth bothering with, but I wasn't going to refuse his help. Three other people were coming toward us now, too, not carrying anything, but they spread themselves out between me and Olive and ferried the water in our three containers up the line.

The smoke had almost stopped.

A few minutes later I could see Lena waving to me from the doorway, shouting, "That's enough!"

The man who had brought the pot seemed annoyed at having to stop, and he insisted I fill the wastebasket one more time. I did, and he carried it up the slope to the basement door. I picked up my shoes and followed him. The rocks and spiny pine needles pricked at my feet, but I was barely aware of them, my heart still shot full of adrenalin going thump thump thump. I realized that most of the front of my uniform was wet with lake water.

The Pratts were sitting on the sill of the open door leading into the basement. They were both covered with smoke and soot. Around them, the restaurant customers, staring, speaking to each other in low voices, made an uneven semicircle.

"How bad is it?" asked the man who'd brought me the pot.

Mrs. Pratt stood up, rubbed her hands up and down her pants, but that probably just made them dirtier.

"It's all right." Her voice was hoarse and croaky, and she cleared her throat. "Mostly smoke. Smouldering, that's what it was, mostly. Go back inside." She gestured with her black hands toward the restaurant. The customers, shaking their heads, disappointed, perhaps, turned and straggled back.

Charlie stood up. "We should close the restaurant, Gladys."

"We don't need to close the restaurant. It's almost lunch time."

"We should close the restaurant," Charlie said, trying to wipe the soot from his face but only smearing it around. "For the day, at least."

"No."

"Even you should—"

"No. Damn it. I won't."

"Jesus, Gladys."

She caught sight of Lena and me, and she said angrily, "And you two. Get back inside. They could be stealing us blind in there and you stand around here gawking."

Lena's grip on my arm was tight, urgent, pulling me away.

"Come on," she murmured. "Come on. We have to go."

"Elke. Wait." It was the only time I ever heard Mrs. Pratt say my name right. She was waving her hand at my waist. "Your apron. Give me your apron. Tell Olive to give you one of hers."

I untied it, handed it to her. She wiped her hands and face on it, turning it black. We were expected to launder our own aprons, and I was about to ask her, if my clenched teeth could get the words out, if she expected me to wash that one, too, but Lena's grip was getting frighteningly tight on my arm. She almost pulled me off my feet to lurch me away with her.

"You'd think," I whispered furiously as we went around the corner of the building, "she could at least have thanked us—"

"Basement Bobby was in there."

"What?"

"Basement Bobby. Olive went in. She saw him. He was dead."

I sagged against the building. The sun seemed exceptionally bright, hurting my eyes. My shoes must have fallen from my hand because I was aware of Lena picking them up and handing them to me.

"Olive thinks he set the fire," she said. "The only burned things were where he was. She thinks he must have wanted to burn the whole place down, but the rags and stuff there didn't burn well, just made a lot of smoke. That's what got him, the smoke."

"Oh, God." I could feel my own lungs struggle for air. When I inhaled it was like pressing a twenty-pound weight up on my chest.

"Come on. We have to get back to work."

"We can't! My God! His body would still be there, right under our feet!"

"What do you think Gladys'll do to us if she comes up and finds we've closed the place and sent the customers away? Elke, you got only three more weeks here to go. You want to risk it?" She was pleading, still tugging at my arm. "It won't do Basement Bobby any good if you get yourself fired."

"She won't fire me. She needs me."

"Then she'll find another way to punish you. You haven't even been paid yet, have you? Come on, Elke. Please."

Numbly, I let myself be led back inside. Lena brought me a new apron, a full-length bib one that covered most of the wet parts of my uniform, and she tied it on me as I stood there in the lobby like a child being dressed. I'd begun to shiver, though I don't think it was from being wet. Lena had brought a towel along, too, and she wiped my feet with it, then pulled the shoes from my hand and slid them onto me.

"Wait here," she said. She ran off to the kitchen and came back a moment later with two glasses of milk. She handed me one. "Drink this," she said. "It'll help."

We stood there, facing each other but looking, in a dazed way, only at the walls, drinking the cold milk. It burned my throat.

In the restaurant the customers who'd been outside with us were milling around the till, waiting to pay. I took their bills and made myself say that, no, there didn't seem to be much damage, and, yes, we'd been grateful for their help. They were happy, laughing and chatting with each other, strangers who'd been united in common cause. Two of the women exchanged addresses.

Somehow I got through the lunch rush. My ankle was throbbing from where I'd slipped on the rock, and I could only hope I hadn't sprained it. It was the busyness that kept me going, kept me from thinking about anything other than who had ordered the steak and who needed water glasses and who was ready for dessert and who was waiting at the front to buy a postcard.

The Pratts didn't come back to the restaurant, but Olive did, going into the kitchen instead of sitting down at a table. She shook her head when I asked if she wanted something to eat. She was pale, squeezing and pulling at her fingers, which trembled as though she had some illness, and she said that Maud had gone off in her truck to the RCMP detachment. It was probably Maud, not the Pratts, I thought, who had seen the necessity of that.

"He's with God now," Olive said. "That poor boy."

"He sure didn't have much of a life here," Lena said.

"Gladys told him he had to shoot the dog," Olive said. "Faith heard her yelling at him. Maybe that was the last straw."

"Too bad dogs don't go to your heaven," Lena said.

"Why?" I asked.

"Heaven is just for people," Olive said.

"No, I mean, why did you say that about dogs and heaven? He didn't shoot Here Boy."

"Of course not," Olive said. "But Here Boy was ... with him. In the basement. They were lying there beside the furnace curled up together."

And it was hearing that that finally made me cry. The tears ran down my cheeks and I couldn't stop them, and then Lena began to cry, too. Only Olive was strong, patting us both on the shoulders, and saying, "Shhh, it's okay. They don't have to suffer any more now, neither of the poor creatures."

∞

When Kendy came on shift at four, she had obviously not heard the news. She'd been out somewhere, and the car that had brought her back wasn't one I recognized. By the time I'd seen her and run outside to tell her what had happened, she'd already trotted off to the cabin.

She was just picking up an order pad from beside the till and sliding the cardboard backing through her apron band when I came out of the kitchen. She looked especially nice today, wearing half a dozen bluebells pinned in her hair and the heart-shaped earrings Sean had bought her in Whitehorse last month. Her pale skin didn't tan well, but it had a rosy, healthy glow.

She pointed at my bib apron, grinned. "Hey! You do the cooking this morning?" She raised her head a little, sniffed. "Smells like smoke. Burn something interesting?"

"Oh, Kendy." I could feel my throat tightening at the words I would have to say.

"What?" She stared at me. "*What?*"

"Basement Bobby is dead. It looks as though he set a fire by the furnace, and we got it put out, but they found him down there. With Here Boy."

Kendy's hand went to her mouth. "Oh, God."

"We wanted to close the restaurant—even Charlie wanted to—but the old bitch wouldn't let us."

"He can't be dead. I just talked to him yesterday."

"I'm sorry, Kendy. I wish I could have told you before you came on shift."

She leaned back against the till. "I just ... Oh, God. I can't believe it."

"Olive thinks maybe it was because the Warthog told him he had to shoot Here Boy. Anyway, he must have wanted to burn the whole place down with him."

Kendy gave a wild laugh. "He should have. He should have. He should have." She laughed again, so loudly and unnaturally a man at the closest table looked up at her and frowned.

"Shhh," I said.

"Shhh," she echoed me, still laughing. "Shhh. Oh, yes, shhh. We have to shhh. God forbid we don't shhh."

"Look," I said, taking her arm, turning her away from the customers. "Go away for a hour. I'll stay on. The Pratts won't know.

They haven't showed their faces here since it happened."

"Where is he?"

"I ... suppose he's still down there. Maud went off before lunch to get the RCMP. She should be back soon. I don't think she had to go all the way to Whitehorse. There's a detachment closer than that."

"I want to go see him."

"Oh, Kendy, no. The Pratts have probably locked the door, anyway. We have to wait for the police."

But she had turned and was running out. I could see her go past the front window, heading to the side door.

The man who had frowned at her got up and came over to me. He was young, barely older than I. "Is she okay?" he asked, his voice solicitous. "She seemed awfully upset."

I almost told him. I had to turn my head, press my teeth onto my tongue to stop myself.

"It's all right," I said tersely. "She'll get over it." *She'll get over it.* As though it were some small disappointment, something the rest of us already had put behind us.

He handed me a card. "If she's troubled, tell her to come to see me. I can help. I've helped many like her."

The card said, *Brother Fabian's Serenity Commune, Whitehorse.*

"Fabian. Like the singer," I said stupidly.

He smiled. "Yes. Like the singer. Tell her, okay? Give her the card."

If there was one thing I did right that summer, it was dropping the card into the garbage when I went back to the kitchen, although it wasn't until years later that I read the lurid details about Brother Fabian's cult, the way he recruited pretty girls like Kendy.

When she hadn't come back to the restaurant after an hour, Laura asked if I was intending to work the whole shift for her. "I don't know," I said. My endurance had certainly improved while I'd been here, but I doubted I'd be able to go for eighteen hours straight.

When I took an order at one of the tables by the windows overlooking the lake, I saw Kendy standing on the shore. She was picking up rocks and throwing them as hard and far as she could into the lake.

Watching her, I felt myself wanting to cry again, for her as much as for Basement Bobby, because I knew she'd tried to befriend him when the rest of us had shied away, repelled by his coarseness and his anger. I remembered how I had encountered him on the path, how his surliness had made me never try again. But Kendy had. She was the kind of person who would have laughed at his sullenness and made him feel he was no different from anyone else at the lodge.

A woman was tugging on my arm. "Miss! We've been waiting forever to order."

I started, my eyes automatically leaping to the Pratts' table. But today it had been empty since the morning.

"Sorr-EE," I said, hearing in my voice Mrs. Pratt's sarcastic inflection. It wouldn't have been there if she had been in the room. Maybe she'd been right all along—I'd needed to be watched. Maybe if she hadn't watched me I would have snapped at the customers, or started screaming, throwing things, stealing money, shoving plateful of French fries into the faces of impatient bus passengers—

I took a breath, made myself smile at the woman.

"It's just, we're in a hurry," she said apologetically, making me feel ashamed.

When I handed Laura the order from the woman's table I noticed Maud's truck parked in front, and then I saw the police car pull in. Right behind it came a black car that looked like a regular station wagon but that was probably used as a hearse. It didn't park in front where the police car did but pulled around to the side. The RCMP officer got out of his car, put on his hat, pulled his shoulders back in a quick stretch, and followed the hearse.

It had started to rain, a slow, easy drizzle. It seemed appropriate, but I was thinking of Kendy by the lake, hoping she would at least go to the cabin now.

It was about half an hour later when Laura gestured me back to the window, and I could see the policeman returning to the car.

The Pratts were with him. They had cleaned the soot off themselves and changed their clothes, and they were both talking at the officer, gesturing repeatedly to the side of the lodge. I could hear the faint mumble of their voices through the glass but couldn't make out any words. Not that I needed to. I could imagine what they were saying. The officer had opened his car door and had propped one foot on the sill. He kept nodding, but I could tell from the way he was drumming his fingers on the top of the door that he was eager to leave.

The hearse pulled back into our view, going slowly, barely moving, as though the driver knew we were all watching and was doing it out of respect. Maybe he was. Maybe he'd heard what the Pratts had to say and was making them think about it a little longer.

The officer took advantage of their distraction to slide into his car and slam shut the door. When he backed up he didn't make any effort to do it slowly. His rear tires spat gravel at the Pratts as he headed away. Back to his detachment. Detachment. I almost laughed.

I realized suddenly that Kendy was standing out there, too, watching him go, her hair and uniform damp and sticking to her.

Then the Pratts noticed her. Even through the window I could hear the anger in Mrs. Pratt's voice. She looked at her watch, gestured toward the restaurant. Kendy didn't move. Mrs. Pratt grabbed her arm, began pulling her to the front door. Kendy let herself be tugged along, not giving in but not resisting strongly enough to stop her feet from moving. Charlie stood there watching them both and waving his arms up and down in a way that would at any other time have been comical.

I went to meet them at the front door.

"It's okay, Mrs. Pratt," I said. "I told her I'd cover for her."

"You don't make the decisions around here!" Her eyes were wide, fierce-looking, a feral yellow in them. I'd never seen her look quite like that before, beyond angry, a few steps into cornered desperation.

She gave Kendy a shove into the lobby. Kendy turned, looked

at her with an almost listless stare. "It's your fault," she said. "It's your meanness that killed him. You can live with that for the rest of your life."

Mrs. Pratt's hand shot out, slapped Kendy hard across the face, jerking her head to the side. Water droplets flew from her hair.

"You shut up. You shut up that goddamned, ugly mouth. You shut up." She was rising up a little on her toes, then sinking back, then raising herself up again, as though she wanted to pump more red into her flushed face.

I pulled Kendy away, past the reception desk. I found the towel Lena had used on me and dried her off as best I could. She stood there as passively as I had, drained of volition, of resistance. I rubbed the towel through her hair and then combed the damp strands out a little with my fingers. The bluebells she'd clipped in looked limp and pathetic, so I took them out.

"Go back to the cabin if you want," I said. "I can manage for a few more hours."

"No," she said dully. "It's okay."

Charlie came in, stood gaping at us. Behind him I heard the Warthog snap, "Charlie. Get back out here. I told you to lock the basement door. You want the tourists to go snooping around down there?"

⸙

Charlotte didn't want any of us to go the memorial service that the priest at the Catholic mission had offered to hold.

Kendy had talked Charlotte into coming down to our cabin after their shifts, and it was my day off, so it was one of those rare times the three of us could sit down together. Charlotte had never really wanted to before, and even now I could tell she was wishing she weren't here.

"What do you mean, we can't go?" Kendy cried.

She handed me the joint. A friend in Vancouver had just sent her "a farewell supply" crammed into a matchbox. Because it was such a warm evening, the air still sweet and fresh from the rain, we were sitting outside the cabin, leaning against the pine trees. A small brown bird over our heads was singing its heart out: come to me, come to me, come to me.

Charlotte took her time answering. Her slowness in speaking was something we had never gotten used to, because our talk was so fast, full of interruptions and eagerness. Charlotte would think everything over so long before speaking that we'd wonder if she might have fallen asleep with her eyes open.

Finally she said, "It should be only for his own people."

"And friends," Kendy said. "Shouldn't it? I thought I was a friend."

I handed Charlotte the joint, and she took a long pull, held it, giving her even longer to answer. "Why should you want to come? He tried to kill you."

I could tell Kendy was as shocked as I was. For once, we were the ones who had to think for a while before answering.

"Because he set the fire, you mean," I said. "When we were all in the lodge."

"I wasn't in the lodge then," Charlotte said.

"I wasn't, either," said Kendy.

So that left me.

"Well, I don't think he was intending anything of the sort," Kendy said firmly. "He hated the lodge. It was the building he wanted to destroy. And he picked the safest part of the day, really, so far as people in the place went. Most of the overnighters had checked out and gone. The restaurant was at its least busy time of the day. He thought everyone would have enough time to get out."

"Have you ever seen a fire?" Charlotte asked. "It goes like boom, an explosion. You have only a minute."

I couldn't stop myself from envisioning it, what might have happened, the thick, blinding smoke pouring suddenly through the kitchen and restaurant, the fire exploding under our feet, people panicking, not finding the small door to the lobby, the next small door to outside—

"Still," I said, forcing the image away, "I doubt if he was thinking of anything beyond just, you know, ending it for himself. And

Here Boy." Thinking of the dog made a lump come to my throat. Even now it does, oddly. Because the dog was innocent, I suppose, because the dog had no choice about how to live and to die.

"Maybe," Kendy said, "he was hoping to get out. Maybe he didn't intend to kill himself at all. He just wanted to burn down the lodge."

We thought about that, passing the joint around.

"Or maybe it was an accident," I said. "Maybe he was smoking and fell asleep."

Kendy started to say something, but then shut her mouth when she saw Charlotte was smiling a little, just at one corner of her mouth.

"Olive told me," Charlotte said, eventually, "that the morning before the ... *accident* ... someone stole a gas can from the service station. And later Maud found Bobby siphoning gas out of her truck. He took off when she saw him but she said from the way he was running the can must have been at least half full. And they found it beside him in the basement."

"Oh," I said.

The joint was down to a stub, and Kendy went inside to get the clip. When she came back she said, "Well, still, I'd like to go to the service. I won't if you really don't want me to, but I'd like to."

Charlotte scratched a twig at the ground, making cross-hatched patterns.

"Whites were no friends to him," she said. Scratch, scratch, scratch. "He worked here for room and board. What a slave earns."

"All whites aren't the same," Kendy said. "We weren't cruel to him. We're not like the Pratts. We're not like his father, either. Besides, from what I could gather, his mother's family wasn't much better to him."

I caught my breath. Why did she have to say that? Charlotte was Basement Bobby's cousin.

Charlotte laughed, a hard little bark. I sat there thinking of all the bitter answers she could make. What she did say, at last, didn't seem like an answer at all, but when I thought about it later I could see that it was.

"I knew him his whole life."

Kendy looked down at the ground. I suppose, as Charlotte must have intended, Kendy and I both thought of how long *we* had known him.

We were silent for quite a while. Finally Kendy leaned over and picked up a small piece of white wood lying at the base of the pine tree closest to the cabin. She turned it over, put it back down.

"Bobby told me once that some of his people who live farther north believe that if you find a piece of driftwood on the tundra you have to turn it over, to expose the other side to the air. It's your gift to the wood, to the spirit of the wood, its consciousness."

Charlotte snorted. "He shouldn't have told you that."

"Why not?"

"It's bullshit."

"Why is it bullshit?" Kendy persisted. "Because he made it up or because you don't believe in it?"

Charlotte stood up. She was just a dark shape against the westerly sun.

"Go to the service if you want. It's in a white man's church. It won't mean anything."

Elke

Late August, 1965

Dear Registrar:
    Thank you for allowing me to pay my tuition in installments and also for confirming my acceptance into the student residence. . . .

                                    (Miss) Elke Schneider

I had been crossing the days off the little calendar I had drawn on the blank last page of my psychology book: four more days to work. On September 2, my twentieth birthday, I would be leaving.

There was an odd silence around the lodge. Basement Bobby's name was never mentioned, by any of us, even though Kendy and I both had to walk past the blackened side door leading to the basement at least twice every day. Whether Kendy would have gone to the memorial service for him or not I didn't know, because she was on shift when it was scheduled. Olive was on shift then, too, but she went, simply walked out of the lodge with Faith, borrowed Maud's truck, and went.

When I asked her how it was she shrugged. "Okay. Only five other people came."

"Was his father there?"

She nodded. "He cried."

"Did Charlotte go?"

She shook her head. "I didn't know anybody else there."

"Was it hard for Faith?"

"It was her first funeral. She got real upset."

Poor Faith, I thought. Basement Bobby, from what I had seen, had generally ignored her, but, still, he was probably the first person she knew who had died. Plus, Faith was on the cusp of adolescence, and perhaps already her feelings about boys had started to confuse her. I remembered myself at her age, my frightening sexual interest in the bucktoothed neighbour boy whose main attraction was his proximity.

The lodge had been fiercely busy in the middle of August, everyone hurrying a holiday in before the season was over, but now business had slowed to a trickle. I was actually trying to find things to do to look busy. The Warthog was her usual grim and predatory self, ready to pounce at any sign of error or idleness.

But it was Kendy now who got the brunt of her attacks, Kendy who was still paying for what she had said in the lobby. I couldn't walk past the spot without a shudder, remembering the way the water flew out of Kendy's hair from the force of the slap. Of course, I couldn't walk into the cold room without a shudder, either, remembering how the Warthog had thrown me against the shelves and given me the huge bruise on my ribs that lasted for weeks, how she had threatened me with worse if I followed Alice.

Alice. I'd received only two letters from her, although she said she'd written more. I told myself I was being paranoid, that the letters had simply been delayed or lost, but now I tried to hand my outgoing mail directly to the freight driver. Alice's last letter had said that her boss was paying his staff their travel home, so she would fly back from Anchorage, which meant she would be taking the bus past here. I'd have an hour to see her, tomorrow, when the bus stopped at the lodge for lunch. Fortunately, I wouldn't be on shift then.

Four more days, I thought, taking the money from the day's last customer. Charlie stuck his nose in, looking for the Warthog, perhaps, but ignoring me, as he'd done all month. What he *had* been doing, though, was sidling up more and more to Kendy, and I was worried about his increasing boldness.

"I can handle him," was all Kendy said. Still, she had originally agreed to stay on an extra week after I left, and I was nervous about her being alone. Sean and the rest of the DOT crew had pulled out two weeks ago.

Lena and I locked up the restaurant, and I trotted back to the cabin with my flashlight, following its pointing finger of light as though my feet had not memorized the path. But the long twilights of June and July had passed, replaced by the truer darkness which people who didn't live here could think of all year as "night." I knew Lena was standing at the front door watching me until I was out of sight, even though I'd told her I didn't think it was necessary any more. I did intend, though, to ask her or Laura to walk Kendy back to the cabin at night after I'd gone.

It wasn't until I was at the cabin and had turned my flashlight out that I glanced up. The northern lights took my breath away, covering the whole north sky with rippling sheets of white and green and red. I hadn't ever seen them this dazzling here, though I was used to them from home. I had been astonished when Kendy told me she had never seen them before, that they didn't exist in Vancouver. Maybe that was the first time I'd thought there would be things other than people I would miss when I moved to the city.

Four more days. This might be our last chance to see the aurora. I wondered if I dared to wake her.

To my surprise she was still up, reading. Since Sean had left, she'd zipped through my dull textbooks as if they were comics and then borrowed every book she could from Olive and Maud.

"I couldn't sleep," she said. "I wanted to finish this." It was a romance novel, with a barely dressed woman fainting into the arms of a square-jawed man. Kendy was brilliant, but she was an undiscriminating reader.

"Come outside," I said.

"Why?"

"Just come."

She got out of bed, and we stood on the doorstep looking up at the sky.

"I'm going to miss you," Kendy said at last.

I was pleased, and surprised. I had assumed someone like Kendy could paper her walls with people like me.

"I'll miss you, too," I said. "But we'll both be in Vancouver. We'll both be at UBC. We'll see each other."

"Yeah, well. You know. We'll get busy with other things, and when we do get together we'll remind each other of this place, and that won't be exactly wonderful."

I hadn't thought of that, but I supposed she was right. Plus, I'd be in residence, and Kendy would be living off-campus in a house with four other people, so it might not be that easy to make time for each other. The thought of that made me swallow at the sudden lump in my throat.

"Maybe we'll be like old soldiers," I said. "You know, getting together to reminisce about the war, and nobody else will understand."

Kendy laughed, gazing up at the sky. The light seemed to be reflecting in her face, making it shine, opalescent.

"In German," I said, "we have a word, *Schlüsselerlebnis*. It means, like, a key experience, something ... transformative. Maybe this summer was a *Schlüsselerlebnis*."

"Jeez, I'd rather not think the Pratts are that important. The future better give us better *Schlüssel*-whatevers than this."

"It should, shouldn't it?"

"In thirty years, what will you be doing?"

"Thirty years!" I said. Who knows? Anything except waiting tables."

"What else then?"

I thought about it. "I'd like to be a scholar."

Kendy hooted. "A scholar! A *scholar!*"

I was a little annoyed. "Well, what about you? Who will you be in thirty years?"

"I'll be an old married lady. My husband will be a rich and successful doctor. I'll have three rich and successful kids."

"Oh. But, no, I mean ... aside from that."

Kendy laughed. She knew her answer had disappointed me. "More likely," she said, "I'll be dead. My brain burned up by the evil mary-d'you-wanna."

Burned up. Basement Bobby. Maybe Kendy thought of him then, too. We lapsed into silence. The lights that trembled and swirled through the sky looked sadder now, something to do with winter and death and goodbyes.

⊗

Alice got off the bus. We hugged and exclaimed over each other, saying we'd each lost weight, which was true. She was wearing short cut-offs, which I recognized as the remnants of the jeans she'd worn when she first came here, and a white blouse knotted under her breasts. She'd let her perm grow out, and the longer hair looked better on her.

She wanted to go into the lodge, but I pulled her down to the lake and gave her one of the peanut-butter-and-honey sandwiches I'd smuggled out for us the night before. We sat on the rocks with the water lapping at our feet and the sun on our faces and brought each other up to date. I'd already written to her about Basement Bobby, so I was glad I didn't have to tell her about that. She barely remembered him anyway.

"Well," she said, reaching for another sandwich, "I just wish you'd have come with me. Dawson City was something else. I might go up there again next summer. I nearly collapsed from exhaustion, mind you, and we had to wear these skimpy costumes and let the men grab us, but ..." She lowered her voice. "I cleared almost two thousand dollars. Isn't that amazing? Mostly from tips, of course. Where else could I have made that much in two months?"

"It *is* a lot."

Probably because I didn't volunteer my own income she said, "You haven't been paid yet, have you? Jesus, Elke. I can't believe you'd trust those sleazebags to keep your salary for four months."

I couldn't tell her that I'd accepted the arrangement mostly because Kendy had. But even if she hadn't I wondered if I would have had the nerve to ask the Pratts for a regular paycheque.

"Well, as the Warthog said, there's no bank here for me to put it in, anyway."

"You could have sent it home. I bet you don't even know your salary. I bet all you got from them in writing was the same wishy-washy letter I did just telling you your starting date."

That was true. A chill of fear trickled down my spine. "Well, they *have* to pay minimum wage. That's got to be over a dollar an hour, right? Six days a week, nine—usually ten—hours a day, overtime for the tour buses—"

"Overtime." Alice snorted. "I wouldn't hold my breath on that one." She licked some honey off her thumb.

I brushed the crumbs from my sandwich off my lap. "Well, it's too late now to change anything. Guess I'll find out in a couple of days."

Alice stood up, stretched. She'd lost quite a lot of weight, I realized. Her bones were too visible. She picked up a rock and skipped it expertly across the water.

"It's so quiet and beautiful down here," she said, watching a flock of geese circling to land on the far side of the lake. "Too bad the lodge has to ruin it. Maybe Basement Bobby *should* have burned it down." She paused for a moment, then said, "That sounded rather awful. Sorry."

"That's okay. I've had the same thought myself."

Alice had just joined the queue getting back on the bus when Mrs. Pratt came out of the lodge. I'd been crossing my fingers that the two of them wouldn't meet, though Alice had said cheerfully that she'd looked forward to it and only because I begged did she agree to "go quietly." I didn't think Mrs. Pratt had seen her arrive, but perhaps now it was me standing by the bus that had made her look more closely. She could have stayed in the lodge for five more minutes, but, no, here she came, not hurrying, her arms folded across her chest. It wasn't a posture I'd often seen her use, and among my many panicky thoughts was one warning me she might be cradling a handgun or meat cleaver.

"Why, Gladys!" Alice said. She might have been greeting her dearest friend.

Mrs. Pratt gave a twitchy smile that made her look as though she'd been chewing on piece of barbed wire. "Alice. Well. Come to ask for your old job back?"

Alice laughed. "No thanks. Though I would like the week's wages you still owe me."

"Ha. More like what you owe me."

"Well, I did pretty well in Dawson. Made a few thousand."

The Warthog shrugged.

"And none of your many friends there managed to find me and beat me up after all."

"I thought they had. You look like hell."

I could see Alice flinch, not much, but enough to amuse Mrs. Pratt.

"So do you." It was weak, but more than I could have mustered.

The last passenger had boarded now, and the bus driver was looking at Alice. Hurry up, I thought at her. Get on, get away.

"Well, take care then, Elke." Alice put her foot on the bottom step. "Make sure they pay you what you deserve."

I shrivelled, feeling the Warthog's stare skip from Alice to me. Why couldn't she have kept her mouth shut? I knew she'd been only trying to help me, but it was as though she had lobbed a grenade from a departing vehicle and forgotten that friends as well as enemies might get hit with the shrapnel.

The bus pulled away, heading west, to Alaska.

"You been telling her I'm going to cheat you, is that it?"

"No," I said. "No, of course not."

⚛

"So, will you miss us?" Charlie pursed his floppy lips and blew a thin stream of smoke into my face as I refilled his coffee.

"I guess I might," I said. I'd have said anything now to avoid antagonizing them. I could imagine the Warthog sitting in the office this minute, going through her records, writing out my cheque.

I began cleaning the table to his left, careful not to turn my back on him. My last day, and one hour to go.

"Hey," he said, pushing a quarter across the table toward me. "Put it in the jukebox. Pick what you want."

I'd rather have shoved the coin up his nose, but I made myself smile and reach for it and say, "Okay. Thanks."

No Johnny Cash. I pushed the buttons for all the rock 'n' roll, forgetting how many I could choose and not caring. "Satisfaction."

Twice. "Pretty Woman," thinking of how Kendy would exclaim "Roy!" whenever anyone played it because she had gone to his concert last year and gotten his autograph. "Surfer Girl," by the Beach Boys. "I Want to Hold Your Hand," by the Beatles. "Travellin' Man," by Ricky Nelson. "Wipeout," by the Safaris. "Great Balls of Fire," by Jerry Lee Lewis. "Satisfaction." Again.

Faith was watching me choose. "You already picked that one," she said.

"I know," I grinned.

She smiled back, but it was a sad and wistful look.

"*Promise* you'll write," she said.

I already had promised, but I told her again I would, though I had a guilty feeling already, thinking that one or two letters would be it, because, as Kendy had suggested, I would want to put this whole awful summer behind me as quickly as I could. I was too young to understand that it mightn't be that simple, life happily shuffling one on to the next adventure.

Faith kept poking A-12, though she knew I'd used up the quarter and I doubted she was really interested in Jimmy Dorsey.

"You'll forget about me," she said mournfully. "I wish I could go with you."

"Your time will come. When Kendy and I were your age we didn't have any choices, either. We had to just study and wait and do what our parents said."

"But you weren't up *here*. You were Outside."

"I was only half Outside. I was in northern BC."

"But now you're going to university. In the city."

"You will, too, someday. If you work hard."

I hoped I was right. But if I could get there she could, too. For poor kids, we were a privileged generation, I knew, the high schools and universities expanding to welcome us, as they had never done for our parents, who watched—as my mother did—with pride or—as my father did—with jealous resentment.

"Work hard at school, you mean," she said.

I was puzzled for a moment, and then I realized that the work she had seen me do didn't involve studying. "Yes, of course," I said.

"Though you'll probably have to take summer jobs to help pay your way." I took a chance and said, lowering my voice, "I wouldn't recommend this one."

She giggled. "Maybe I'll be rich," she said. "I won't have to have a summer job."

"Don't count on it, kid."

Mrs. Pratt came into the restaurant then and sat down opposite Charlie. She was wearing a stiff, new dress she must have bought in Whitehorse last week; it was white with blue violets sprinkled through it and had a demure lace-edged collar that softened her face a little, but she had cinched the belt so tight she reminded me of pictures of amoebae about to split in two.

She was carrying a file folder—my release papers, my presidential pardon, my keys to the prison door. I hurried to clean the two dirty tables, to hand their bills to the three men identically dressed in dusty, black business suits who were pushing away their dessert plates and lighting up cigarettes and reaching for their wallets. I glanced at my watch. Five more minutes. They would be my last customers.

Kendy came in, gave me a wink, picked up an order pad and went into the kitchen to go over the day's menu with Laura. I took off my apron, folded it over my arm. Mrs. Pratt stood up, walked slowly over to me at the till.

"Well," she said. "So tomorrow you're gone."

"I guess so."

She opened the folder, took out a piece of paper with a cheque stapled to it. She folded the cheque back so I couldn't see it, and pointed at the paper. "You need this for your income tax," she said. She handed it to me.

I folded the cheque open, looked at the big block printing.

Two hundred fifty dollars.

I felt dizzy. A mistake. Surely it was a mistake.

"Two hundred fifty dollars," I said faintly. "For the whole summer?"

Mrs. Pratt licked her lips, wasn't looking at me. "What'd you expect? A million?"

"No, but ... I was here four months. I ... I thought it would be more."

"Well, it's not." She flicked the back of her fingers against the paper I was holding. "Tax had to come off, in case you didn't know. And your room and board."

"Room and board."

"Room and board. You think you get all that for free? You're not exactly a light eater, are you?"

I took a deep breath, willing my hand to stop shaking. I had to stay calm. "But—Alice got over two thousand dollars, for only two months."

"Not from me, she didn't. She worked in a bar, wiggling her ass at a bunch of drunks. Besides, is it my fault you weren't good with the customers? If you didn't get a lot of tips, don't blame me."

"But ..." I kept staring at the cheque, fighting back my panic. Two hundred fifty dollars. That was all. Two hundred fifty dollars. It wouldn't even pay my tuition. I was supposed to be starting classes in little more than a week. Unless my father agreed to help me, which seemed doubtful, university might be as distant a dream for me as for Faith.

"But what?"

"There was a lot of overtime. Maybe you forgot to include the overtime."

"What are you talking about, overtime?" She gave a bark of laughter. "You worked a normal shift. If you girls helped each other out that had nothing to do with me."

"But you told us to—"

"None of my other girls ever complained. They were grateful for the work."

She leaned over and reached under the cash register into the glass display case and lifted out one of the trays of jade jewellery. There wasn't much left: three necklaces, each with a small green pendant; four pairs of earrings; a bracelet with a broken jade clasp marked down to twenty-five cents.

"I always let my girls take something before they go. For free. Here. Pick something."

I could only stand there and stare at the feeble litter of trinkets.
"Hurry up," she said. "Unless you don't want anything."

And, to my shame, I reached into the tray and picked up one of the necklaces.

I think I even said thank you.

I did. I said thank you.

I should have smashed my fists up under the tray and knocked it into her face. I should have screamed every ugly name I could think of at her. I should have thrown the coffee cup on the counter against the wall. I should have, should. Should have been someone other than Elke Schneider, who had been brought up to be nice and say thank you when someone gave her something.

When I stumbled out through the lobby I threw my apron onto the horns of the moosehead. Oh, aren't I brave, I thought, as sick with helpless anger at myself as at the Pratts.

⊗

When Kendy came off shift, she found me sitting beside my packed suitcases, crying. I showed her the cheque. She put her hand to her mouth and gasped, sinking down onto her mattress.

"Oh, my God," she whispered. "So I'll be getting about the same."

"She said she had to make deductions for our room and board. But that can't amount to hundreds of dollars. Not for ... for this!" I gestured at the cabin. "And we were only allowed to eat what was going to get tossed out that night. We'd have done better to pitch tents by the lake and cook our own food on a campfire. And when I asked her about overtime she just laughed."

"I can't believe it. I can't believe it's so little." Kendy's hand dropped heavily to her lap.

"What can we do?" I wailed. "We worked so hard! When I told her Alice made over two thousand dollars in two months, she said, well, that was mostly tips. But, God, my tips won't even pay my fare home. I have to use the traveller's cheque I brought with me."

"It's wrong. I know it's wrong. But there's nothing we can do now, here. We have to wait until we get home."

"And then?"

"Well ... sue, maybe. My dad will know."

"Sue! It would mean hiring a lawyer!" I'd never actually met a lawyer, but I'd heard their profession spoken of, in a frightened whisper, the way a nun might speak of the devil and then cross herself.

"We can't let them get away with this," Kendy said. "It's theft."

"We shouldn't have let them keep our salaries until now. If we'd known this is what we were getting we'd have left after the first month. You said it would be okay!" It wasn't right of me to say that, but I needed someone to blame, someone who, unlike the Pratts, was capable of feeling guilt.

Kendy looked away from me. I could see how much I'd hurt her.

"I'm sorry," I said, ashamed. "It was my fault, too. We trusted them to be fair."

Kendy sighed. I could tell she was close to tears herself. "This is our last night together. We were supposed to be happy."

"We'll be all right. Besides, maybe they won't dare do it to you. You know how the old bitch is a little afraid of you. She knows you might make more of a stink."

But I never did find out what Kendy got paid. I left on the bus the next day, and I haven't seen her since.

Part II

2 0 0 0

�

Gladys

Early May, 2000

Dear Editor,
   It makes me so mad to see my tax assessment up again
this year when any idiot can see property values are down. . . .
                           Mrs. Gladys Pratt

When I get out of the car I see the hedge pruner is still at it, even though he said he'd be finished by three. Well, he better not expect to be paid extra. Forty dollars is what we agreed on, and forty dollars is what he'll get.

As I go up the back steps he gives me a frowning look, and my foot stops dead as it lifts to the next stair. For one awful moment I think he is Basement Bobby. That same surly stare, that whole face with its look of hardening concrete. But then my heart starts beating normally again, and I shake my head at myself, knowing Basement Bobby has been dead now almost forty years.

But it's not the first time I've seen him. Once when I was walking along the beach at Kitsilano a few blocks from here I saw him coming toward me, and it was all I could do to stop myself from turning and running. Then once I saw him at Safeway, pushing a cart as ordinary as you please. You'd think I was losing my marbles.

I lug the groceries up into the kitchen and put them away. I see I've gotten a litre of milk when I still have an unopened one. Maybe I *am* losing my marbles. I'm turning seventy this year. Is that when they're supposed to start rolling away? But seventy these days isn't old.

Rodney has been saying that the house is too big and expensive for just the three of us, but I know what he's really saying is that if I sold it I could go into some condo or nursing home and he could keep the leftover money. And there would be a lot of money. Even though house prices are down from last year, this place must still be worth about twenty times what we paid for it thirty years ago, when we sold the lodge and Rodney got married. He and "the wife," as he calls her, put up half the down payment and I put up the other half. This was a dumpy part of Vancouver then, though it's become fancied-up and trendy now. The house seemed like a palace. It still looks pretty good—a huge living room and a kitchen I had remodelled last year and two bedrooms upstairs and a whole other suite downstairs for Rodney and the wife.

Rodney had wanted an ocean view, but I wasn't about to pay thousands more just so he could look out at water. I'd had enough of that at the lodge. But if Charlie hadn't run off by then with that Glenda woman he'd probably have agreed with Rodney. He always agreed with Rodney, mostly just to spite me, I think. An ocean view would be a good investment, he'd have argued, although what he knew about investments you could engrave on a pinhead. Well, he hasn't got much of a view where he is now, not unless you like looking at the roots of daisies.

I go into the living room, turn on the TV to watch my soaps, but then there's a tap at the front door, and I can see through the front window it's the pruner. I open the door, holding his cheque, but I don't give it to him until I've had a good look up and down the boxwood hedge. It's not as even on top as the last gardener got it, but then he charged twice as much. This one is probably glad to get paid at all, since he doesn't speaka da English. I found him from an ad in the paper. A woman's voice on the answering machine said, "Give number. I get back at you." She was probably the best talker in the house.

He still reminds me of Basement Bobby. It gives me a chill. His eyes, I suppose, and that down-pulled look to the mouth. The whole general shabbiness of him. Maybe it's because of who he reminds me of that I don't say anything about the uneven hedge and give him his cheque. He mumbles something and shuffles off. I usually get a receipt, but he probably wouldn't even know the word.

I get myself a beer, which I've grown fond of the last few years, sink down into my recliner and watch one of my programs, and then suddenly it's five o'clock and I hear the back door opening. I shove the footrest down, quickly, and pull myself to my feet—if I don't hurry she'll have gotten downstairs by the time I get through the kitchen. Rodney's wife. My daughter-in-law. Thirty years and I still find it hard to think of her that way.

She's taking her coat off but has already started down the steps. It's like this pathetic game, where if she gets to the bottom of the stairs before I reach her she's home free, she doesn't need to come up if I yell down to her. Rodney has always wanted to have another door put in so that there's a private entrance to the downstairs suite, but I absolutely said no. The house already has three doors. What do we need another one for? Just so burglars have another way to get in? We had a big fight over that one, Rodney and me, but he knows when I'm not going to back down.

She looks so much like her mother. That same solid, chunky body and the greying hair pulled back into an unattractive pony-tail, her face getting that droopy look some middle-aged women get. Though I never did. My face got wrinkles but it never got droopy. I think it makes me look younger.

If I look for it, I can see her father in her, too, although I don't remember him well. George Logan. You could have knocked me over with a feather when Olive finally told me he was the father. I'd always assumed, from the kid being so dark, that it must have been some Indian up there.

"Faith," I say. "Come up for a minute."

She looks at me, then down the stairs. There's an annoying sag to her posture that makes her stomach stick out. When she was little she used to be so pop-up perky, and didn't I always say that was never going to last? Now she looks like someone who's landed butter side down her whole life.

"Well ... Just for a minute," she says. "I have to get supper started."

She follows me through the kitchen into the living room and sits down on the sofa, looking at her watch as though she has this big, important life to get to.

"So," I say. "How was work?"

"Fine," she says, the same answer she always makes.

Faith has just started a new job, clerking in some kitchenware store. She doesn't much like it, being on her feet all the time. She used to work for the same software company that Rodney works for. She got him his job, in fact, just last year, and I suppose if I had to I could admit it wasn't fair that he started out in sales making almost twice her salary although he knew bugger-all about computers whereas Faith had already worked there for five years. And then *she's* the one to get laid off. Okay, he's a man, but it was also because he is who he is and Faith is who she is. She's plodding and plain, and Rodney has a zip and energy to him that makes him seem handsome even though he's inherited nothing special in the looks department from either Charlie or me. It's too bad he's so, well, flighty, they might call it if he was a girl. He has trouble sticking with any job for long. It's not that he gets fired, not usually, anyway. It's that he gets bored and quits. This job has lasted longer than most.

"It's tonight Rodney has to fly to Toronto?" I ask. "You taking him to the plane or is he leaving his car at the airport?"

"I'm taking him." Faith glances at her watch again. "He should be home by now."

She's just finished saying that when I hear a car door slam, and then Rodney coming up the back stairs.

"We're in here," I yell.

He comes up into the living room, looking a little flushed, his thinning hair ruffled like he's been scratching at his scalp all afternoon. He's tall, a little over six feet, and when his face isn't clenched tight over some worry or other he has nice, regular features and clear skin. He's lucky with his skin. Even when he was a teenager, he didn't get those pimples like most of the boys. He broke his nose playing football, though, and it still has a white scar and a list to the left. Lately he's had to wear double-vision glasses, and they drive him crazy. He's always squinting through them, like he's doing now, lifting and lowering his head to get things focused.

"Any mail?" he asks.

"Nope," I say. "Sit down. Take a load off."

"No time," he says, drumming his fingers on the big black briefcase he's balancing on the back of the armchair. "I have to pack. Faith? You got supper ready?"

Faith leans forward and presses a hand onto the arm of the sofa to push herself to her feet. It's like she has to un-Velcro herself from the damn cushion. She's wearing that ugly old brown cardigan over a green dress I remember being loose on her once upon a time. Now she looks like a package busting out of its wrappings. Even through her pantyhose I can see her varicose veins. Her legs have long ago forgotten what ankles are supposed to look like.

"I just got home," she says. "I haven't even been downstairs."

"Well, get moving then, hey?" Rodney says. "I got no time to waste."

"Sit for a minute," I say.

"Gotta go," he says. "Faith?" He makes some open-palmed gesture at her that seems to mean she'd better stop dawdling, and she lumbers off in front of him. Good Lord, but I wish sometimes that woman would show some spunk. If Charlie had ordered me around like that I'd have given him a whack.

They're both at the kitchen entrance already when I remember. "The hedge trimmer was here today. You owe me twenty dollars."

Rodney sighs, says something under his breath, but he knows they owe me half of all the expenses and that I don't like to wait for it. I wish I'd asked the man for a receipt, so Rodney could see I wasn't cheating him. He jerks out his wallet, hands over a twenty. I shove it into the pocket of my slacks, although I know I shouldn't without recording it in the accounts book first, because I forget about it and then think he hasn't paid me.

"The man, the hedge trimmer," I say, "for a minute there I thought he was Basement Bobby."

And immediately I wish I'd kept my mouth shut.

Rodney turns back to me, his eyebrows pushing down and forward so far they're shoving his glasses halfway down his nose. "For Christ's sake," he snaps. "Will you stop with that stuff? Who was it you saw last week? Lena? And the week before, one of the bus drivers? You'd think you'd just sold the damn lodge yesterday."

I'm wincing inside, but I don't let him see it. "Watch your mouth, Rodney. I don't yell about the people you see."

"Maybe because I really see them."

"People look like other people. So what?"

"So it makes you sound senile, that's what."

Faith is pulling at his arm. She hates when we get like this.

"Senile! I'll give you senile!" I act outraged, even though it's not the first time I've heard that word when he's talking about me. But I can't let him see me getting used to it.

"Get a grip, Gladys," he says.

Gladys. Ha. He can never pull that one off. He says it when he's mad, when he thinks he's impressing me with how grown-up he is, but it always backfires, just makes him embarrassed. He should quit trying. He looks down now, can't meet my eyes. Ha.

"My grip is just fine, thank you." I crunch my hand into a hard fist, hold it up between us. "See?"

Faith is dragging him off into the kitchen. I can hear him saying something cranky to her, about her, about me, I don't care to listen. I turn up the volume on the remote, and when I glance around they've gone. If I wanted to, I could go to the top of the stairs and hear what they're saying, since Rodney has never learned to keep his voice down, but the novelty of eavesdropping has worn off over the years. Besides, I know only too well what they think. Rodney wishes I'd drop dead. Faith wishes we'd both drop dead. Then she could sleep twenty-four hours a day.

I lean back, push down on the recliner's arms so the footrest shoots out, and flick up and down the TV channels, but there's nothing there I want to watch. But I don't turn it off. It's company, Olive said once.

Olive. Olive would understand about my seeing Basement Bobby. The last time we got together all we did was talk about the lodge, although neither of us ever called them the good old days. I can still see her sitting there on the sofa across from me, right where Faith just was. As usual, Olive and me, we argued a lot, but, as I had to keep reminding her, she was looking at those Yukon days from the point of view of my employee and I was looking at them from the point of view of the boss.

"Still," she said doggedly, "you were too hard on everybody. Those girls."

I snorted. "*Hard* on them. They were there to work, not party."

"They didn't get to do much partying."

"That's because I was *hard* on them, apparently."

"There was that one from Toronto who was crying practically the whole summer."

"And that was *my* fault?"

"You were so mean to her. She was doing her best."

"What about the one I found stealing from the till? The little bitch had just shoved twenty dollars in her pocket. Who knows how much she got away with before I caught her?"

"That was just one girl."

"Huh," I said. "I did what I had to do. If you'd been the boss you'd have done the same."

And so our argument circled around to the beginning again, and then Olive sighed and said she'd better get going, because Faith was driving her home to Surrey and Olive didn't want her to have to drive back here in the dark, as though the dark were full of monsters.

I shrugged. "Go then."

But she knew I liked to have her visit. Maybe that was one reason I wanted to keep Rodney and Faith in this house, because it would make Olive come over, to make sure her precious Faith wasn't being beaten to a pulp or something by Rodney and his mean mother. Once I told her that if she'd raised Faith with half the orneriness she herself had she wouldn't have had to worry. Well, that got me one of her more impressive tongue-lashings. Made me appreciate for a while that Faith was as bland as she was.

Olive had been furious when she found out Faith was pregnant and even more furious when she found out who'd done it. I think she wanted to kill every Pratt she could find, but Olive was nothing if not practical. Once she realized there wasn't a damn thing she could do about it, that they had to get married and that was that, she calmed down. Funny, how I'd told Faith once when she was a kid that this was exactly the future in store for her, but I didn't dream it would be my Rodney who'd be the one to knock her up.

I was no more thrilled than Olive, that's for damned sure. Of all the girls he could have had he picked dowdy little Faith. Neither of them with a brain between them about birth control. Nowadays, of course, it's a quick trip for an abortion and get on with your life, but back then there was no choice. I have to give Rodney credit, I suppose, for not just taking off, even though a part of me wished he'd do just that. Maybe he was too scared of Olive. She'd have hunted him down and hacked off his valuables.

When Faith came to tell us they'd set the date, I looked at Olive and said sourly, "So. We're going to be related."

"Lord," she said. I think that was the only time I'd ever heard her say that word and sound irreverent. Taking the Lord's name in vain. "In vain"—that was about the size of it.

So there we were. For all our wanting to get away from the lodge we got ourselves stuck with people who'd always remind us of it.

Even this house still reminds me of the lodge. Not because it's full of old souvenirs, unless you count the three of us, but because it was was built and paid for and still partly runs on money from the lodge.

There's my half, which is about eighty percent of what Charlie and I made up north and which he was too stupid or guilty to go after in the divorce. Besides, I deserved it. I'd done eighty percent of the work. Then another part was Olive's money from God knows how many years at the lodge and some of which she gave to Faith for the down payment. And then there was Faith's inheritance—old George Logan invested what Charlie and I had paid him for the place, and he'd done well, too, so Faith got a nice chunk when she turned eighteen. She wound up being worth a whole lot more than Rodney'd expected, and he made sure it all got put into both their names. Too bad for her, really, because, except for the bit they put into the mortgage, Rodney frittered it all away on one get-rich-quick scheme after another.

Another bit of lodge money came in just two months ago. That was money I'd just as soon not have seen. It was the cheque that Faith got when the lawyers settled her mother's estate.

Olive, who was healthy as a horse, dropped dead of a heart attack while she was digging around in her back garden, planting daffodils. Daffodils. I can't look at the damned things now without feeling mad at them. Sometimes I wondered if Olive and I even liked each other, but she was still the best friend I ever had. I could talk to her. She knew that no matter how much we might have hated it, those years in the Yukon had sunk permanently into our brains. She had her haunted dreams, too, about the year Basement Bobby killed himself and tried to burn the lodge down, that awful year that ...

Kendy. There. I've made myself think her name.

Olive thought she knew all about how hard I was on the girls. But even she didn't know about Kendy.

If I *was* hard on the girls, it was for the lodge. Everything was for the lodge, to keep it running. I don't think anybody understood that, how I couldn't let up or the whole thing would grind to a halt. So none of it was personal.

Except for Kendy. With her it was personal.

I thought that once I got my revenge I'd stop hating her. But it didn't work out that way. What happened to her was bad enough to make me feel pretty guilty, but I still didn't feel ... satisfied. I thought I got even with her for what she did with Charlie, but it didn't feel even. It felt more uneven. I still hated her. Still *hate* her. All these years later. If she walked into the room right now and I shot her dead I'd still hate her. I don't quite understand it.

Especially since it wasn't even her Charlie left me for. It was a tarty, fat, divorced clerk at Zellers he met a year later in Vancouver. But somehow, in my mind, it still has to do with Kendy. She gave him ideas, I guess that's how I'd put it. She began to make him think he could have someone else, someone better than me. Though for Glenda to be better than me then I'd have to have the looks and brains of an earthworm.

What still annoys me the most is that he left me and that I

didn't leave him. Why didn't I? I'd like to think I'd have gotten around to it. But there was the lodge to think about, and Rodney.

I got so mad at Olive once when we were watching this TV show about these pathetic losers who kept giving money to a con man way past the time they should have seen they were just throwing good money after bad. Olive said it was kind of like me staying so long with Charlie, how it was because I couldn't admit I'd made a mistake in the first place. Well, Olive didn't know what she was talking about. I'd admitted I'd made a mistake. Especially after that summer with Kendy, boy, had I admitted it. Charlie and I stayed together for another year and a half, but by the time that summer was over all I felt for him was contempt.

⚔

It's while I'm standing on the Skytrain platform downtown waiting to go out to the senior's centre in Surrey where I used to meet Olive that I see Upstairs Bobby. Bob. I see him only in profile, but it makes me catch my breath. He still has that curly black hair, a little grey now but still thick, and his mouth has that same little smile to it as he stares across the tracks. He's wearing a long, dark brown coat open to show the suit and tie underneath, and that almost makes me laugh. Maybe it's the suit that makes me feel I can go right on over to him. I'll say something about it, something like, "Well! You're the last person I ever expected to see all dolled up like this."

I walk over slowly, keeping my eyes on him, past the dozen or so other people hunched around us on the platform with that dead look people always get on the underground stops. The aboveground ones, it's different, they seem a little more alive, looking out at the sun or rain or traffic, but down here their faces shut right down.

I'm beside him now. I reach up, tug lightly on his coat sleeve. "Bob?" I say.

I've been so quiet that I've startled him, and he takes a quick step away, turning to stare.

"Pardon me?"

It's not him, it's not him. What's wrong with me? This man looks about forty, and Upstairs Bobby would be old, he'd look old.

"Sorry," I mutter. "I thought you were someone else."

"That's okay." He gives me a little smile, but his eyes are cold. Crazy old lady, he's thinking, crazy old lady.

I move away from him back to where I was standing before, feeling a sudden annoyance at the boy holding a skateboard who's moved into my spot. I go stand close to him. It seems important to go back to exactly where I was. The boy frowns at my closeness and moves away.

When the train comes I make sure I go into a different car than the man I talked to does. The whole way to Surrey I feel stupid, telling myself I better not tell Rodney about this one or I'll get the "senile" lecture again. But it's not my fault the past sticks to me like iron to a magnet, and I can't shake it loose.

I get out at the Surrey Place stop and walk the block to the seniors' centre, where I know the afternoon whist games are about to start. The place is pretty fair sized, in some kind of pentagon shape, with about ten activity rooms, but I hate the way most of the building smells of cigarette smoke because there's some old farts who won't give it up no matter what the by-laws say. It reminds me of Charlie, that stale smell. I head past the receptionist, a doing-her-good-deed teenage volunteer, down the wide central corridor to what they call the Bingo Hall, though it's mostly card games they play there and it's one of the smaller rooms.

Even before I get to the door I'm cursing myself for coming. It was just my missing Olive that brought me here, and what did I think, anyway? That this would bring her back or something?

I get paired up with a hunched-over woman I've played against before. Seems to me she used to have a regular partner, too. We're like the old decks of cards, getting shuffled, getting lost, going missing.

She's nowhere as good as Olive, who always seemed to know when not to waste a trump because I still had an ace. If it had been me that dropped dead into the daffodils Olive would have been a prize catch around these tables.

Well, at least I didn't get paired up with old Margaret, who has these times where she will just stop in the middle of a game and stare at something over your shoulder. Everybody just puts up with it and waits until she's ready to go again, but it makes me so mad. She does it on purpose, to try get attention. Olive used to say Margaret couldn't help it, that they were just little spells that hit her. Spells, my foot.

Shuffle, shuffle, shuffle. The man at our table has such twitchy hands that more cards go flying as he mixes them than go into the deck. We three women keep having to go retrieve them, sometimes from other tables. He's a menace. He reminds me of those martial arts movies where the bad guys throw something that looks like a playing card and it takes someone's head off.

Olive read a novel once, she told me, where someone called old people "the results." The results. That's about the size of it.

"Your play, Gladys," says the woman beside me.

"Yeah, yeah," I say, but she's caught me daydreaming and probably taken great delight in it because I'm always the impatient one who tells the others to get a move on.

The suit is spades, but I don't have any more, and I don't have a trump, either, so I have to sluff, throwing down a four of diamonds, and my partner exclaims, "Why don't you trump?"

I grit my teeth and don't answer. Olive would never have asked something so stupid. Olive's brain would have clicked over in its mathematical way and figured out just what my hand must look like.

When the game is over I don't stay for lunch. Nobody asks me to. At the outside door I run into the old biddy who's like this motion-detector alarm—you get within a few feet of her and off she goes and the only way to shut her up is to walk away—but today she's got somebody else cornered so she ignores me. I trudge back out to the Skytrain station, feeling rotten. I'm not going to come here again. Without Olive it's all been spoiled.

It's raining lightly, like a mist, but I don't put my hood up. I don't mind getting my hair wet. I had a perm a few weeks ago, and one of the reasons for suffering through that is to not worry if it gets wet. I've spent half my life putting curlers in my hair and getting fed up because the slightest dampness would make it go straight as a ruler.

The train is crowded now, and I have to stand. I tell myself it's because I look so young that nobody offers me their seat. The ride seems to be particularly rough, as though the car had a flat tire. I hang onto the post by the door and put on that vacant, straight-ahead stare that the other passengers have. I don't want to see anybody from the lodge. I don't want to see Upstairs Bobby again.

The last time I really saw him was the summer of 1966. It was May, I think. This time of year. I hadn't seen him since I'd made that humiliating pass at him, which was before Basement Bobby died.

He came into the lodge that May and asked if he could see where it had happened.

"You don't want to see that," I said.

"Yeah. I do. I don't know why, but I do."

So I had to take him around to the side of the lodge, to the door that still had a charred look to one of the boards in the jamb. We went down the stairs. It was dark, mouldy-smelling. I'd brought a flashlight, which was lucky because of course Charlie hadn't replaced the dead bulb dangling over the furnace.

It gave me the creeps down there. I shone the light on the bare floor beside the furnace and said, "That's where we found him."

I was the one who'd had to clean everything up. Well, me and Olive. I didn't think it was a good idea to order the others to do it. So Olive and I had gathered up the bits of charred clothes and magazines, the broken beer bottles, some warped plastic things we didn't want to identify, and folded everything up into the burned-out mattress and hauled it all to the dump. Then Olive went back the next day and washed up some of the soot. I didn't think she'd done a great job, but I could hardly complain.

Upstairs Bobby squatted down, put his hand on the bare concrete floor. I shifted my feet impatiently. I didn't know what he wanted to find here.

"The poor kid," he said, his voice husky. "What a life he had."

I wanted to say all kinds of things about how his life wasn't that bad, and how we're responsible for the things we choose, and even how no matter how mad we got we shouldn't try to burn down a hotel full of people. But I had the sense to keep my mouth shut. I didn't know what he might have been told, how it was evil old Gladys's fault because she'd yelled at him about his damned dog.

After a while he got up. I kept the light on the floor so I wouldn't have to look at him. I moved the beam toward the stairs, as big a hint as I could make about how much I'd like to get out of here.

I was starting up the steps when he put his hand on my arm. I turned. There was enough light from the open door for me to see his face. It was red-looking, his eyes all watery.

"I'm sorry about everything, Gladys," he said. He ran his hand quickly across his cheeks.

"You got nothing to be sorry for," I said.

"I do. Not just about the kid."

"What else is there?" I was playing dumb, but my heartbeat clicked up a notch.

"I've been thinking about, you know, what happened between us last time."

"Nothing happened."

He gave a sad little laugh. I was getting a crick in my neck from having to look at him so crookedly from the steps, but my feet seemed unable to pick themselves up and move.

"Maybe that's what I'm sorry about. That, you know, it's not possible."

"Because ... of Charlie," I said, not making it a question, not giving him a chance to disagree.

"Well, yeah."

We stood there for a few more minutes, and then I heard a car door slam in front of the lodge, and I said, "Customers," as though that would be an answer for us, and I guess it was, because I turned and went back up the stairs, and Upstairs Bobby followed, his head down, not speaking, back to the restaurant, where we sat down beside Charlie and ordered lunch.

I tried to find him. Later, after Charlie left me. But he'd quit his job, and the office in Whitehorse had no forwarding address. When I went up that last time to hand the keys over to the new owners, I even stooped so low as to ask Charlotte if she or her family had any idea where he'd gone, and she gave me a look that could have stripped off my skin and said she hoped he was dead.

Dead. I suppose he might be, by now. I loosen my grip on the post by the door of the rattling train car and feel my body get shuddered from side to side. It seems like too much of an effort to hold on, to hold out, against that much shaking.

Gladys

Late May, 2000

I hear a funny noise downstairs. I turn the TV volume down and listen. Faith has the flu and stayed home from work today, but it doesn't seem like her usual thudding and clomping down there, and not her snoring, either, which can sound like a goddamned lawnmower hitting the tall grass.

I go to the top of the stairs, call, "Faith?" but there's no answer. My heart starts to pick up its beat a little, and I grab the spray can of Robber Repel I bought in the States and start slowly down the stairs. I'm not supposed to go down there unless I'm invited, it's one of their big rules, but there are times for rules to be broken.

The suite down here is pretty nice, mostly because Rodney spared no expense to put in the latest and greatest. The bathroom has two sinks and two separate showers, and he had the east wall taken out to add a Jacuzzi, which I don't think they ever use, but there it is. Last year he had new cupboards and a cutting-board island thing installed in the kitchen. The living room furniture is all matching brown and orange, most of it leather, the sofa and chairs facing the huge TV screen that takes up most of one wall. They never invite me down to watch it, but I don't care. I got my own TV upstairs, thank you very much.

The noise, I can hear now, is coming from behind the closed door to the master bedroom, and I lower my Robber Repel because I can tell now what it is. Crying. Faith is crying.

I stand there a moment listening to the pathetic snuffling and then decide there's nothing *I* can do about it, so I start back up the stairs, but I barely take a step when the door opens and Faith comes out. I don't know whether it's because she heard me call or because she was coming out anyway, but she just stands there looking at me with her eyes and nose all red and in need of a wipe. She's got her hair pinned up on top of her head like some kind of limp rooster comb.

"I thought I heard something," I say, showing her the Robber Repel.

"Only me," she says.

The way she's just standing there when she could go back into her room makes me think she might want to talk to me. Talking to me isn't ever anything Faith showed much interest in, but that wasn't my fault. I'm willing if she is. Besides, I'm curious. What's she got to cry about? What's Rodney done now?

I take the last two steps back to the bottom of the stairs. This close I can smell the staleness of her bedclothes and her breath that sure isn't minty-fresh. And she's got the flu, I remind myself, leaning back a bit, trying not to breathe the air she's wheezing out.

"Everything okay?" I say casually.

She takes a deep sniff, puts her hand up to her nose and rubs at it. I'm relieved to see the hand contains a tissue.

"I've just been ... missing Mom."

"Oh." That catches me off guard.

"It's like it just happened yesterday."

I shrug, running my finger along the door jamb and raking up some ancient cobwebs. Faith never cared much about a clean house. Not like Olive.

"It'll take a while," I say. I'm no good at this.

"I was a disappointment to her."

"She never said so to me."

"Well, she wouldn't, would she?" She makes it sound as though Olive would never in a million years have told me what she really thought. I have to bite my tongue from making some sarcastic answer.

I shrug again, look at the cobweb I've rolled into a tiny ball between my fingers.

"She wanted grandchildren."

Well, there are a lot of answers I could make to that. Such as, Olive sure didn't want the *first* grandchild, although when it died she cried and carried on like it was the end of the world. Such as, it wasn't just Olive you've cheated out of grandchildren, and if you stopped thinking only about yourself for a minute you might remember that. Such as, well, not being able to get pregnant is one thing you can't blame Rodney for. He had the tests, and he's fine.

But I don't say any of those things. I take the high road, as my mother used to say. She's been dead for twenty years. She was a nasty old thing—and a nasty young thing, too, for that matter—but even so I suppose I miss her. It doesn't seem fair, to miss the mothers who didn't love us the same way we miss the mothers who did, but there you are.

"Olive was a good person," I say, and I feel pleased to have found those words, because they aren't sarcastic and they don't lie.

"She had such high hopes for me. She worked so hard to save money for me. She made sure my dad kept me in his will. All so that I could have my chance, could go to university. And I never even finished high school."

"University. Huh. It's not what it's cracked up to be. All that money and studying and you don't get a good job out of it these days, anyway."

"If I'd gone I'd have done all right. I could have been a teacher. Or a doctor."

"Doctor!" I give a snort. "I doubt it."

Faith blows her nose into the tissue. I turn my head so I don't have to see it or be in the line of anything that misses.

"I kept in touch with some of the girls who waitressed at the lodge. Louise became a doctor. She said I could do it, too."

This is all news to me. "What do you mean, you kept in touch?"

"I asked them to write to me, and they were real nice about it, most of them, considering I was just this dumb kid. Some of them kept in touch for years. Ellen still sends me a Christmas card."

"Ellen. Louise." The names are only vaguely familiar. "Who

else did you write to?" I try not too sound too interested.

"Patty. She was the one who came to the lodge a few years later with her husband."

"If you say so." I can remember Patty, a snippy little thing, but if she came by the lodge with a husband later I don't remember that. Of course, she might not have wanted to see me. Which doesn't exactly hurt my feelings.

"And Corrine. And Margaret. And Elke."

"Corrine. Margaret. And who?"

"Elke."

I shuffle through my memory, but I can't dredge up anybody by that name. "*Elk*-ee?"

"You and Charlie called her the deer."

That still doesn't help. I had names for quite a few of the girls. I shake my head.

"She was there with Kendy."

It feels like I've waded out and suddenly the land's dropped away and there's only water under my feet.

"Oh, yes," I say. "Maybe I do. Elk-ee." My chest has become tight with dread

"And, let's see, Ruth. She went into engineering, which was really unusual for a girl—"

"And Kendy? Did she write to you?"

Faith gives me an odd look, and I know I must have sounded eager, anxious.

"I remember her," I add, "because she had such pretty hair." Will Faith buy that? I watch her out of the corner of my eye.

"Yeah," she says. "I remember. But she never wrote to me."

"Anyway," I say, relieved, nudging the conversation back to shore, "you want to go to university so bad, you can still go. Who's stopping you?" If I hadn't wanted to change the subject so much, I'd have thought twice about what I was saying.

Faith gives a sniffly kind of laugh. "Oh, sure. At my age."

And then she starts to cry again.

Oh, Jeez. I don't know how to comfort people. My parents weren't big in the comforting department. "Get over it," was about as much sympathy as they ever gave me. I never in my whole life gave someone a hug unless it had to do with sex. But I look at Faith with her face going all red and watery again and I think, well, it must be what she expects, a hug, like the people on my soaps get when they cry.

I go over to her, clumsily put my arms around her, but not that tightly because I remember she still has the flu. "There, there," I say.

I'm feeling rather proud of myself, learning to do this at my age, but Faith has gone stiff as a board and she looks up at me with an expression I know immediately is fear.

I gave her a hug and said "There, there," and I scared her! She pulls away from me at the same time as I back away myself.

I drop the bit of cobweb I'm still rolling between my fingers and turn abruptly and head up the stairs. I don't know whether I want her to say something or not, but she doesn't.

Fear. I'm getting angry now, slamming the kitchen tap on and washing my hands with soap. *Fear.* I grind my hands into each other, as though there's something between them I'd like to squash, but I don't know what it is.

⚌

This is the third time I've done this jigsaw puzzle. It's at least two feet square, and not easy, with small pieces and lots of sky and red-roofed Italian houses. Rodney got it for me for Christmas, and I thought it was a pretty stupid present, especially when he told me it was something one of the secretaries at work had brought in to give away because her kids were too young for it. A secondhand Christmas present, I'd thought, how nice.

So when I found myself spending hours every day on it I couldn't very well tell him I was sort of enjoying it, and when I finished it I took it apart and started over, to make him think, on those rare times he came into the second bedroom upstairs, that I'd never really gotten going on it. One of these days I'm going to have to break down and go buy myself another one, but I can do this one a few more times. Doing it over again makes me feel like I'm getting better at something, even if it is completely useless.

I fit another piece of sky into the left corner, yawn, stretch. That stiffness in my shoulders is getting worse. I suppose I'll have to go to the chiropractor again, even though I hate the way he folds my arms up and then more or less jumps on me. I don't know if it does any good. I just go because my regular doctor is an idiot. The last time I went to see him I was worried about this little pointy growth on my arm, and he said, oh, that was just a tag and old people get them.

"A tag?" I said. "What do you mean? Like a name tag?"

He laughed. "Yup. When they grow long enough you write your name on them so if you drop dead in the mall they can identify you." He laughed some more.

Like I said: an idiot.

It's early afternoon. Sometimes I have a nap at this time, but I don't like to give in to it, even when it's hot like today. Last summer I wanted to get one of those air conditioning units you stick into the window, but Rodney said the house didn't have the right wiring. I don't know whether to believe him or not. Of course, it's nice and cool down there in the basement.

I lean back in the big armchair I had moved here from the living room when I got the new recliner, and close my eyes. I know I'm going to doze off, but if I stay in the chair it doesn't feel like a real nap, not one of those lazy siesta-type things people my age are supposed to enjoy.

There's water. There's always water. I know this, that I've been here before and that there's always water. Someone is shouting. At first I think he's saying, "Fire!" but then the words blur. I strain to hear. The water laps at my feet. I'm barefoot, and it's like a tide starting to come in, my legs are getting wet. The man shouting is running along the other side of the lake. I squint and shade my eyes against the westerly sun, try to see who it is, to hear the words. It's not a man. It's a woman, running. It's Kendy.

I jerk awake. My hands fly to my feet, to brush away the burning water.

God. What a dream. I get up, slowly, shaking my head to get rid of the fragments. I pick up a piece of the jigsaw, a piece of sky, and try to fit it in, but my hand has an odd tremor and I let the piece drop. I go to the window with its view out into the back yard of the big arbutus tree with its flaking bark that everyone seems to admire but that I think is just messy, and I lean my forehead against the glass. My breath makes a faint fog on the pane. It clears at exactly the moment when I exhale again.

Kendy. Why can't I forget about that damned girl? There were dozens of them at the lodge over the years, some worse than others, and they've all mixed up together in my head into some mushy notion of "waitress." But I can't get Kendy into that place. No matter how hard I try. I remember everything.

Once, a year or so ago, when Olive and I were arguing about some damned thing to do with the old days, how I'd never give her enough laundry soap or something just as stupid, she sighed and said maybe we should heed the lesson of Lot's wife, that there are things in the past we shouldn't turn around and look at or they would paralyze us.

I don't want to turn around and look at Kendy. She just comes to me. I can't help it.

It was her second last day. She was on the evening shift.

I've told myself so often that I didn't know what was going to happen, but I did. Of course I did. I wasn't spelling it out to myself, but when I saw the clues I couldn't help but add them up. I guess I told myself that if it wasn't anything I was doing myself, that if someone else did it, it couldn't be my fault.

The first hint I had was when I found my bottle of sleeping pills on the middle shelf of the bathroom. I always put them on the bottom shelf. I remember standing there, holding the bottle, frowning. When I counted the pills I knew I hadn't just put the bottle on the wrong shelf. I'd kept track of how many pills I'd need to get me through to the end of summer, and there were half a dozen missing. I felt a slow chill go along my spine.

But I didn't know what his plan was, not really, not until the end of Kendy's shift. Charlie had gone into the kitchen and was trying to make small talk with Laura, who was basically ignoring him. His going into the kitchen was unusual, but I didn't think anything of it. I was keeping my eye on Kendy as she added up the day's receipts and tried to get the till to balance.

Charlie came out of the kitchen with three glasses of milk, balancing two in the palm of his left hand and holding the other in his right. He handed that one to Kendy. He gave one to me, took a swallow from the third.

"From Laura," he said. "Sweet dreams."

I think that was the moment I understood. I've gone over and over it in my mind, and I know that I had the urge to reach over and take Kendy's glass from her. So I must have known.

But I let her drink it, slowly, Charlie watching her with something in his face I couldn't look at.

"I'll finish the till," I said to Kendy. "Go to bed."

Why did I say that? Who was I trying to help?

Kendy looked surprised and said, "Oh, okay. Thanks."

She took her apron off, put on her jacket and headed off to the cabin. Laura went out to the front parking lot with her, as she'd taken to doing, and watched her until she was out of sight. With Charlie in the restaurant she must have figured there was no particular danger, but I suppose she thought her distrust of him would be too obvious if she didn't follow the routine.

Laura came back inside, and we finished up at the till and closed the restaurant. It had been so slow we could almost have closed up in the afternoon. But it had given me the opportunity to make Kendy wash the walls, although Laura was right in saying there wasn't much point if the lodge was closing for the winter in a week, anyway. I didn't say that making Kendy wash the walls wasn't just about clean walls.

When we went back to our apartment, Charlie was full of energy, excited. I could smell it on him. He paced around the living room, rubbing his hands up and down his pants.

"I don't know what's wrong with me," he said. "I just feel so restless."

"Go for a walk."

He mustn't have believed his luck, hearing me say just what he wanted to hear. And, oh, I knew. By then I had no excuse.

I watched him go. I remember quite clearly how I looked at the back of his head and thought his ears stuck out more than they used to, like two big doorknobs.

I lay down on the bed, not taking my clothes off, and stared up at the ceiling, my eyes tracing around and around the watermarks in the middle of it. I tried to think about next summer, about repainting the ceiling, the walls. Light green, I thought: I'd seen a show home in Vancouver with light green walls.

I suppose I lay there for almost half an hour. Too long. Long enough. Then I got up, put on my jacket, and went outside. It was a clear night, the moon almost full, the stars brilliant.

A couple of times when I was a girl I would lie in the front yard on nights like that and look up. Once my dad came out of the house, drunk, and stumbled over me before I could get up and out of his way, and he cursed and gave me kick to the thigh that left a bruise the size and shape of his boot.

Was that something I remembered that evening, or only now? Maybe I'm trying to stick in one of those oh-poor-me memories like they sometimes do on TV shows when they want you to feel sorry for somebody bad.

With the moon out it was bright enough that I didn't need a flashlight to find my way down the path to the cabin. I was halfway there when something rustled in the bushes beside me and then flew up. My heart just about flew up there with it. I was never any good at the outdoors, even in the daylight. Whatever it was flapped away into the dark.

I could see the light now from the lamp in the cabin.

I was close now, just a few more yards. I moved slowly, carefully, putting my feet down toes-first, wincing when I stepped on a twig or dead leaf.

I went around to the door. It was open about half a foot, more than I needed it to be to see in.

The first thing I noticed was that the rectangle of wood nailed onto the jamb inside was lined up flush to the frame and that there was about a quarter inch of nail visible. It didn't take a genius to see that it would have been easy to flick something—a knife, a twig, a piece of cardboard—into the crack and push the bar open. I supposed he'd come down this afternoon sometime and let himself in with our key and loosened the nail.

He was standing there completely naked. Just standing there beside the bed. His big penis up and pointing at Kendy.

She was lying on her back on the bed. Her uniform buttons had all been undone and the uniform peeled back to the sides. Her right arm had been pulled out of the sleeve, by the look of it to make it possible for her bra to be unhooked and pulled off that shoulder. It was wadded up somewhere in her left armpit. Her panties were off, lying on the floor beside her shoes.

He'd arranged her like that, I knew. I could feel my nails press themselves into the wood of the door frame. I shoved the knuckles of my other hand into my mouth to stop myself from crying out.

I couldn't tear my eyes from Kendy on the bed. I thought she was beautiful. I have to admit that to myself. I have to admit that, no matter what revulsions I felt, I looked at her and thought she was beautiful: that long, slim, white body with the high breasts and nipples that he might have sucked into the shape they were in, the pubic hair the same colour as the red-gold hair spread out on the pillow.

She moved a little, bending one leg up and turning her head. A moan, a sigh, a word, I don't know what, came from her mouth. She licked her lips several times, grimacing, like there was a taste in her mouth she was trying to get rid of. The arm that was out of its sleeve lifted up and across her body, as if she might be trying to turn herself over onto her side, to face the wall.

And Charlie jumped up onto the bed, quicker than I thought he'd have been able to with his erection to unbalance him, and straddled her, to stop her from turning. He laughed.

"No, no," he said.

His weight seemed to bring her more to consciousness, and she moved feebly under him, her arms and legs lifting and then falling like they were too heavy to be raised. She was saying something, her voice thick and slurred, and trying to sit up.

"Don't, Charlie," she said. "Don't. Please."

I pressed my fist hard against my teeth. Don't, Charlie.

But I only stood there and watched. I watched him take his hand and line his penis up and push and push, grunting, until it was inside her. She was crying, trying to twist herself away, but she couldn't stop him.

I was running back, stumbling, scraping my elbow into a tree, falling once, heavily, as I tripped on a root, running as though I were terrified of something chasing me, looking around to see what it was, where it was.

When I got back to the lodge and into the apartment I ripped my clothes off and got into bed. I pulled the blanket up to my chin and lay there on my back in the dark, listening to my heart hammering away, long past the time it should have slowed back to normal. Something skittered on the roof, and I stared up at the ceiling as though my staring could make me both see it and make it go away.

Serves her right. She was asking for it. She wasn't some pure little virgin. Serves her right.

"Serves her right." I was saying it out loud, over and over.

Finally I heard Charlie come in. I turned to face the wall as he got undressed and crawled in beside me. It was only a few minutes before I heard his breathing deepen into snores. I lay there for another half hour before I got up and took one of the few remaining sleeping pills.

⊗

The next morning I found Charlie had taken the truck and gone off to Whitehorse, leaving me a note that said he was going to see about the insurance stuff and might have to stay overnight. It was all an excuse, I knew that. We were settling the insurance just fine through the mail, and he didn't know a damned thing about it, anyway. I could just see him driving in tomorrow half an hour after the bus had left, pretending to be sorry he'd missed saying goodbye to Kendy.

I'd done the paperwork several days ago for Kendy's cheque, for two hundred and seventy-five dollars, exactly what I owed her and what I supposed she was expecting because she'd have found out what the other waitress got. What did Faith say I called her? The deer? I don't have much memory of her. She wasn't a memorable sort of person.

So now I started all over. When I was finished, I cut up Kendy's cheque and wrote another one for four hundred and fifty. It damned near killed me. Maybe it was a good thing Charlie was away. If he'd walked in just then I'd have used the scissors to cut off what he used for a brain. All my careful accounting all summer wasted.

I decided that if Kendy asked why her pay was more than the other girl's I'd say something about it being a bonus because she was such a good worker. It would make me puke, having to say that, but I wanted this over and done with.

I began to wonder if Kendy would come in at all for her afternoon shift, since she didn't show up to have any lunch. I was just thinking about asking Maud to stay on for a few more hours and then closing up early since business was so slow, when Kendy showed up.

Her face had a kind of dead, whitish look to it, like someone who'd forgotten to wash off all her cold cream. It wasn't hard to see something had happened to her. Laura stared at her and asked her a question, but Kendy just shook her head. I stayed out of her way, but I kept my eye on her. After she'd been on shift for an hour or so she started to look a bit less like a zombie, but not much.

I knew that if I avoided her until the last minute she'd think something was odd, so I let her bring me my supper and said, trying to sound hearty, which was a stretch at the best of times, "So. Last day, eh? You all packed up?"

"Pretty well."

"We can close up early tonight. Ten o'clock, maybe, unless we get some late overnighters. No point staying open when the place is empty."

"Whatever you say."

I was glad she didn't thank me. I'd never had many dealings with guilt, and I didn't want to get chummy with it. I'd pay her and give her a piece of jewellery and that would be the end of it. I'd never see her again.

I was so anxious to get it over with that I called her up to the till at nine-thirty and handed her the cheque and the tax receipt stapled to it.

"Congratulations," I said. "You made it through the summer."

She reached for the cheque, slowly, took it. When she looked at the amount her hand went still in the air. The paper hung halfway between us, like something neither of us wanted, like something smelly she'd picked up off the kitchen floor.

I reached under the counter, pulled out the tray of jade jewellery. "And I always let the girls choose a piece of jewellery to take. Here." I held the tray out to her.

All day she'd been avoiding looking at me, but now her eyes were on me so intensely I felt I almost needed to reach up and brush her gaze away. I had to grit my teeth to look right at her. When she didn't reach for any jewellery I set the tray down on the counter.

"Okay, you don't want any, that's fine with me," I said, making my voice sound cranky and impatient, the way I thought she'd expect.

"You know, don't you?" she said.

"Know what?" I looked her right in the eye. "What are you talking about?"

"You know what he did."

"What who did?"

"You know." She lowered the hand holding the cheque, and she clenched her fingers into a fist. I could see the cheque and the receipt crumpling.

I nodded down at them. "You wreck those you're not getting other ones."

"Maybe it was your idea."

"I don't know what you're talking about."

"You bitch. You vicious, ugly bitch."

For once I didn't know what I should say, and maybe I did the best thing by saying nothing. Kendy wrenched the apron from her waist and threw it on the floor, the order pad hooked to the band coming free and skidding away into the kitchen. I kept my eye on the cheque, to see if she'd toss it on the floor, too, but she shoved it into her pocket. I was hoping she'd throw it away, but maybe then I would have worried about what else she might do down the road. This way, we were done. She'd been paid.

She grabbed her jacket and walked out.

Laura came out of the kitchen holding the order pad. "Is she all right?" she asked.

I shrugged. "Who knows?"

Laura set the pad on the counter and followed Kendy outside. I could see her stand there looking down the path until long past the time Kendy would have safely reached the cabin.

⚙

I must have been dozing. The phone has jarred me awake, and I shuffle off to the living room to get it. My back is stiff, and my left knee aches so much I have to limp. The worst of all this getting-old stuff is remembering the body I used to have that never hurt.

It's Faith. "I'll be late. There was a meeting that went overtime so I won't be home until after six."

I remember how yesterday I went down to her bedroom when she was crying and how I tried to put my arms around her and how she pulled away.

"So you'll be late. Why should I care?"

There's silence for a moment, and then she sighs, "I just thought I'd let you know."

"Okay. You let me know. Goodbye."

Yesterday after she pulled away from me I thought the look on her face was fear. But now I think it was something else. Revulsion.

Maybe I'm still just thinking of Kendy.
I don't know any more.

Elke

Early June, 2000

Dear David,
    I'm so sorry, but your father and I think it best, since
we sent you a thousand dollars just last month, that we
not send more so soon. . . .

                                      Mom

I keep looking at the woman sitting across from me. There's something familiar about her.

She is probably an adult student I had years ago; there were so many, and it shouldn't surprise me not to remember them all, but this face seems to nag at my memory in a different way. It might be a face I knew when it was much younger. It has a hard-edged rectangular shape, although saggy with age at the bottom, its wrinkles almost all running vertically. The woman must be in her seventies. She sits with a slight osteoporotic hunch, but her body seems lean and wiry. She has short, permed hair dyed an ill-advised black, which makes the white at the roots more noticeable.

Her eyes meet mine, flatly, and I look quickly away. There was nothing of recognition on her face.

Well, what does it matter if I have met her once upon a time or not? I turn my eyes to the map of the Skytrain route near the top of the train car, as though I need to remind myself how many stops there are until mine in Burnaby.

The train slows, grating on the track, for its stop at Broadway, and people stand and shuffle to the door across from me. The woman I've been watching gets to her feet, easily, not having to lean forward. She's in better shape than I am. She takes hold of the pole by the door, and then nudges her foot, almost a kick but not quite, against the shoe of a woman about my age.

"Faith," she says. "Our stop."

Faith.

The instant my eyes flick to the seated woman I recognize her. Olive. She is Faith grown up into Olive. My hand reaches up to press at my chest where my heart has started a mad pounding, because I know now, even before my eyes lift to the standing woman, who she is.

Gladys Pratt.

I would have known her immediately, I think, if the wart on her cheek were still there. I can see the small scar now where it has been removed.

The train has stopped. The doors open. Olive—no, it's *Faith*, little *Faith*—has gotten to her feet and follows Mrs. Pratt out.

And, not thinking about it, my body behaving without orders from my brain, I leap up, snatch my briefcase from under the seat and bolt through the door a few seconds before it closes.

The two women are heading along the platform toward the stairs, and I walk fast, almost running, to get close behind them.

I am almost unable to breathe from the rush of memory. *Her shouting, loud and humiliating: not good enough, not good enough, not good enough. Her slamming me against the racks in the cold room, threatening me with worse. Her handing me, finally, a paycheque so small it barely covered my travel—*

Another train is coming. I can't see it but I can hear the jostling of air, the rattle of the rails. Mrs. Pratt is walking along only two feet from the edge. I have the terrible urge to push, to push her onto the rails. I could pretend I stumbled—

The train whooshes up alongside me. It hasn't run over a body. Mrs. Pratt is heading down the stairs.

I follow, keeping a greater distance between us now in case I have another frightening urge, perhaps to shove her into the traffic or batter her unconscious with my briefcase. I make myself smile, as though these are amusing fantasies, but the truth is that I am shaken by the ferocity of my feelings on the train platform. I wanted to do it. I wanted to hurl her onto the tracks. It felt as though something big and black had surged up and out of me, something that had been gaining speed for years.

They have gone to wait at the bus stop on Broadway. I go and stand close beside them, still not sure of what I am intending.

When they get on the #10 westbound bus I get on, too, right behind them, fumbling for change because I do not, like most of the others at this stop, have a transfer to show the driver. I am so close to Mrs. Pratt her frizzy hair touches my forehead. If I dared, if no one were watching, I could spit on her. I can feel the saliva building up in my mouth, and I swallow it quickly back.

Everything I am doing, thinking, seems new to me, coming from some tenebrous place I don't recognize. I am a retired university professor and a psychologist. My husband is a lawyer. I am not a person who thinks about shoving people in front of trains or spitting on them in buses. A part of my brain has gone quite clinical, the way it does with the few clients I still see, and it steeples its metaphorical fingers and says, Hmm, interesting; I wonder what she will do next.

What I do next is sit down on the seat behind Mrs. Pratt and Faith. Across from me the folding centre doors mutter shut. The bus starts up. I feel as though I have boarded a flight with an unknown destination. My only luggage is my briefcase holding some academic journals, including one carrying the Toronto interview with the psychoanalyst Julia Kristeva in which she speaks of her concept of *étrangeté*, of how we all carry within us an essential strangeness. The journal seems an inadvertently appropriate thing to have packed, I think, as I hug the briefcase to my chest and lean forward, willing the two women to speak. I don't think they've said one word since they left the train.

At last, Mrs. Pratt says something. "Maybe we should go to the other Sears."

Faith murmurs something I can't hear.

"Of *course* we have to keep looking," Mrs. Pratt says. "Rodney doesn't like any other brand."

Rodney. There is a vague familiarity to the name, but I can't place it.

"I don't know why he can't buy his own," Faith says, in a mumbly small voice that bears little resemblance to that of her chirpy childhood self nor to that of her mother.

"He's *busy*, for God's sake. When does he have the time?"

Faith murmurs something again, and Mrs. Pratt answers sharply, "Because Rodney's job is important, that's why."

And then I remember. Rodney is her son. The cooks would talk about what an uncontrollable child he was and how glad they were he hadn't come up that year.

Faith has said something else I couldn't hear, and Mrs. Pratt snaps, "Well, it's not up to me, either. I'm not his wife."

Wife. Dear Lord. Faith must be Rodney's wife. I press my fingers over my mouth to stop my exclamation of surprise, of dismay. Faith who had such ambition, who had wanted so much to go to university, to have a life of her own: here she is chained forever to the Pratts. The only thing worse than working for Mrs. Pratt would be having her for a mother-in-law.

"... for himself," Faith is saying.

"I used to buy all Charlie's clothes. If I did it, you can."

Charlie. Another wave of ugly memory washes over me. I think of him terrifying me in the cabin that night, the way he would sidle up against me in the restaurant.

Used to, Mrs. Pratt said. Does that mean he's dead? I hope so. If I ran into him on a train platform he might not make it to the stairs.

They don't say anything else that I can hear, and, like most of the other people on the bus, they begin watching a man who has just gotten on and who is wearing a jacket that looks like a cut-off top of a bathrobe. He is having an angry and wild-eyed argument with himself, his hands gesturing viciously at the air. He is a re-assurance to us, perhaps. Here is what crazy is, and it's not us, not yet.

Two stops later Mrs. Pratt and Faith get up and shuffle to the folding door in the middle of the bus. I get up, too, with no plan except, I suppose, to keep following them. But I know that I will have to be careful now, that I won't be able to walk close enough behind them to eavesdrop.

The door rattles open, and we get out.

The day started out cloudy and cold, but the sun is blazing now. This is the Kitsilano area, where a lot of students live, and we're the only ones on the streets wearing coats. I take mine off, drape it over my arm, but my suit jacket still makes me look over-dressed, professorial, the briefcase out of place, too, among the nylon backpacks. Faith has on a yellow, belted cloth coat over a blue dress that catches her unflatteringly at mid-calf, and Mrs. Pratt is wearing a green jacket with a hood. One of the drawstrings has wrapped and knotted itself around the hood so that it looks like a small strangled head on the back of her neck. I can't seem to take my eyes off it.

We walk for about three blocks, me close enough, I hope, to hear anything Mrs. Pratt has to say in that loud and domineering voice that has changed not one bit from what I remember. If they turn around they might, at most, recognize me from the train, but I won't look particularly suspicious.

If someone were to ask me what I am doing, I don't know what I would answer. I'm following them, I might say, the kind of response which, if received from a client, I would find annoying, though I would then ask patiently, but why are you following them? I don't know, I would have to answer now. I do know there is a certain existential excitement to this, some pleasure. I suppose I will analyze that feeling later.

Faith stops suddenly, then bends down to take off one of her pumps and shake a pebble from it. I almost run into her before I can stop, too, pretend to look for something in my jacket pocket. Mrs. Pratt turns around to see why Faith is lagging. I catch my breath, rummage more earnestly in my pocket, but they are both already walking on. I walk on behind them. When does following someone become pathological, become stalking? Is it a question of motive, of intent? Of frequency?

Abruptly, they head down the walk of a large, well-kept, older, two-storey house with a veranda on the front. I don't know what I was expecting, but the house startles me with its agreeableness, its yard full of rhododendron bushes and holly trees. It is the kind of house I might like to live in, and do, in fact.

I want to follow them up the walk, into the house, but of course I can't. I stop, fumble with my jacket while I note the house number, and keep walking. *Étrangeté*, my heels click out the syllables on the sidewalk: *étrangeté, étrangeté*. I go to the end of the block, then come back, turning my head toward the house only as any casual passerby might.

❈

I am supposed to be editing an article we have accepted for *The Northwestern Journal of Psychology*. I agreed to sit on the board before I realized it was not exactly the honour it seemed. The other editors are still full-time professors, so it falls to me, here at home, to do most of the work. You have the *time* now, they say ingenuously, as though, once retired, one is obliged to work. Perhaps they simply remember me as I was at the beginning of my teaching career, a dogged sessional, willing to do anything to assure them motherhood and a doctorate degree were not incompatible, anything to join the runners on the tenure track.

I can't concentrate. The mild tinnitus in my right ear, which I can usually tune out easily, flicks at my brain with small, distracting chirps.

I lean back, fix my eyes on the wall opposite me, on the poster-size reproduction of Caspar David Friedrich's *The Wanderer Above the Mists*. My husband, Andrew Campion, gave it to me a year ago, saying it seemed appropriate for a psychologist's office, and though I didn't like it at first I do now.

In the painting a man, clothed in black, his back to the viewer, looks from a high, rough crag down on a rocky, mist-draped landscape. He seems to stand on the edge of reality, an observer with his feet planted in his world but with his gaze beyond and above it. There is much ambiguity, both rootedness and alienation. I have sometimes found the picture helpful in centring my own thoughts: because I can see only the back of the man's head I am free to create his expression, which I variously imagine as either thoughtful and meditative or lonely and alienated. I have tried to imagine him smiling and happy but have never quite managed it.

The picture does nothing now to help me compose my thoughts, which keep slithering away from the work on my desk. Aside from this article there are ten others the journal couriered over yesterday, with a note from Ted, the editor-in-chief, entreating me to get them read and back to him in a few days. Each submission is supposed to have at least three readers, but judging from how seldom I have received one already evaluated I suspect I am usually the sole reader. I also suspect Ted simply passes my comments on as his when he sends an acceptance or rejection. I enjoy this work, unpaid and professionally unprofitable though it is, but just because I am past the days of doing something because it will advance my career doesn't mean I don't still feel an academic's intellectual territoriality. I must talk to Ted about this, someday. Really I must. It is hard when I am no longer physically in the department, in the loop, even though the loop often felt like a noose.

I get up and pour myself a brandy and pace around the house, picking up papers and books and carrying them around for a while, then setting them back down in the same place. I have a craving for, of all things, a cigarette, although I haven't smoked for twenty years and then not enthusiastically. I open the sliding door onto the large back deck and sit down on one of the vinyl-padded chairs to let the sun fall on my face. The deck is cleverly angled to be completely private. It faces the ravine behind the house, and it is the thing I like most about living here, that thickly wooded slope whose trees are antennae for the murmur of summer winds, tuning out the distant fuss of traffic and making me forget sometimes that I am in the middle of a city. An echelon of geese flies overhead, calling encouragement to the leader.

I close my eyes, try to focus on the smell of the heliotrope in the planter box beside me, on the lucid complexity of a robin's song from the pear tree.

But my thoughts seem unable to pull themselves away from those four months so long ago. I am aware of the tricks of memory, the way they can unexpectedly open floodgates, but I am not used to it happening to me. And it is not as though I have repressed knowledge of those unpleasant days. I have, over the years, thought about them, though rarely. I left. I went to university. I graduated. I married. I had children. I taught. I got on with my life. In the mind's constant triage, choosing between what to remember and what to forget, I'd have thought those months in the Yukon would have mostly been selected out.

So this rush of pure, vengeful hatred I felt for Mrs. Pratt, and feel again this very moment, is a disquieting surprise. But I don't try to suppress it. It is interesting, the intensity of it.

I wanted to hurt her.

I have, apparently, not forgotten nor forgiven.

I should probably talk to someone about it.

There is Andrew, of course, but he is away in Europe for a month, and, besides, he is busy; he is a lawyer. Overall, we have had a happy enough marriage, although when the children left I suppose we felt, as many couples do, the removal of that coercive bond, trusting now only friendship and habit to keep us together. Even friendship and habit have been strained for the last few years, however. I have had to be very patient with Andrew, careful not to impose my problems upon him. No, I will not tell him about what happened.

Then there are the children: my oldest, David, is twenty-five, in Portugal now, travelling or perhaps studying; I am not certain. He is poor at keeping in touch, and the occasional e-mail is usually to ask for money. He nurses some old grudge against his father, some disagreement which neither of them has fully explained to me. Since I am the only parent he communicates with at all, I have tried to be consistently supportive, but it has not been easy. Sean is my other child, married and successful and living in Toronto, an architect. Neither of the boys are the sort of people I could talk to about what I am feeling. They are not yet of the age, for one thing, to have discovered that life is not linear, that memory lays snares in the brain to step into years later.

Sean's wife, Gail, I had hoped would become the kind of daughterly friend with whom I might share such confidences, but Gail has no time for anything in her life except her work. I admire her for her ambitions but wish guiltily she had fewer of them. I think for a moment of Faith, who has apparently become for Mrs. Pratt the most obedient of daughters-in-law, and I am annoyed to find myself nudged by envy.

If it's a counsellor I want, there is Jane, at the university, who is also more or less my closest friend, and we have in the past exchanged casual therapy sessions; but I would feel awkward telling her something like this. We became friends rather late in our careers, and our early lives, for some reason, were rarely mentioned. I may have alluded to my difficulties with my father—who resisted so strenuously my going to university that he made my first years there unnecessarily miserable and impoverished—but usually what Jane and I talk about are ideas and academic intrigues, and I do not want her sharp, interrogative mind probing at an old injury whose depth and density I may not understand myself.

If I want a more objective therapist, there is Ben, Jane's office mate, who actually specializes in anger theory and anger management. He is a fervent adherent of the forgiveness school, and with his clients uses flash cards that say things like "Choose to let go" and "Anger mostly hurts yourself" and "Take another look" and "Try empathy."

Anger management: is that what I want? For that matter, is forgiving what I want?

The person I'd really like to talk to is Kendy.

The thought of her fills me with such sudden longing and affection that I feel a tightening in my throat. I take a big mouthful of brandy to swallow it away. Kendy is as vivid in my mind as if we had seen each other only yesterday. I suppose I have idealized her, but I do think I have never met anyone since with whom I got along so well. And if she hadn't intervened that night with Charlie— I shudder.

When I came to the university—leaving my mother crying and cupping her hand to her cheek in that painful gesture I can never forget, hearing as I climbed the bus steps my father's words which I can also never forget: "If you go, don't come back"—one of the first things I did was try to find Kendy. She'd told me she was staying off-campus in a house she had rented with several friends, so as soon as I settled into the residence I called the number she'd given me. But the girl who answered the phone said that, although Kendy had indeed moved in with them, she'd suddenly decided to drop out of university and move out.

"Drop out of university!" I exclaimed. "But ... she can't! She's so smart."

"Yeah, well."

"Do you know where she is, where I can find her?"

"I suppose she might have moved back home. Or in with Lance. I think he was her boyfriend."

"Lance. Do you know his last name?"

"No, I don't." The girl was impatient, I could tell, wanting to get back to the party going on in the background.

"Well, her parents, then. Do you have their address?"

"Look. I hardly even know her. She was here, she moved out, now Ingrid has her room. I gotta go."

If her attitude seemed brusque and dismissive to me it was also an attitude I would assume soon myself, in that survivalist way of university students confronted with overwhelming change. Even today, perhaps especially today, I can appreciate such pragmatic existentialism. She was here, she moved out, now Ingrid has her room.

I did make some further effort to find Kendy, even though I barely knew how to use a phone or phone book. I had no idea, for example, that in the yellow pages at the back I could have looked under Chartered Accountants and perhaps found her father listed. I phoned the first five Kennedys in the white pages, but when a woman told me angrily to stop wasting her time I gave up. Besides, I remembered what Kendy had said about us drifting apart once we got to the city, about how we would only remind each other of an unpleasant time in our lives. She knew where I was staying. She could have called me. She mustn't have wanted to.

I pick up the phone book now and look up "Kennedy." There are several pages of listings. And I can't remember her real first name. Or she might have a married name. Or have moved away.

She's gone. I lost her thirty-five years ago.

I finish my brandy and go back inside. My small black-faced and blue-eyed Siamese, who sped up the tree beside where I was sitting and leapt onto the deck, now gallops inside a few seconds before the sliding door clicks shut. Of course he will want out again in five minutes.

I go back to my study, which is really just one of the four upstairs bedrooms. Andrew uses one as his home office as well, though he was gracious enough to give me the bigger one, with the large window looking out at the ravine; but that was only sensible, since my department office had been minuscule and I also needed a place to see my clients. Patients, they used to be called, but now they are clients. I still see some, the few who seem impervious to my suggestions they move on. Their neuroses are mild, their finances comfortable. We have a gently mutual need, perhaps.

I pick up a pencil, make myself start to read the article I'm supposed to be editing. The magazine will be publishing it in the fall issue: "The Semiotics of Rejection Signaling," by someone from Berkeley called Dr. J. Samuels. This article at least is interesting; I've had to deal with far too many I thought more suitable to *The Journal of Irreproducible Results.*

> While much has been written about young women's non-verbal behaviours to signal *interest* in males, it is also the case that nonverbal methods are used to signal *disinterest*, to end a courtship behaviour.
>
> The most common of these signals of disinterest from women involves use of the *gaze.*[1]

Ah, the footnote, that sly, adventitious growth on academic discourse. They're like little ulcers, Ted complained once, worrying about word count. I replied that I'd once heard a doctor refer to such swellings as "proud flesh," and Ted gave me a lewd look and I realized, blushing, where the expression must have originated. Still—proud flesh: it was an apt description of the footnote. I ignore this one and read on.

Avoidance of eye contact was frequently observed. Women did not return the gaze of the man but made eye contact with other people or looked elsewhere in the room. Sometimes the woman would turn her head pointedly away from the man as he was speaking to her. There was also the ceiling gaze, in which the woman looked upward for a prolonged period, and the hair gaze, in which the woman pulled her hair across her face and stared at the ends.

Some women, on the other hand, were observed to stare directly at the man, but with pronounced frowns, for a long time, until the man looked away. In other ...

I change the last "the man" to "he," but it seems a feeble effort. I sigh, lean back, look at *The Wanderer Above the Mists*. The viewpoint, I realize for the first time, is not that of a painter with his feet on the ground but from a point in space level with the wanderer's head. Perhaps that is part of what gives the picture its unsettling power. The importance of the gaze, Dr. J. Samuels would say. Not just at what but from where.

I pick up the cat, who likes to sit on my desk like a tidy white loaf, and carry him around the room, letting him sniff at the bookcases and filing cabinets. He purrs and purrs. These excursions are his favourite thing.

Gladys Pratt. The way she slammed me against the shelves in the cold room. The way she would sit there, sit there, sit there, and watch and accuse and berate. The way she never said my name without a sneer, the way I was just "the deer," the stupid deer, the way she cheated me, I can still feel the cheque in my hand, the disbelief and then shock making me dizzy, and then seeing her today having an everyday life. It isn't fair and I want to punish her.

The cat feels something wrong about the way I am holding him. He jumps down.

My heart is beating fast, as fast as it did when I first recognized the woman. Get a grip, as my sons would say. Get a grip. I take hold of the corner of the filing cabinet, take several deep breaths. There.

I really have to talk to someone about this.

I think again about calling Jane, but I can't make myself do it. I can't face having her see me lose control. When I struggled so long in the department for a permanent position, I wanted to be perceived as strong and disciplined and patient; "Let Elke do it; we can count on her," my colleagues, including Jane, would say, and even if the work was drudgery I would smile and take it on. When my position came up for review I overheard one of my assessors say, "Elke is, well, *trustworthy*, but not especially creative." It took a long time for my hurt over that remark to subside. So what if I am not *creative* in their sense? *Creative* is an exculpatory word, used to indulge unkindness and laziness and selfishness. I kept my head down and kept smiling and bided my time.

Bided my time. It is something I seem to have spent much of my life doing. Biding my time until I could leave the farm, until I finished my doctorate, until my sons were grown and I could resume my career, until Andrew came back to me.

Is that what I have done with Gladys? Bided my time? Surely not. Surely I have not had such deliberateness. She has been a footnote, and barely that, to my life. But I never imagined our paths would cross again. Why am I so disturbed and angry and strangely excited by seeing her again? Because whatever I might have bided my time for is now here?

I *must* talk to someone. But not another psychologist. I smile, remembering suddenly the man I was once counselling who, after a hostile and sulky silence in response to a question, snapped, "Why should I try to answer that? I'm paying you for answers. You shrinks pretend you're so wise and non-judgemental but really you don't have a fucking clue." For one wonderful moment I believed he was absolutely right. But, like a cleric at a sleepless midnight who stares into godlessness, I had to suppress that insight or lose my profession.

But it's not distrust of my profession that keeps me from calling Jane. It's pride. That stiff-upper-lip pride. I am Elke the stoic one, the controlled one, the dependable one. I do not have the luxury of problems that are not external.

Who, then, can I talk to about this?

Suddenly I think of Alice. Of course. Alice was at the lodge, at least for a bit. She would understand. We haven't been in touch much over the last years—she lives in Calgary—but we have had the occasional meetings and phone calls. I last saw her at my mother's funeral three years ago, when she happened to be home visiting her brother. Home: the farms still having that enduring claim on us.

I'm surprised when she, not her machine, answers the phone.

"Alice! It's Elke. I just had to tell you who I ran into today."

Alice laughs, sounding a little breathless. She runs a small picture-framing business from her house, and I get the feeling she has raced to the phone expecting someone more rewarding. "Jimmy Neufeld," she says.

"Silly girl." Jimmy Neufeld was a merrily brainless lad on whom we both had crushes in Grade Ten. "Nobody as lovely as that, I'm afraid. Gladys Pratt. You probably don't remember her, but—"

"Gladys Pratt! Are you *kidding?* Of course I remember her! The wicked witch of the Yukon! You ran into her? With your car, I hope."

I laugh and tell her the whole story, making it funny, embellishing the moment when Faith turned around on the street and I tried to hide myself behind a tree. Alice is giggling, throwing in nicely vicious remarks that make my homicidal urge on the train platform seem quite appropriate.

"And you think Faith is her *daughter*-in-law? God, the poor thing. She was such a little sweetie. Olive was really proud of her. Wonder how she likes this."

"Faith looks just like Olive now."

"God, how too, too weird. Like, it doesn't seem quite *fair* that Gladys can be down there in a nice house and having a happy old age, does it?"

I laugh, but uncomfortably, because Alice has articulated only too well what I have been feeling.

"If they're down here in June," Alice continues, "it must mean the Pratts sold the lodge. I figured they'd be up there forever."

"Well, it shouldn't take too many years of cheating your staff to be able to retire."

"Not the whole staff," Alice says. "Just the summer girls. And Basement Bobby, of course."

"Basement Bobby! I haven't thought of him in years. Poor guy. He never had a chance."

"I thought he was kind of cute. If you could get past the attitude. But he only had eyes for Kendy."

Kendy. We haven't mentioned her name to each other for years. I'm relieved that it's Alice who's done it, who's given me this easy segue. "Yeah. Kendy could do that to people. She'd be amused to hear the old Warthog is still walking around. Too bad we never kept in touch."

"Hey, I bet I forgot to tell you—I met her at a Chamber of Commerce marketing conference a year or so ago. She was giving a talk about her business. She runs some winemaking franchises, out of Vancouver, I think. Kennedy Wines. Ever heard of them?"

"No." My heart is giving itself extra beats. Kendy is here. I can find her. "You sure it was her?"

"Yup. I went up to her after her talk and said, 'The Yukon, 1965, right?' and she gave me such an alarmed look, like I'd discovered some evil secret or something, that I had to laugh. Then she did, too. 'Alice,' she said. I was impressed. She remembered me."

"Why shouldn't she? You remembered her."

"Well, yeah. True."

I've said the right thing to please her, I can tell. After all these years we can still be flattered by being told we are as memorable as Kendy.

There is a small beep on the line, and then Alice says, "Oh, wait a sec, I need to see who this is," and, not waiting for my agreement, she puts me on hold. When she comes back, she says, "Gosh, I really need to take this call. Do you mind?"

"No, no, of course not," I say, even though I do mind, a bit.

But I am aware that people trying to run businesses full-time do not have as much leisure to chat as I do. It was one of the humbling lessons I had to learn after I quit teaching—just because I suddenly had an open schedule didn't mean that the people I might have liked to spend it with had one, too. Even this odd preoccupation with Mrs. Pratt now is probably the result of my having too much time on my hands. Is it just some diversion for me, some excitement because I am bored? If I had lectures to prepare or essays to mark or meetings to go to I wouldn't be letting my mind linger over her, and I certainly wouldn't have had the time or energy to leap up and follow her off the Skytrain.

I go to the kitchen and peel myself an orange.

"Kendy," I say softly to the cat. "Alice has found Kendy."

I wait until I've finished the orange before I go to look up Winemaking in the Yellow Pages. There it is. Kennedy Wines. There are four locations, one in Burnaby, only a few miles from here. I put my finger on the ad, think of how she must have been here for years, close enough to touch.

I pick up the phone, put it down again. Would she even remember me? She chose not to contact me when I came to the university; why would she want to hear from me now? Alice said when she mentioned the Yukon Kendy looked alarmed. The lodge had been only a marginally less odious experience for her than for me. Why would she want to be made to remember it, to meet someone she'd known just in that place?

Calling her would be a mistake. It would only make us both uncomfortable. Let sleeping dogs lie.

I go back into the study, sit down and stare for a while at the blank face of the computer monitor. I pick up the article by Dr. J. Samuels, flip to the third page, start reading.

> Another nonverbal rejection behavior adopted by the women involved self-grooming activities. Unlike grooming activities used flirtatiously, such as primping or flipping of the hair, rejection behaviours involved activities more usually done in private. Such behaviours might involve personal hygiene. These included cleaning their nails or picking their teeth.

I cross out the second last sentence as redundant and circle the two different spellings of "behaviour," smiling a little as I imagine Dr. J. Samuels trying to appease us with Canadian spelling but not thwarting the computer spell checker.

The cat jumps onto my lap, where he treads and kneads and fidgets, turning around and around, unable to settle. He falls off, jumps up, tries again. Someone called this Irritable Lap Syndrome.

"For Pete's sake," I say, as his bum goes past my face for the twentieth time. I lift him off, and he says something reproachful but goes away.

No matter how long I stare at the page in front of me I seem unable to do anything more than tap my pencil on it. I shift on my chair, readjust its height, push the pillow in the small of my back higher. Irritable Chair Syndrome.

Finally I give up, go back to the living room, put a Rolling Stones tape in the player. I turn it up loud. If Andrew were here he would frown and say something unkind; he does not have a sentimental attachment to the rock 'n' roll of his youth.

"Satisfaction." I pretend I am surprised to hear it on this cassette, but of course that's not true, even though I haven't played the tape for years.

Let sleeping dogs lie. What was it my father used to say that amused me when I little, about sleeping dogs? Why let them lie, he said, if we can make them tell the truth.

After a while, I turn down the volume and call the Burnaby outlet of Kennedy Wines.

Elke

Late June, 2000

Dear David,
 Thanks for your rather desperate fax. Though I am not at all happy about this, I'm transferring another thousand dollars to your account in Lisbon. . . .

          Mom

She's late.

Of course, I was here half an hour early, walking up and down the paths along English Bay in front of the restaurant before going in and getting a table with a view of the water. Four huge freighters are anchored in the bay today. The beach is rather pleasantly devoid of people, only a few resolute joggers out facing an unusually strong and cold wind bringing in real waves from Georgia Strait, whose swells are usually gentled by the breakwaters of the gulf islands and, farther out, the long cushion of Vancouver Island.

The waitress comes by with the coffee pot and asks me if I want to order, but I tell her I am still waiting for my friend. She gives me a look I might think pitying if I weren't recalling my own waitressing days, which allowed no time for interest in the personal affairs of customers. Another server comes out of the kitchen with a tray balanced skillfully on one palm, and she delivers the order to a table beside me. Trays, I think: what a good idea. I remember how I had to stack plates up my arm, pile coffee cups on top of each other, how I once spilled all the coffees on a group of tourists who, bless them, were more forgiving than Mrs. Pratt.

I check my watch again. We *did* say four o'clock, didn't we? It's a quarter after. We had to book three weeks ahead to find a day when Kendy was free and in town; have I, after all that, gotten it wrong?

And then there she is.

Her red-gold hair is lighter than I remember and cut shorter, falling to her shoulders in a way that suits its slight natural curl. Her face seems virtually unchanged. As she gets closer, I can see the hint of bagginess at the eyes and the chin, but her skin still has the small-pored smoothness of a teenager's, and there are none of the menopausal wrinkles around the mouth that I sigh at in my own mirror. She is wearing loose, velvety, grey slacks and a beige cloth coat with black buttons that match the silk scarf puffing gently out from under the collar. A businesswoman: well-groomed, slim, alert. It crosses my mind that she looks much like Alice, who is also a businesswoman. It is a look I admire because I could never quite achieve it; an academic disdain for fashion at my university encouraged a rumpled shabbiness, but I never quite achieved that, either.

So here she is. At last. Kendy: married twice, now divorced, no children, parents both dead, a commerce degree completed ten years ago, a townhouse with an upscale address on False Creek, a winemaking business she bought three years ago.... Her half of the hard-edged facts we have exchanged on the phone to prepare ourselves to meet the women we now are.

She sits down opposite me. A faint minty perfume has accompanied her.

"Elke," she says. "You haven't changed a bit."

I laugh. "Of course not. We didn't even need this."

I gesture at my throat, at the jade pendant by which I had told her she would recognize me, but I'd forgotten the stone was so tiny as to be invisible across a room. I'd even forgotten I still had the necklace, buried at the bottom of my jewellery box, until we asked each other for a way of recognizing each other. It was the only thing I still had from the Yukon, and it seemed like a clever choice. But when I put it on I remembered how I'd come to have it, and I felt the same shiver of distaste I can see on Kendy's face now as she looks at it.

"God," she says. "You weren't kidding. It really is. From the lodge."

"Yup. From the leftover tray at the end of the year. Didn't the Warthog offer you something from it?"

"I didn't take anything. I might have tried to strangle the bitch with it."

Well. I am simultaneously taken aback and delighted at the vehemence of her response. We are still comrades, united in our hatred of the oppressor.

"Oh, Kendy. It's good to see you."

"You, too."

I reach up and unclasp the necklace, shove it under my plate. "I'll leave it for a tip," I say. "Good riddance."

The waitress comes to take our order, and we make a point of looking at her and saying friendly things, trying not to seem like the usual customers who treat her as invisible, but I can see she is only impatient at our slowness. I order the fettucine; Kendy orders a carafe of wine, the Greek salad, and, as an afterthought that makes me smile, a side of French fries.

"We should have had the hamburger deluxe," I say.

"Hamburger deluxe! We must have served a million orders of hamburger deluxe. I never see it on the menu any more."

"It has classier names now, that's all."

"Probably still comes well done," Kendy says. "Remember well done?"

"Lord, yes. The code for inedible."

"On the way over I was thinking of the cabin. Remember the cabin? That horrid hovel? I've seen doghouses twice as big and better furnished."

"My cat's *litterbox* is twice as big and better furnished."

We laugh, leaning back, then forward, in that surprising bodily synchrony people can have when they share an emotion.

"You know what else I was remembering for some reason?" Kendy says. "The moosehead."

"The moosehead. God. It was so ... repulsive, wasn't it? But my dad was into all that hunting stuff, too. Stuffed animals were status symbols."

"For some of us they still are." Kendy must see my eyes widen at the "us" because she adds, "Not *me,* of course. But I have clients who still have dead animals on their walls. I don't have the luxury of chastising them. Not like you academics do."

There is a barb in that remark, but I decide not to let it snag me. "Ha," I say instead, lightly. "You should have met some of my students. Any attempt at chastisement and they'd have sued me."

To my relief, Kendy smiles. "Ah, the young. They're so litigious."

The waitress brings the carafe of wine. Kendy pours herself a glass. I notice a small tattoo on the inside of her forearm, something blue and red, perhaps a dragon. Kendy sees me looking and says, "Oh, that. From my self-mutilation period."

I am suddenly ashamed to have nothing equivalent to show, no unaccidental scars, no self-inflicted experiments.

Kendy raises her glass in a toast. "Well," she says. "To the bad old days."

I raise my coffee cup. "I feel as though we're twenty, meeting up at university in September to celebrate our freedom."

Kendy takes a swallow of wine that is more a gulp than a sip. I notice how well-manicured her hands are, the nails cut short but gleaming with a clear polish, the perfect half-moons all visible. Lunules, they are called, I remember irrelevantly, perhaps because my own nails don't seem to have any.

When Kendy sets the glass down it is almost empty. I am surprised to realize she is nervous, a little edgy. "I *am* sorry I didn't call you," she says, repeating what she already told me on the phone. "My personal life was just such shit."

"You don't have to explain," I say. "I was just disappointed you'd dropped out. You were the smartest person I ever met."

She laughs. "You met me at my peak. After that, what the demon weed didn't muddle the mescaline did."

"Ah, the demon weed. I did miss that. You were ahead of your time."

"A head. An old joke but true. But the dope ... mellowed things. I sort of floated through most of the bad stuff."

"You just seemed extraordinarily self-assured."

"Self-assured." She frowns. Her mood seems suddenly to have darkened. "I was foolish. The proverbial young and foolish." She pushes her hand, hard, through her hair over her right ear. "Anyway. So you saw the Warthog. Tell me again."

So I tell her again, filling in the story I had distilled to a few sentences over the phone, not afraid to admit to my homicidal response to Mrs. Pratt, not afraid to sound a little deranged at the way I followed her. Kendy leans forward as I talk, an avid glitter in her eyes that I find hard to look at. Her minty scent seems to grow stronger.

The waitress brings our meals, and we start to eat, but with less interest than we give to my story.

"So you think Charlie's dead?" she interrupts.

"Well, she said she *used* to buy all his clothes. Past tense. It could mean she was just talking about when she was Faith's age."

Kendy runs her finger over the rim of her wineglass until it hums. "It should be easy enough to find out for sure," she says.

I get a prickle up the back of my neck.

"I suppose so," I say.

"And if he's not dead we can kill him."

I blurt out a silly, fluttery laugh. The prickles at the back of my neck are heading down my spine.

"I hated them both so much," Kendy says. "You've no idea."

"So did I. But you were a good waitress. At least they valued you for that."

"Huh. They didn't value anything except themselves. By the time I left I was wishing Basement Bobby *had* burned the damn place down."

"Basement Bobby! Poor old Basement Bobby. And Here Boy. Remember Here Boy?"

"Indeed I do." She leans forward. "You know, the day after they died I was so angry and upset that I found some of Here Boy's shit and kneaded it into Gladys's burger."

"You didn't!"

"Well, yeah, I didn't. I mean, I *did,* I had it all ready, I was on the way out of the kitchen, and then some kick of sanity or cowardice or fear that I might actually poison her made me take it back, and Laura made me another burger. She didn't even ask why."

I start to giggle. "She probably knew. She probably thought it was a good idea."

"Maybe she did. Maybe she'd served Gladys worse things. I saw this TV program once where security cameras showed cooks and servers spitting and even peeing into the food."

"Lord." I look at my fettucine, try to recall if our waitress had looked disgruntled.

"I should have given it to her. And to Charlie. I wish I had."

"What did they finally pay you, anyway? I hope it was more than my two hundred fifty dollars. I can still remember how I nearly fainted when I saw that."

Kendy picks up a French fry, which she has bathed in salt, puts it down again.

"I got four fifty."

I try not to gape. Kendy was there only a little over a week longer than I was, and she got paid almost twice as much. I take a mouthful of fettucine, but it tastes stale. I make myself swallow. I can't believe I am annoyed about this, after all this time, annoyed at *Kendy*, for God's sake. I should be glad she got a fairer deal. And the amount of money is so trivial now. What's two hundred dollars? The people at the next table are probably spending that just on their meal.

Kendy is watching me, and I know I have not disguised my feelings. "Well," I say, "that's something at least."

"Something," she says. The way she says the word makes me uncomfortable. Am I imagining that chip of sarcasm on the first syllable?

Surely we aren't going to give in to such pettiness. Nothing would have made Mrs. Pratt happier than to imagine this moment between us, to think she could have caused it.

"Can you imagine Faith as the Warthog's daughter-in-law?" I ask. "What a life."

It is the right thing to say, because Kendy seems to relax and pokes her fork into another French fry. "Yeah. Poor thing, eh?" She pauses, then gestures at me with her fork. "You know. What we should do is get in touch with Faith. Invite her to lunch or something. Find out the situation. Pick her brains."

"Mmm," I say noncommittally.

"Really. Why not? What's the harm? We both liked Faith."

"Well ... yes. But we'd have to do it without the Warthog finding out. I'd hate to get Faith into trouble."

"Why should it get her into trouble? We can just tell her the truth: you saw her on the Skytrain, she reminded you of her mother, you have these good memories of her, blah blah, you want to get together for a chat."

"I suppose so. I just don't want to, you know, use her."

"We wouldn't be *using* her. Besides, she might be as interested as we are in getting even with the old bitch."

"Is that ... I mean, is that what we want?" I ask. "To get even? Is that the point?"

"It's *my* point. *I* want to get even."

But at least they paid you better, I want to say. But I don't. Kendy has as much right to hate the Pratts as I do. And I wanted her as an ally, didn't I?

"Well?" Kendy asks bluntly. She snaps a glance at her watch. "Are you in?"

"*In.* It sounds as though we're planning to rob a bank."

"Just to steal back what they stole from us."

"I don't know, Kendy."

"Yes, you do."

Yes, you do. As though it is obvious, as though there can be no doubt.

A tremble of excitement goes through me. "Okay," I say. "I'm in."

⊗

Of course I had misgivings. Of course I *have* misgivings.

Several times I picked up the phone to call Kendy to cancel, but I could never finish dialing. "You're the one who started this," I could imagine her saying impatiently.

There had been a hard edge to her that I hadn't expected.

There: I've admitted it to myself. Despite my pleasure in seeing her, despite my old warmth for her that rekindled so effortlessly, there was something about her that disappointed me, that unnerved me, that made me sad. I remembered her as filled with light and grace and ease, I suppose, and I don't like to think of her now as, well, someone like me, brooding over old injustices.

Perhaps I have observed in her only the inevitable souring of age, or perhaps she was always as she is now, and I just couldn't see it in her then. Or perhaps, as she suggested, her light and grace and ease were simply the gentle chemical dishevelment of marijuana. As I pick up my purse on my desk I glance at *The Wanderer,* and I imagine the obscuring mists are marijuana smoke. The thought amuses me enough to get me out the door with somewhat lessened anxiety.

I drive to Kendy's store in Burnaby, where we have arranged to meet before going to see Faith at the Vancouver mall where she works.

The store is small and crowded at the front with merchandise for sale: labels, corks, racks, books on winemaking, fancy decanters, T-shirts and ties with grape-leaf designs. On one wall is a large seascape, in pale shades of grey and blue and white, and it has an oddly three-dimensional effect, the waves seeming to curl right out of the painting. I notice the artist's signature. Lily Briscoe. The name is familiar, but I can't think why.

The smell of wine is so strong I can imagine becoming intoxicated if I had to stay here long. A couple at the back is bottling a red, she siphoning it into bottles and he operating the machine that plugs in the corks. Friends of Andrew's do this and have brought us some of their wine when they've come to dinner. Perhaps they made it here. I would find it more interesting to watch the couple if I weren't fretting over what Kendy and I are about to do.

Then there she is, pulling into the parking lot in a big Chevy Suburban. She waves at me through the window, comes in and hands some papers to the gangly young man behind the desk, and they talk for a minute about merlots and cavignacs and a spoiled order. The man nods and looks at her earnestly, and I realize he must be her employee. What kind of a boss is she? Does he sneer at her behind her back the way we did about the Pratts? It doesn't seem likely. When he smiles at her he looks totally charmed. I look at her hair, that paler red-gold than I remember, and I wonder if it has gently incorporated grey over the years or if it has been artfully tinted that way. My own hair is almost completely white. Andrew has suggested that I colour it, which dismayed me a little. He wouldn't dye his own hair.

When Kendy and the clerk are done she comes over and takes my arm and grins. "Ready?"

"I guess so," I say. I like the way she's taken my arm.

At the door she pauses, straightens a large sign in the window advertising a chardonnay at twenty percent off. She frowns at it, asks, "That better?"

"Looks fine. A little lack of symmetry can be eye-catching." My voice doesn't quite pull off that exaggerated home-decorator tone it was going for.

Kendy keeps looking at the sign. "You probably think this a strange place for me to have ended up."

"Not at all." Damn. I must have sounded patronizing.

"Brainy Kendy running a wine store. Doesn't it seem just a bit, well, *wasteful?* A bit *déclassé?*"

I can feel myself flush. "Why should it? If you enjoy this work that's all that matters." Even *more* patronizing.

She shrugs. "The work's okay." She pushes open the door. "It's the first time I'm my own boss. I met someone at a party who was selling the business, cheap, so he could follow his bliss to Australia or somewhere, and the next morning I woke up to him telling me his lawyer was drawing up the transfer papers. Either I got the most amazing deal or I was the best fuck he'd ever paid for."

I laugh. I'm not going to let her shock me. "At least he was leaving. In my department you had to keep working alongside the people you'd had ingratiatory sex with." I'm making it seem as though I could have been such a "you." Kendy would snort if I admitted Andrew was only the second man I'd slept with. The first, a sad exchange student from Ireland, seemed so disheartened by that fumbly experience that he flew back to Dublin two weeks later, leaving me not even a note let alone a chain of wine stores.

We walk out to her Suburban, which she calls "Ernie the thug," explaining that she needs a vehicle this size because she is always delivering supplies of some kind from one store to the other.

"I was thinking of getting a GMC Yukon," she adds. "But the name put me off."

In the back seat I notice two plastic-wrapped and unframed paintings, seascapes, apparently by the same artist who did the one in the store.

"It's interesting work," I say.

"Yeah. I like her stuff. Sometimes I just sit and look at it when I'm trying to work out some problem."

"I have a painting like that, too." I buckle my seatbelt. "The artist's name is familiar somehow. Lily Briscoe."

"She gets that a lot. It's the name of the artist in Virginia Woolf's *To The Lighthouse.*"

"Ah, of course. Is that her real name or did she change it for career purposes?"

"Her real one, far as I know. Maybe she was compelled to her profession the way my doctor was compelled to his. Benjamin Casey."

I laugh. "Ben Casey! How lovely."

"*Nomen omen,* as the Greeks would say. It might be nice to be so ... aimed from birth. Not all that fumbling around trying to find out what to do with our lives."

"Maybe there was a fictional Gladys Pratt. Maybe there was a greedy, cruel innkeeper in Dickens called Gladys Pratt."

Kendy pulls her lips to the side, gives an almost inaudible grunt. I wish I hadn't mentioned Gladys Pratt, not just yet, hadn't invited those sour memories so soon into the van with us.

Kendy maneuvers expertly out of the lot, turns onto the street. In half an hour we will be meeting Faith. Kendy wanted to be the one to contact her, even though it seemed more logical that I do it, so Kendy set up the meeting. Maybe she didn't trust me not to bungle it. Faith was delighted to hear from her, Kendy assured me.

I don't doubt that. It's Kendy and myself I doubt.

"You're still game for this, I hope," Kendy says, keeping her eyes on the road. "You look a little squeamish."

"Squeamish! I hope not. We're just having an innocent drink after work with an old acquaintance. Aren't we?"

"Right. An old acquaintance. Who lives with another old acquaintance." She changes lanes, faster than I would. In the car in front of us, the coat of the woman in the passenger seat is caught in the door and flaps against it and the road. *Undercarments,* someone once called such unfortunate items. I seem excessively relieved for the woman when the car turns into a restaurant parking lot.

"You're sure Faith knows she's not supposed to tell Mrs. Pratt about this?"

"Yes, yes, I'm sure. And are you *still* docilely calling her *Mrs. Pratt?* Jesus."

I laugh a little, both hurt and embarrassed. "I'll try to stop. It's just, you know, the old habit. I'd be terrified of slipping up and calling her Warthog."

"Too kind a name for her subspecies."

"Well, the name no longer applies now, anyway. She's had the wart removed."

"Maybe the wart had *her* removed." Kendy reaches up to adjust her rear-view mirror, reminding me, irrelevantly, of how people often have to do that because their spines compress by an inch or more during the day. "Remember how she'd scream at us if we didn't clean the tables or wash the dishes fast enough?"

I groan. "Remember how she'd expect us to work when we were off shift when the tour buses came in?"

"Tour buses. Yuck. Remember how she assaulted you in the cold room after Alice quit?"

"I think I still have the scars. Remember the time she slapped you, after Basement Bobby died?"

She doesn't answer for a minute. Then she says, in a lowered voice, "I might have deserved that, actually."

"What?"

"I was relieved when people were saying it was her fault

because she'd told him he had to kill his dog. But I think that if anybody was to blame it might have been me."

"What do you mean? How could *you* be to blame?"

She clears her throat, doesn't take her eyes from the road even though we are stopped at a light. "I think he ... well, he fell in love with me. He couldn't stand it that I'd be leaving. He wanted to— oh, it was just too dreadful—he wanted to marry me. He wanted to come with me when I left. I had no idea he'd get so ... involved. If I had I'd never ..."

"Never what?" But I have a sinking feeling that I know what she will say.

"Never have given him, you know, blow jobs. I was so silly about those."

I remember what she told me after she had done it to Charlie. It had been for practice.

Basement Bobby would have been practice, too.

I almost tell her to stop the van, to let me out. What am I doing here? What other unpleasant surprises will she spring on me? Kendy was the only good thing about that awful summer, and now even that memory has been cheapened.

And it makes me wonder why she is so eager to pursue this plot with Mrs. Pratt. With Gladys. The two nastiest things she did to Kendy, cheating her out of her salary and slapping her, turn out to be, in the first case, not exactly true, and, in the second case, something Kendy thinks she more or less deserved.

"You should have told me," I say.

"I was ashamed to."

We ride in silence for a while. I watch the road, as though I have to memorize landmarks, as though I will have to find my own way back.

Perhaps I am simply being puritanical. How do I know Basement Bobby was just for practice? And if she hadn't done the same thing with Charlie, God knows what he might have done to me.

I make myself smile and turn to her. "Hey. You weren't responsible for what happened to Basement Bobby. Suicides always make survivors feel guilty. I doubt if there was anything you could have done to stop him."

She smiles back, for the first time taking her eyes from the road to glance at me. "You're a psychologist," she says. "I'd forgotten."

It's not exactly the reply I might have hoped for.

At the mall, Kendy parks in the underground lot, and then I follow her to the elevator. We go up to the ground floor. The pub where Faith said she would meet us is just to our right, and I can see the kitchenware store where she must work. I was sure we would be late, but it is a few minutes before four.

"I'm so nervous," I say. "What will we talk about?"

"We'll play it by ear," Kendy says.

"We have to remember Faith's mother just died. You said it was just about the first thing she told you on the phone. We have to be sensitive to that."

"Yeah, sure. Stop worrying."

We go into the pub to see if Faith is there already, but in the dim light I can make out only three occupied tables. At one of them a young blond woman sits staring at the ends of her hair, apparently looking for split ends, and ignoring the young man across from her who is trying bravely to summon her interest; when she does look up it is not at him but at a table across the room. Rejection signalling.

We go back out into the mall, and then I see her. She's carrying her coat over her arm and wearing a green suit jacket with too-big shoulder pads and a matching skirt at calf-length. Her grey hair is pinned back severely on both sides with thin silver barrettes. Her large mouth opens into a wide smile as she spots us, and she waves.

"Olive," Kendy whispers.

"Amazing, isn't it?"

We exchange clumsy and cluttered greetings and exclamations about how we haven't changed one bit.

"Kendy says you saw me on a *bus*," Faith says to me. "You should have *said* something."

"I did. I told Kendy."

And then we all laugh, as though I've said something hilarious, and move into the pub.

"Hi, Faith," says the bartender.

Faith seems both pleased and embarrassed at the recognition. "We all kind of know each other," she tells us. "Those of us in this section."

We sit down at a table with a guttering candle in a glass jar covered by an acrylic net charred around the top.

"So how long have you worked in the mall?" Kendy asks, shrugging her jacket off. She's wearing a beige sweatshirt with a small logo for Kennedy Wines above her right breast.

"Just a few months. I had a job I liked better at a software company, but I got laid off. Rodney still works for them." She glances at me. "I suppose Kendy told you I married Rodney Pratt."

"Yeah," I say.

"I nearly dropped the phone when I heard that," Kendy says.

The waiter comes, and when Faith orders a beer Kendy and I do the same.

"So tell me all about the Pratts," Kendy says as soon as the waiter has turned away. "Charlie? Gladys?"

"Charlie died. He and Gladys had been divorced for a while by then, though. And Gladys, well, Rodney and I share a house with her."

Kendy allows a quick glance at me. "So Charlie's dead. Can't say I'm sorry to hear that."

I hold my breath, wondering what Faith will say to that. It's possible she actually liked him.

But Faith gives a guilty little grin. "I wasn't especially sorry, either," she says.

The waiter brings our drinks. Kendy insists on paying for us all. It's been a long time since I've had beer, and when I take a swallow I'm reminded of why I don't much like it. Kendy drains half her glass before putting it down.

"And Gladys," she says, leaning forward over the table. "Tell me about her. What's she like now? Mean as ever?"

I wince.

Faith sighs, looks down at her hands clamped around her glass.

"I suppose she is. Still the same mean old Warthog." She gives a snort of laughter, and it sounds so comic, as though she were imitating a warthog, that she giggles and says, "Sorry, sorry. I knew you used to call her the Warthog. I thought it was so funny."

"She had names for us, too," I say. "I was 'the deer,' I guess because she thought I had a silly name. I don't know what she called Kendy."

"Oh, a lot of things," Kendy says. "A lot of things."

"When I was a baby," Faith says, "she used to call me Stub. Not so's Mom could hear, but she knew." When she says "Mom" her face twists a little, but her voice doesn't waver. "I guess Gladys thought I looked like a cigarette stub."

Kendy shakes her head. "She specialized in nasty. So, if she hasn't changed, how come you share a house with her?"

"Rodney, well, he's smart, but ... he has a hard time holding onto money. And the house is in her name, even though Mom and I paid for a lot of it. I've asked Rodney enough times if we could have our own place, but he says we can't afford it. And Gladys, well, she wants to keep us there." If there is bitterness in her voice it is heavily overlaid with resignation.

"Let me get this straight," Kendy says. "You paid for most of the house. But it's in Gladys's name. And she's using that to make you stay there?"

"Well ..." I can see Faith is regretting telling us so much, wondering, perhaps, how the conversation has galloped so quickly to such revelations. "It's not so bad. We have our own suite in the basement."

"Doesn't sound like a great arrangement to me." Kendy's voice sounds angry. She has finished her beer, gestures to the waiter for another. Faith orders one, too, and I quickly take a gulp of mine so that I won't look as though I am having trouble keeping up.

"We've been talking just about me," Faith says. "Tell me about yourselves."

So we do, both trying, I think, not to make what we have accomplished in our lives sound particularly special, and we add little deprecatory details. I can tell it annoys Kendy that what seems to impress Faith the most is the fact my husband is a lawyer. Kendy has told us nothing about her past husbands.

"You're both so lucky," Faith sighs. "I mean, I know it's not just luck—"

"Yes, it is," Kendy interrupts. "That's all it is. Luck. Accident."

"Even people who appear lucky might not be happy," I add. They both stare at me as though I've said something nonsensical. I smile, trying to appear wise or at least enigmatic but almost certainly not succeeding, and look away across the room. The young blond woman is gone but the man is still there, slumped in his seat and apparently talking to his drink.

"But you've both done so well," Faith persists. "You own this successful business, Kendy, and, Elke, your husband is a lawyer...."

I resist returning Kendy's glance. I *am* essentially retired; perhaps a husband who is a lawyer *is* my biggest asset now. I remember Kendy and me at the lodge thinking helplessly about my wages, how when Kendy said the word "lawyer" I felt the fear and impossibility of even speaking to one.

"If you don't like your life, Faith," Kendy says bluntly, "you can change it."

An alarm bell sounds in my head. Before I can think of what to say, Kendy continues, "You don't *have* to live in a house with a mother-in-law you dislike. You don't *have* to live with Rodney, either, for that matter. You don't *have* to stay at your job."

"Well, now, Kendy—" I manage, before she interrupts me.

"But I'll bet they both need your income, don't they? I'll bet they'd be lost without you. That gives you a lot of power, Faith. And if you've kept any receipts for when you bought the house a good *lawyer*—" she glances pointedly at me "—could get you a good settlement from its sale."

"Now wait," I plead, looking from Kendy's face rapt and faintly eerie in the fluttering candlelight to Faith, whose mouth has fallen open into a little ellipse. "Faith, Kendy doesn't mean this seriously."

"Why not?" Kendy frowns, shrugs, lifting her hands palms-up into the air. "As for the job, well, hell, there's always a turnover at my stores. You could probably pick up something there. I'll bet the pay is better and so are the working conditions. You just have to like wine. You like wine, don't you, Faith?"

"Sure. Sure I like wine."

I am suddenly furious. We have been with Faith less than an hour, and already Kendy is trying to change her life. Faith is no match for her. Kendy promised she wouldn't use Faith for whatever mischief is simmering in our heads about Gladys. And what is Kendy getting *herself* into, for that matter? Is she serious about the job offer? She is inviting Gladys into her life; every time she looks at Faith she will see the past, the lodge, the Pratts.

I reach across the table, put my hand on Faith's arm. She starts to jerk away, and then laughs in confused embarrassment, as though she has forgotten what such a touch can be for.

"Don't make any hasty decisions, Faith. Really. Kendy may be sounding more sure than she intends. You can't change your life overnight." I feel a sharp pain in my ankle, and I realize Kendy has kicked me. I feel like kicking her back, but instead I glance pointedly at my watch. "Actually, I have to get going. Kendy, since you're driving ..."

Faith immediately gets to her feet. "Oh, I'm sorry. I've kept you."

"Of course you haven't," Kendy says, giving me a black look. "Sit down."

But Faith is pulling on her jacket. "No, I have to go, too. Gladys will be wondering where I've gotten to."

"Let her wonder," Kendy says.

Faith giggles. "I won't tell her where I've been."

"Good for you."

They are both sounding so childish I want to shake them. But to them I must look the critical parent, frowning and saying no, mustn't, don't.

"We'll have to do this again sometime," Kendy says. "What do you think, Elke?"

"Sure," I say, knowing no other reply is possible. They will meet again, I am fairly certain, with or without me. And since I am responsible for all this I had better be there to see it doesn't get even further out of control.

"Call me at the store," Faith says. "It's, you know, easier."

"Gotcha," Kendy says.

We wave goodbye to Faith and then head down to the parking lot, neither of us speaking. I imagine Kendy is doing what I am, marshalling arguments and accusations.

We're in the car before I turn to her, say, "Kendy, look. I think this is—"

"I know. I'm sorry. It got a bit out of hand."

"Oh. Well. I'm glad you agree."

She stares at me with those pale blue eyes that seem, in the dimly lit van, almost luminescent. "But, Elke, I could see it. I could see how we could get our revenge on the Warthog. She's still this cranky old bitch, right, and what she wants most is for her son and Faith to dance attendance on her. So we get in the way of that. We get Faith away from her—"

"But we agreed we wouldn't use Faith!"

"Did she look happy to you the way she is?"

"She's lived this way for about thirty years. We can't just swoop in and say, here, here's a different life for you. Especially when our motives are so ... tinged."

"Tinged." Kendy makes a face.

"And you—so cavalierly offering her a job. Even if you really do want to help her—and that would be admirable, I admit that, it would be admirable—you don't know what you could be getting into. You don't know anything about who Faith is now."

"I know more than I know about most of the people I hire."

"But think about who she's married to, who her mother-in-law is, who's influencing her. And Faith's a Pratt now. I can't even hear that name without a shiver going up my spine."

Kendy sighs. "Faith isn't a Pratt. You saw her. She doesn't have Prattness in her."

"Prattness." Now I am the one to make a face.

"Anyway. We haven't committed ourselves to anything. We just know more than we did. *You* have any suggestions about what to do next?"

I think about it for a while. "Maybe we should just drop it." I concentrate on rubbing at a spot of dust on my coat sleeve.

"I thought you wanted this. Or was that someone else sitting across the table from me saying, 'Let's get even'?"

I fiddle with the seat belt clip. "No, that was me."

"So is it this scenario you don't like or the whole concept?"

"Well ... I don't know. Maybe both. It's just ... all the research confirms that seeking revenge is physiologically and emotionally the worst way to go. It increases stress and anger. Forgiveness is the healthier alternative. There's something to that proverb about how one who seeks revenge should dig two holes. We may hold grudges because it gives us a feeling of being in control, but—"

"Yeah, yeah. The bottom line is that you want to let it go. You want her to get away with everything she's done."

Her shouting, loud and humiliating: not good enough, not good enough, not good enough. Her slamming me against the racks in the cold room, threatening me with worse. Her handing me, finally, a paycheque so small it barely covered my travel—

And suddenly another memory hits me like a blow to the stomach, literally pushing me back against the seat of the van.

It is the first night Andrew and I make love. We have planned it, have gone out to dinner first, I have washed and perfumed my sheets, put low-watt coloured light bulbs in my bedroom lamps, and when Andrew steps naked out of the bathroom and poses playfully before me saying, "Ta-da!" I see Charlie Pratt, only Charlie Pratt. I start to cry, curl up into the corner of the bed, say, "I'm sorry, I'm sorry," but I can't stop crying, and Andrew stands staring at me, appalled, his desire fled. I don't tell him what has happened, am too aghast myself, but he is patient, and later we do make love, but it has been ruined, I cannot forgive myself, cannot—

"What's wrong?" Kendy asks. "You look sort of green."

"Green. Green like jade."

Charlie is dead. But Gladys is still here. She could have stopped him. She is the only one left to hate.

"Jade?"

"I mean, no, I don't want her to get away with everything she's done. I guess I do want ... revenge."

"Attagirl."

"Revenge. The word sounds so dark. And in my profession, you know, we aren't supposed to consort with it."

"We don't have to call it revenge. We can call it justice."

"You'd make a good psychologist."

"I would. Find me one."

We laugh. It makes the air in the car somehow easier to breathe. Kendy's teeth are very white, with slightly extruded incisors. We can handle anything, those teeth seem to say.

"I wish we didn't have to involve Faith, though," I say. "Maybe we can do something else, something simpler."

"Like push Gladys in front of a train."

My laughter turns shrill. "Everyone gets to have death," I say. "We need something more original."

❖

When I get home I find two messages on my machine. The first one is from Andrew, and I groan. I am usually home at that time of the afternoon. The connection is exceptionally clear, and I have to remind myself he is calling from Brussels, not just from his office downtown.

"Elke. Pick up. Are you *there?*" There is an edginess in his voice, and I wince. Sorry, I mouth at the machine. "Are you there? Pick up.... Okay. I don't know where you could be. Anyway, the conference is over. Waste of bloody time. Levin wasn't there. I don't know what Drake expects me to do here for three more weeks without the Oland papers. I'll have to phone Copenhagen. Okay. I'll call you again when I get the chance. Bye."

I smile, put my hand on the receiver, though I know I can't call him back unless it's important. He will be either out or too busy or asleep.

I think again about that night we first made love. I never had that reaction again, never again saw Charlie Pratt at the foot of my bed, for which I suppose I must credit the useful blanket of repression, that same blanket I am always trying to pull off my clients. Andrew never spoke of that night again, either, imagining, I suppose, it had something to do with the Irish exchange student of whom I had told him. Andrew might have been pleased to think of himself as the one to introduce to me sex that was not traumatic.

Our sexual life has been satisfying, even exciting sometimes, when he would win a case and be in a kind of wild, celebratory fervour. Until four years ago. Everything I say about Andrew seems to append that codicil: until four years ago. That was when we stopped having sex, when he stopped even touching me, as though I repelled him.

It felt as though he had moved a mistress into the house. What he did move in was almost as hard to deal with: a deep depression that descended, for no apparent reason, virtually overnight. I was afraid to leave him alone. He turned from a confident, aggressive extrovert to a man who would sit in the dark and refuse to speak.

He seems better now. The doctor has found a drug that works, though Andrew won't discuss it with me. Perhaps he is ashamed; perhaps he thinks that, despite my protests, I disapprove of the reductionist simplicity of the serotonin drugs, of the neurological explanation overtaking the narrative one, the historical one, the subconscious one. Jane feels that way, and she warns me repeatedly about the drugs, about rebound reactions, about how the tests have not been rigorous. But it's not that easy for me. Jane has never found her husband in his pajamas, weeping, in his car in the middle of the night, saying, "I can't go on. I can't."

I play his message again. He sounds brusque and impatient but also full of energy. Like his old self. He is better, I keep assuring myself. Stop worrying.

Still, I won't tell him about Kendy and Gladys. I have tried, even before his depression, not to burden him with anything but my daily sameness, and even though the drug may no longer make that necessary it is a habit I am afraid to break. I have always had great empathy for those clients who feared that any word or gesture might trigger a spouse's rage; for me it was not his rage I feared to trigger but his despair. I know, rationally, it doesn't work that way, that, as I told Kendy, we are not the cause, but there is a guilt that comes from just being there when it happens.

The second message on the answering machine starts to play. It is Kendy. She must have called from her store right after she dropped me off.

"Whatever we do," she says, "I want her to know it was us. No stabbing-in-the-back stuff. She has to know it was me."

Gladys
Early July, 2000

Dear Glenda,
*   You've got a nerve, I must say. Even if I HAD saved any pictures of Charlie I sure as hell wouldn't send YOU any.*
*   Gladys*

I saw Olive today.

She was in the drugstore, fingering some vitamin bottles. Why was she buying stuff here instead of Surrey, was all I could think. I dropped the ankle brace I'd picked up and walked up to her.

"Hey, old woman," I said. "Too late for vitamins at our age."

She turned to stare at me, and then of course it wasn't Olive. This one had a droopy eyelid and her nose was too big. And she wasn't dead. The being dead part hit me like a ton of bricks. Olive was dead.

"Thought you were somebody else," I muttered and turned away. I think she said something to my back but I didn't listen.

Was it worse to see people from thirty years ago, looking like they did then, or to see dead people, looking like they did just before they died?

When I get home I make myself a cup of tea, using the loose leaves instead of a bag, thinking about how Olive would sometimes read my tea leaves. Once up at the lodge, I remember, she saw trees and then corrected herself and said, no, it looked more like a fire, and some animal beside it, lying with its four legs up in the air. And two weeks later Basement Bobby tried to burn down the lodge. It was downright spooky. I'm no good with the tea leaves, though. When I tried to read Olive's all I ever saw was people running.

I plop myself down in the recliner and drink my tea. The leaves stick to my tongue. I should have used a tea bag like a civilized person. When I finish the cup and try to read my leaves all I can see are people running.

I hear a car door slam in the alley. It's probably the woman who gives Faith a ride home sometimes. I crank myself quickly out of the chair and go to the landing at the back door where I left the vacuum cleaner plugged in. I do the same spot about twenty times before I hear her key in the lock.

When the door opens, I put my hand over my heart and shout, "Lord, Faith, don't sneak up on people like that." I turn the vacuum off.

"Sorry," she says, not sounding sorry at all. She's been strange lately. Broody and kind of lippy. It must be the Change.

"How was work?"

She shrugs off her coat. "Same as usual."

"Yeah, well. That's what they pay you for."

I know she wants to get on down the stairs, and I know the machine is blocking her way. The cord plugged in from the kitchen is stretched across there, too, about thigh-high.

"I'll move that in a minute," I say. "I just need to do this bit."

I turn the switch back on, give the machine a few prods into the corner by the door. Faith stands there, looking tired and like somebody beat her up. No matter how expensive her clothes are, that woman drags everything down to shabby the first time she wears it.

As soon as I turn the machine off, Faith gets her foot on it to push it aside.

"I thought I saw your mom at the store today," I say. It's the first thing I can think of that I know will make her answer me.

"For Heaven's sake, Gladys," she snaps.

"Don't use that tone with me."

"Unplug the cord. I have to get downstairs."

"Olive wouldn't like you using that tone with me. She'd give you a good whack on the head."

Faith looks at me. A little redness spreads across her cheeks. "Don't talk about her like that. My mother never once hit me. Never once."

"Figures," I grunt. "I thought it said to in the Bible. She always liked that Bible. Spare the rod and spoil the child."

Faith tromps off into my kitchen, and the next thing I know the cord comes whizzing by and zooms itself into the ass end of the machine. It always scares me a little the way it does that, like it shouldn't have that much energy if it's not plugged in.

Faith gives me another surly look and then stomps off down the stairs. I think she's gained another ten pounds this last week. All those empty chocolate boxes in their garbage. I don't know how Rodney can stand it, having his wife get so thick and lumpy. Me, I weigh almost the same as I did when I was a teenager. But fat lot of good that did me in the husband department. *Fat* lot of good. *Skinny* lot of good, it should be.

Olive told me once I didn't have a sense of humour. I was reading this novel then, one of those Stephen King things, and for some reason I remembered a line from it. "Humour is almost always anger with its makeup on," I told her.

Well, that surprised her. I must have sounded downright profound.

I think that was the last book I ever finished. Now I'm too impatient. All that reading and reading and trying to get all the characters straight and by the time you finally do it's over. So I don't bother any more. No matter what Oprah says. If God had meant for us to read books he wouldn't have given us TV. Ha. Too bad I can't say that to Olive. But maybe she'd think I was serious. If you ask me, *she* was the one without the sense of humour.

I put the vacuum away and crack myself another beer. Rodney will be home in half an hour. I'd like to get him alone and tell him Faith is acting up. But he probably knows. I've heard them yelling at each other downstairs. It's the "at each other" part that worries me. Faith is yelling back. At one time I thought I'd like to have her show a little spunk around Rodney, but now I don't know. Things were better as they were. Predictable.

I lie down on the couch and flip through the TV guide, looking for what's good tonight. I can't figure out the channels any more, though. What it says in the book isn't what I get. And

Rodney still hasn't fixed the way there's printing at the bottom of the picture. I hate that. Why do I need to read what they're saying? Some moron thought that one up.

I take another gulp of beer and close my eyes. A car with its radio on so loud it shakes the whole house goes by on the street. Boom cars. Another moron invented those.

It's Upstairs Bobby. Bob. He's looking at me like I'm the best thing he's seen in his whole life. He holds out his hand to me, and I take it, and I step onto his boat, a small one, like a canoe. It rocks under my feet, and I give a girly shriek, and he laughs, holds my hand tighter and pulls me toward him. He puts his arms around me, and we sink down onto the board seats. There's thunder in the skies, and some wind, but it's a hot day, and I'm so happy to be with him I kiss him right on the mouth. He pushes his hand slowly through my hair. I feel this desire, this desire—

I sit up, confused, blinking. There's a noise.

Upstairs Bobby. Upstairs Bobby was here. I can see his hand reaching out to me. Feel his hand in my hair.

By the time I realize the noise is Rodney and I get to the back door he's already halfway downstairs. If I don't nab him when he's coming in it's damned near impossible to get him back up here.

"Rodney! I need you to change a light bulb."

I can hear him sigh. He's annoyed, but he stops, turns, and comes up.

"Where?" he snaps.

"The bathroom."

"I've showed you a hundred times how to take that shade off the fixture."

"I tried. I'm afraid I'll drop it."

He sets his briefcase at the top of the stairs and follows me to the bathroom. There's a nice smell to him, some new scent he's started wearing, but I know not to comment. He needs a haircut, though I kind of like the way a hank of hair falls across his forehead, like a big black apostrophe.

"How was work?" I ask.

He grunts. That's all I get for an answer.

He unscrews the shade, which is a long rectangular shield over four bulbs. He has to be careful not to drop it as the screws loosen.

"So how are things with Faith? She seems kind of crabby lately."

He snorts. "You can say that again."

"So what's wrong with her?"

"How should I know? Some woman thing, probably. Why don't you talk to her?"

"Me! You think Faith talks to me?"

"Well, somebody should talk to her," Rodney says. "I'm getting fed up with the way she bitches about everything these days."

"You been getting after her too much, maybe," I say.

"Getting after her. What the hell's that supposed to mean? Faith starts acting weird and it's my fault?"

"I didn't say that."

Rodney wiggles the shade out of its track. I flick the switch on so he can see which bulb doesn't light.

"Turn it off, for Christ's sake. You want me to electrocute myself?"

I can think of some smart answers, but I flick the switch off. He unscrews the bulb, and I hand him the one I've set on the windowsill. He shakes the one he's just taken out.

"Just a *min*ute," he says. He puts the old one back in.

"What're you doing?"

"Just a minute, I said. Okay, turn the switch on."

I give him a big sigh, but I do as he tells me, and all four bulbs light up.

"Thought so," he says, smug. "It was just loose."

At least he doesn't accuse me of loosening it on purpose just to lure him up here. Although now that he's figured it out it's not something I can use with him again. Not for a while, anyway.

He puts the shield back on, me handing him the screws. I admire the way his fingers work. They're big and thick but very precise. Charlie never learned to do anything that required fine-tuning. If his fingers couldn't squeeze it or bang it or shake it into working properly he'd throw it across the room.

"Thanks," I say.

"You coulda done it yourself."

I shrug. "I might've broken it."

He wrinkles his nose, sniffs the air. "You cooking something?"

"Nope. Must be Faith burning your supper." I'm not a great cook, but Faith is worse, and we all know it.

"Lighten up on her, will you? It's probably you that's got her so moody. Her cooking's okay."

"Oh, for Pete's sake. Who was it told me Faith's cooking tastes like cardboard boiled in vinegar?"

He shrugs, looks annoyed. I don't know what's gotten into him. If there was one thing we ever agreed on it was that Faith was a lousy cook.

"Remember the time," I go on, "she cooked something so horrible and gassy it gave you burps you said were like throat farts? Throat farts—that was a good one."

Reminding him of the throat farts always got a chuckle out of him, but not today. "That was just once," he mumbles.

"Once? *Once?*"

"I think maybe Faith just doesn't feel appreciated," he says.

"Appreciated!"

"Okay, okay. I'm just saying. I think maybe she doesn't feel appreciated."

"Has she said so?" I ask.

"Not in so many words."

"Huh. Well, she can join the club."

He doesn't answer, just rinses his hands off in the sink and then trots away downstairs, scooping up a handful of strawberries from the bowl on the kitchen counter. He leaves me only five or six. If he hadn't just fixed the light I'd be yelling at him, but I let him go, even though I didn't exactly get enough conversation out of him to make up for the strawberries. I hear him bang a door downstairs, home free now. Home free, home free: the words clang in my head, the way words can do sometimes, until they make no sense at all.

⚘

I've just put my lunch dishes in the dishwasher when I hear the knock at the door.

I look through the peephole and see it's two middle-aged women, one of them carrying a purse the size of Rodney's briefcase. If it's not full of *Watchtower*s I'll eat my dishrag.

I'm heading back to the kitchen when they knock again, long and loud this time, like they know for sure I'm home, and it makes me mad enough that I march back to the door. It's very satisfying sometimes to tell the JWs to bugger off to hell.

I jerk the door open and glare into their faces. Their expressions aren't what I expect, none of those big, fake smiles. One of them isn't smiling at all, and the one that is looks like she's just drunk a glass of milk past its due date.

"Yes?" I snap, ready for their sly trick of saying something sucky sweet about how it's such a nice day or how the roses by the front door are so pretty.

The one with the constipated smile, the one with the purse the size of a suitcase, finally says, "Mrs. Pratt? Gladys?"

I look at her more closely, frowning. She's short and kind of round-looking, hair thick and well-cut but gone all grey, a plain kind of face with a pair of those prissy modern glasses rammed up against her eyeballs. She's wearing an expensive-looking beige cloth coat with a big collar and a belt.

"Am I supposed to know you?"

"I don't know. Are you?"

"I'm busy. What do you want?"

The other one suddenly speaks up, her voice harder. "What about me, Gladys? Do you remember me?"

I squint up at her: she's tall, dressed in some fancy silky suit jacket and pants, and she's younger and better-looking than the other one, with a good figure and even features, though the mouth is kind of big, and a smooth complexion with not much going on for wrinkles. She has these very blue, controlled eyes. Her hair is a reddish-blond colour that I bet comes out of a bottle—

My hand flies up to my throat.

The woman smiles, just one side of her mouth lifting. "I see you do remember me."

"Kendy."

"May we come in?"

She has turned sideways and is sliding right past me, into the hallway. I'm just staring at her, unable to move. The other one out on the stoop seems to figure she'd better sidle in, too, so she nudges her way past me on the other side. But I don't even look at her. Kendy is sprung right out of my nightmares, walking into my house. My heart is pounding so fast it seems to want to flap its way out of my chest.

She's not Kendy. She's like the woman at the store I thought was Olive.

Whoever she is, she has walked right into my living room, and now she sits herself down on my sofa.

The other one slinks into the living room, too, and sits down on the loveseat that's at a right angle to the sofa. She's so tense she's got her shoulders pulled up right to her ears, but the Kendy person is sitting there like she owns the place, leaning back and propping one ankle onto her other knee.

If she's not Kendy, then I'm crazy.

It *is* Kendy. I'd rather be crazy, but I don't get to choose.

They're both more or less facing the recliner, as though they know it's where I usually sit, and now Kendy actually gestures at it and says, "Close the door, Gladys. Come sit down."

My heart is still banging away like mad, but if it's sending my blood around faster it must be all going to my feet, which want to bolt right out the door, and not going to my head, which just feels dizzy.

"Come on, Gladys. Sit down. Join us."

I glance out at the front walk. My mind must be thinking like my feet now because it's telling me to make a run for it.

But I can't leave them alone in the house. It might be just what they want me to do.

I close the door, but don't shoot the deadbolt, and then I come into the living room, stand by the recliner. It's supposed to make a person feel more in control, I heard once, to stand when someone else is sitting, but it just makes me feel like a bigger target. So I sit down, carefully. The leather makes its rattly noise.

"Nice house you've got," Kendy says, looking around. "Must be worth a small fortune."

"What do you want?" I'm surprised at how my voice doesn't shake, how I've been able to make it hard, blunt. My heart slows down almost to normal.

The one that isn't Kendy leans forward, licks her lips and says, "We both feel we—"

"And who the hell are *you?*"

A flush comes over her face. "I'm Elke. I was there the same year Kendy was."

"If you say so." I tell her that because I could see it made her mad that I recognized Kendy but not her. I do remember her now, sort of. Elk-EE. One of the more useless ones.

She clears her throat. "We both feel we have some unfinished business with you, Gladys. Because of the way you treated us at the lodge. There's often value in having people who've been wronged confront the person who's—"

"What are you blathering about? Wronged? I never *wronged* you." My voice sounds sharp and sure because I really don't know what she's on about. I never *wronged* her. I don't look at Kendy.

"You were abusive," Elk-EE says. "Emotionally and physically abusive. You cheated me out of my fair wages after I worked myself half to death for you."

"Half to death. You look meaty enough to me." Ha. That was humour with the makeup *off.*

I see her flush again. Her hands are twitching so much at each other in her lap it's like watching a short circuit. She's no match for me. For all her fancy talk and fancy clothes. Street smarts: that's what I've got and she doesn't.

"Fuck you," says Kendy.

I make myself look at her, at those ice-cold blue eyes. My heart begins to bang away again, but I keep staring, don't let her see how she's affected me. Her eyes hit back at me like hard-thrown rocks. She won't be as easy as Elk-EE to intimidate, but if she thinks that all she has to do is say "fuck" and I'll fall over in a faint she's got another think coming. I can say that word, too, when I need to.

"Get out of my house. Both of you. I got nothing to say to either of you."

"Well, you wouldn't, would you?" Kendy leans forward. "There's not one word you can say in your defence, you miserable, lying bitch. You haven't changed one bit."

"Get out. I'm going to call the police."

"Go ahead. What will you tell them? That you got into a fight with these nice old friends of yours? Do we look that scary? I can see them laughing all the way back to the station."

"They can laugh all they want. You're still in my house. Uninvited. I know my rights. They'll have to throw you out."

"Fine. Call them," Kendy says. "We can have a nice little chat until they get here. Reminisce about old times."

"We got nothing to reminisce about. We were finished with each other a long time ago."

Kendy leans back, props her elbow on the arm of the sofa. Her face has such a smooth, sleek look. Like her skin is made of vinyl or something. "Were we?" she asks.

"Yeah. Your lives so boring now you got nothing better to do than bother an old woman you once worked for?" I wince at the "old woman" but I want them to think how ridiculous they seem. "What do you want from me, anyway? Money? That's a laugh. An apology? I'm not apologizing for one G.D. thing." G.D.? Have I ever said "G.D." in my whole goddamned life?

"It's too late for apologies," Kendy says.

I shrug. I'm still annoyed with myself for the "G.D." Their church-lady look must have gotten to me.

"Al*though*—" the other one starts, but Kendy cuts her off.

"No, Gladys, we *want* something else. Something you might even understand. What we want is revenge. For the ugly things you did to us. And part of that revenge is telling you in advance that you'll have us to thank for the next really bad thing that happens to you. You won't know what it'll be until it happens. But you have it to look forward to. And when it does happen, well, think of us."

It's her calm, even tone, like a waitress reading off the specials for a customer, that sends the chill up my neck. "You can't threaten me. I'll tell my son. I'll tell the police."

Kendy laughs. "Police, police, police. My, haven't you become the righteous citizen? You think they would believe you over respectable women like us? And as for Rodney, well, what if he's part of that next really bad thing?"

Rodney. What does she mean about Rodney? How does she even know his name? I get to my feet, point to the door. "Get out. Get out. You slut."

Kendy leaps to her feet. I can see rage in her face now, and I take a step back, banging my knee into the recliner. She wants to hit me, I know she does, and I raise my arm up a little across my chest. The other one—I forget her name—says something, but I don't listen.

"You'll pay," Kendy says. "God damn you, you'll pay for what you did to me."

"It wasn't my fault. *He* did it. I didn't know. I didn't know he was going to do it."

"You're a liar. You knew. You were there. You watched. I saw you. I didn't realize it until later, but you were standing there big as life, watching. I saw you. Watching. Enjoying it. Wishing you could get in there, too, maybe."

"Shut up. Shut up. I don't know what you're talking about. I didn't know what he was going to do."

The other one, what's-her-name, has stood up now, and she's taken hold of Kendy's arm. "What's she mean?" she asks. "What happened?"

"Charlie raped me," Kendy says. "And she watched."

"Oh, God." The other one, Elk-EE, I remember her name again, puts her hand over her mouth, like some scared little virgin. I realize Kendy mustn't have even told her. Some team they make.

I try to use that, and I turn to Elk-EE, hold my hands out, palms up, make my voice soft and reasonable. "Look, what Charlie did to her was wrong, of course it was. But explain to her, will you, that it wasn't my fault. I couldn't control what he did."

"Charlie raped you?" She's looking at Kendy, maybe hasn't even heard me.

Kendy gives a kind of twitchy shrug. "It was after you left. I should have told you. Sorry."

"Oh, God."

"It's Charlie you should have punished," I say. "Too bad he's dead now." I didn't intend that to sound so flip and cocky.

"You were both to blame," Kendy says. "His being dead doesn't make you less guilty."

"Look," I say. "I know what he did was wrong. I *know* that. I divorced him over it. What he did made me so disgusted that I divorced him. That's revenge right there, isn't it? That our marriage broke up over it?"

There's this thick silence in the room. I've convinced her, I think. I humbled myself in front of her and it made me feel sick to do it, but I've convinced her, I've satisfied her. Now she can get out and leave me the hell alone.

She still doesn't say anything, just stands there shining those hard eyes at me.

I turn back to Elk-EE. "And after all this time—well, we're talking, what? thirty, forty years ago. It's pretty pathetic."

I guess I should have left well enough alone, because now Elk-EE flares her nostrils at me and gets up on her hind legs. She seems to forget about her highfalutin language and yelps, "*Pathetic?* You let that sicko husband of yours rape Kendy? You cheated us. You bullied us. You hit us. You threatened us. And you haven't changed, Gladys. *That's* what's pathetic. You're still the same cruel, nasty, selfish person you were then. So, no, it's not over."

I shrug, as though her words don't matter to me one bit. I think of reciting the old sticks-and-stones piece, but catch myself. They might think I was daring them. They scare me, there's no doubt about it, and I don't want to give them any worse ideas than they already have. Maybe those ideas already have some sticks and stones in them. Why didn't I keep my mouth shut after my little grovel about how I left Charlie? Okay, so he left *me,* I wasn't a hundred percent honest about that, but it was no lie about our marriage breaking up, and I still think that had as much to do with Kendy as with dumb old Glenda.

"I think we're finished here." Elk-EE reaches down and picks up her huge purse. "Let's go, Kendy."

Kendy gives a narrow-eyed look around the room, like she's memorizing it. I try not to imagine what for. She lets Elk-EE take her arm and pull her to the door.

Elk-EE opens it. I can hear a little scrabbling on the front step, and then the bushes rustling. It's probably the damned squirrel Faith has been feeding. Too much to hope that it's the Rottweiler from across the street.

Before they step out Kendy turns back to me and says, "Remember. The next bad thing."

Gladys

Late July, 2000

Dear Glenda,
> *Right. YOU let bygones be bygones. I'd like to shove*
MY bygones right up your ass.

Gladys

I think someone's following me.

I can feel that prickling on the back of my neck, just the way they describe it in books. But when I turn to look all I can see is the usual afternoon mall people, none of them familiar and none of them concerned about me. I stand for a few minutes pretending to be interested in the window of a clothing store, trying to make out the reflections behind me, but there's nobody sinister aiming an evil look at me.

Paranoid, that's the word they use.

But, damn it, I *have* been threatened. That bitch. It's probably all she intended, to make me look behind myself for a while, to worry about what might be lurking in dark corners. If she'd wanted to hurt me she'd have done it the day they came. Not just sauntered out and left me to tell anybody I wanted. An idle threat, that's what it was, an idle threat.

Still, there's that prickle on my neck. I reach up and try to rub it away.

I should have tried to find out more about them. I don't know where they live or even what their names are now. The Elk-EE one wore a wedding ring, so her name is probably different, and Kendy, well, there are hundreds of Kennedys.

I take the escalator to the ground floor, and for some reason this feels safer. It's the big mall in North Vancouver. I used to like the one where Faith works, but I don't go there much any more because I don't want to run into her. She sighs and looks hangdog and tries to make me feel guilty because she has to work and I can wander around wherever I want.

I go outside, find my bus stop. It's barely noon, but it's hot, the sun grating down. A skateboarder swings past in front of me, and he's wearing cut-off jeans so threadbare at the crotch I can see a testicle. His board makes its arc just a few feet from the waiting bus passengers, who give him that wilty look of people who are hot and not thrilled about where they're going. Their faces seem not sweaty so much as glazed with grease.

I get that tingly feeling in the back of my neck again, but I don't give in to it, don't turn around.

My bus comes. It's crowded, but I manage to get a seat near the back beside a large man whose butt pancakes out over half my seat. He gives me a little frown as I plop myself down, maybe onto some of his flab. His face looks kind of like Rodney's, and I give him the same stiff-lipped grin I give Rodney when I know I've annoyed him.

Rodney's been different lately. Him and Faith both. I can hear them talking and arguing late into the night sometimes. And I haven't been able to get either of them up to see me no matter what. I even made a lemon meringue pie last week, Rodney's favourite, but would he come up into the kitchen, even to just pick up a piece to take downstairs? Nope. It's not like he seems particularly mad at me or anything. That I could handle. A good clump of yelling and we'd clear the air. But he's just ... preoccupied. And Faith, too. She won't say a civil word to me, won't come upstairs.

I sigh, shift on my seat, and the man beside me glares at me again. I give him a glare back that lets him know what a real glare is. The bus jerks its way across the Lion's Gate Bridge. A breeze from the water cools us off a bit, but we heat up again going through Stanley Park and downtown and along Howe Street. The traffic is hell, all these damned big motorhomes farting exhaust through the open bus windows.

My stop still is four or five blocks away, but I can't stand the wait, so I get off early, head west on Broadway. Sweat is trickling down between my breasts, and I press my arm across my stomach to help my sweatshirt blot it up. It feels hot and cold at the same time.

I don't want to go home. I stop at some tiny, four-booth restaurant and order a coffee from a waitress so slow and rude I'd have fired her on the spot if I ran the place. I watch her go back to the phone call I've interrupted, listen to her going "Ah-huh, ah-huh," pulling out her gum slowly between her lips with her little finger.

The coffee is actually fresh. I sip it slowly, looking out the window at the people passing on the sidewalk. The air smells of diesel and fried onions. I sit there and think about Kendy, the way she was then, the way she is now.

In a way, it's almost flattering how she's been remembering me all this time, even if it is just because she's been wanting revenge. It was revenge I wanted on her, too, and revenge I got, so now it's revenge she wants again on me. It's almost funny. I just about stop hating her long enough to feel sorry for her. Thirty-five years of wanting revenge on me. Jesus. I only waited a month. If you wait too long you miss your best chances, plus you have that much extra time to carry it around with you.

It was revenge I wanted on Charlie, too, but I never got it. I let myself wait, let myself simmer too long on that stove. By then he'd pranced off behind his big stick to Glenda.

All I did, finally, was write Glenda a long letter telling her she was welcome to the creep. I even told her what he'd done to Kendy. Let's see how you like *that*, Charlie, I remember thinking as I dropped the letter into the slot. And what happens? The letter comes back to me a few days later, marked "Return to Sender." I knew I had their right address. So I was left to stew. Had Charlie intercepted it? If so, why didn't he just throw it away? Had he or Glenda used my old trick of steaming it open and sealing it up again? Whatever it was, they knew sending it back "Return to Sender" would be the more insulting thing. I could have sent it again, without a return address, but I didn't want them to think I cared enough.

I did, though. I cared. More than I let on. Him leaving me was humiliating as hell. Not to be good enough for even a loser like

Charlie. I brooded over the way he had left me until the day he dropped dead. And then it was Rodney Glenda called, of course, not me. Rodney took it pretty well, I thought, but then he had never been that close to Charlie, always thought of him as an embarrassment. I was the one who cried when I heard he was dead. That surprised me, my crying. But it was that whole part of my life I was crying for, I suppose, that whole part I hadn't been able to live any other way because I'd lived it with Charlie. But nobody saw me shed one tear. Even Olive couldn't get me to say more than, "Huh. Good riddance to bad rubbish."

Now that stupid Glenda has written me, like she's my long-lost friend, asking for a picture of Charlie. I just about fell over. Well, she's getting the message now. She's getting the picture, all right.

⊠

Something's up.

Rodney and Faith have come up from downstairs, both of them looking serious and dressed like they're going out, even though it's just after supper Thursday and they should be plopped down in front of their big TV with their slob-clothes on. But Rodney's wearing dress pants and a clean white shirt, and Faith has on her blue dress with the little bolero top, and she's wearing shoes, which she never does in the house. And she's got on some new thick lipstick that makes her mouth seem like two pieces of glued-on red cardboard. Hard to believe she must think it improves her looks.

"What're you both all tarted up for?"

"Nothing. We just ..." Rodney stands fidgeting at the entrance to the kitchen, and Faith hasn't even come up the last step. "Can we talk to you, Mom?"

"That's what you're doing," I say.

I don't let them see they've made me nervous, and I saunter out of the kitchen with my glass of ginger ale and drop myself into my recliner. I can at least be comfortable. I turn the TV sound down, but not to nothing, so that I can still tune in if I don't like what else I'm hearing.

They come into the living room, sit down beside each other on the sofa.

Rodney licks his lips. He's twisting and pulling on his watch band, and every time the little sections retract they pinch his skin but he doesn't seem to notice.

And then he does something I don't think I've ever seen him do in his life before. He takes Faith's hand.

"We've made a decision," Rodney says.

"Good for you."

"Listen," he says. "I'm trying to tell you something. Turn the damned TV off."

So I do. If it matters that much to him. It was just the news.

"We're going to move out."

Whatever I was expecting, that wasn't it. I almost laugh. We've had this argument before, and it seems pretty pointless to have it again.

"Don't be silly. We can't afford two places. You know that."

"We have to sell the house."

"I'm not selling the house! What's the matter with you? This is my house!"

"It's *our* house," Rodney says. His voice is calm, and that makes me more uneasy than if he were yelling. "You know it was mostly Faith's money that helped to buy it."

"Don't get smart with me. The deed is in my name. You agreed to that."

"Because you insisted, not because it was fair."

"Well, I'm not selling my house."

"Okay, don't. You can buy us out. Buy out our share."

"Like hell. Even if I owed it to you, where would I get that kind of money?"

"Then sell. There are all kinds of smaller places you could move to—"

"Nursing homes!" I spit the words at him. "You want to put me in a nursing home! Well, dream on. I'm not going to any nursing home."

He still doesn't get mad. Faith sits there with a glazed, idiot smile on her fat red lips and doesn't say anything. They're still holding hands. It looks so stupid it makes me want to reach over and jerk them apart. They're doing it just to annoy me.

"It doesn't have to be a nursing home. It can be a condo of some kind. Like Olive had."

"She hated that place!"

"No, she didn't," Faith says. "She made friends there. So could you."

"This is my home. You're not going to throw me out of it."

Rodney takes a deep breath.

"We've made up our minds. We're going to move. And we've got a right to get some money out of this house. We'll get a lawyer if we have to."

"This is about the separate entrance, isn't it? Jesus H. Christ. I don't see why you have to have a separate entrance. What's wrong with the way—"

"It's not about that. Not any more."

"Okay. I'll think about it."

"Well," Rodney says. "Well, good."

"I'll get some workmen to give me an estimate."

"This isn't *about* the entrance, Mom."

"The neighbours used some Iranian guy to put in their new porch affair. He was probably cheap. I could ask—"

"Listen to me! I don't *care* about the separate entrance any more!" Rodney gets to his feet. At least he has to let go of Faith's stupid hand. "Don't you get it? We're leaving."

It hurts my neck to look up at him, so I glare at Faith. "This is your fault, isn't it? You think if you move then your life will get suddenly perfect. Well, let me tell you, it won't. You can move to Timbuktu and you'll still be the same person."

"I got offered a better job," Faith says. She looks right back at me. I can see Olive in her, Olive when she was stubborn as a closed door.

"Good for you," I say sarcastically.

"It's in Victoria. We're moving to Victoria. We can get a real nice house there for half what this one will sell for."

"Victoria! On the island! I'm not moving to the island!"

"Nobody's asking you to," Faith says. "In fact, we'd rather you didn't."

I stare at her, let what she said sink in.

They mean it. They really mean it.

And not just to move to their own place but to move to another city. We've lived here for thirty years, argued our way around every damned domestic problem you could think of, and now this. My stomach feels queasy. I reach for the pop on the end table and my hand is shaking.

Rodney sits back down, leans forward, clasps his hands between his knees. I can see sweat on his forehead.

I make my voice low, softening it. "So you want to abandon me here. You want to go off on your exciting new life. And now that I'm old and no more use I get dumped. That about sum it up?"

Rodney looks down at his hands. He's clenched them so tight his knuckles look like they're trying to burst out through the skin. He doesn't answer. It's Faith who does.

She says, "Yeah. That about sums it up."

Her voice is so hard, so cold, so mean. I can see Rodney wince.

"What's gotten into you?" I say to Faith. I keep my voice soft, even though I'd like to jump up and give her a hit across the head. "How can you talk to me like that?"

Rodney still doesn't say anything. I don't know what's gotten into *him,* either, that he'd let Faith talk to me like that.

"It's just time, Gladys," Faith says.

Damn them. How *dare* they?

"I'll fight you on this. I swear I will." I don't bother with the sweet-and-low voice any more. "You want to get a lawyer? Go ahead. You know how much a lawyer charges? There goes your new house. Move out, see if I care. But you won't get one red cent from me. You hear that? Not one red cent!"

I stand up, wave my hands in the air, although I don't know myself what the gestures mean.

"Don't," Rodney says. "Please."

"Please. Please. Well, *please* don't try to throw me out of my home. Because please I'll fight you every inch of the way. I'll make sure you don't get your greedy fingers on one cent of my money. Not one red cent!"

"All we want," Rodney says, "is our share—"

"It's not so easy to throw an old woman out of her home. You'll see. When the lawyers get through with you there won't be anything left of your *share.*"

"Why are you doing this?" Faith asks. "Why can't you just let us go? Why punish yourself, too?"

I give her a long look. "This is all your doing, isn't it? Rodney would stay. It's you who wants to go."

"We both want to go, Gladys," she answers.

"You get him all to yourself, then. That's your plan. You think he'll turn into the perfect husband if I'm not around to be a bad influence on him."

"That's enough." Rodney stands up. His white shirt has big scoops of sweat under the arms.

"She's the one who wants to go, Rodney, so let her. Let her go. See how far she gets. She's bluffing, she wouldn't move across the street without you."

And Rodney smiles, a faint grimace of a smile, and he says, "I'm afraid that's where you're wrong."

"I've already accepted the job in Victoria," Faith says. "It's up to Rodney if he comes with me."

"What about *his* job? You expect him to quit his job?"

"He should be able to get a transfer. If not, well, it isn't as though he's built up a lot of good history with the company, anyway."

I'm shaking, with fury, with frustration, with not knowing what else to say. How the hell did they come to this, to Faith being the one to call the shots?

"Why is *she* the one suddenly deciding? There's a word for you, Rodney. Pussy-whipped. I sure as hell never thought I'd apply it to my own son."

Rodney's face goes red, but he doesn't answer. He turns to

Faith. "Let's go," he says. Then he looks at me. "Don't get in my way, Mom. I'm warning you."

"*Warning* me now, are you? Threatening me?"

And then a chill washes over me. *What if he's part of that next really bad thing that will happen to you?* Is Kendy somehow behind this?

And then I figure it out. Just like that. I know what's happened.

Kendy's been having an affair with Rodney.

If she could do what she did with Charlie she could do it with Rodney. He's a good-looking man. And I couldn't blame him for looking around for something more attractive than Faith. And Kendy's kept her looks all right. It wouldn't have been hard for her, that slut, to get her hooks into him. And now Faith has found out. It's the hold she has over him.

I take a chance. "I know about Kendy," I say to him.

Rodney frowns. "Who's Kenny?"

He never could lie convincingly to me, but he does a good job now. I almost believe him, but then I glance at Faith, and I can see from the way her eyes go wide and she pulls herself up straighter that I've hit on it.

"I know," I say. "That's all."

"You don't know anything." Rodney sounds tired now, like he's sick of this conversation. He's pretending, he's acting bored because he's wondering how the hell I could have found out his little secret.

Faith gets clumsily to her feet, using the arm of the chair to pry herself up. I can hear her actually grunt. No wonder Rodney would take up with someone like Kendy. And now she must have dumped him and he's had to go back to lumpy old Faith.

"Faith's new job starts in two months," Rodney says. "You've got that long to get ready."

Two months.

I sink back down into my chair. Rodney and Faith tromp across the room in front of me. As they go down the stairs I can hear their voices, Rodney's loud and angry now, Faith's quieter, and I think about following them to the top of the stairs to hear what they're saying. But why bother? What would they say to each other that I don't already know?

I'll fight them tooth and nail, I swear to God I will. But deep down I know this time I'm going to lose. One way or the other, I'm going to lose.

Damn them. It's like I dozed off for five minutes and when I woke up everybody'd changed.

⊗

The transit supervisor on the Skytrain asks to see my ticket, which is at least an hour beyond its expiry time because I've just been riding back and forth from one end of the line to the other. I make up some dithery old-woman excuse about how I missed my stop, but then he's all solicitous, or pretending to be, and asking which stop I want, so I say the first thing that comes to mind, which is "Surrey Central," where I used to go to meet Olive. Lucky it's far enough away so that he can't hang around to make sure I do get off there.

The train squeals to a halt at Metrotown, where I got off this morning and wandered around and finally went into a beauty parlour and had my hair done. I can feel it sitting there stiffly on my head like a new hat, and it has that chemical stink I told the girl not to spray on but she did anyway. When I came out of the salon I had that feeling again of someone watching me, but of course when I turned around there was nobody there. I kept expecting to see Kendy, or maybe that other one, Elk-EE. Or any one of the God-knows-how-many girls from the lodge who might still hate me, even though they all went on to their rich and fancy university lives.

Maybe it was a good thing I'd been feeling suspicious because when the young guy with all the zits and the baseball cap on backwards bumped into me and put his hand on my purse I jerked it away so fast and hard he almost fell over.

"Sorry," he said, like it had been an accident.

"Fuck off," I said.

He did, probably thinking they must not make old ladies like they used to. I looked around for a mall cop to report him to, but the kid was long gone by the time I found one.

I should have gone home after that, but I knew I'd just sit there and look at the walls and think, how much longer will I be able to live here? How much longer will this be my home?

I went into Sears and bought a new cardigan, for no other reason than that the mall had too much bloody air conditioning, and I'm wearing it now with the tags and their damned unbreakable acrylic thread still through the buttonhole. Then I bought a new pair of shoes, and I'm wearing them, too, to break them in. They were a mistake, they pinch in the toe, and they've got a Cuban heel I'm not used to. If I had the energy I'd go return them, or at least put on my old runners I'm carrying in the shoebox, but it seems all I can do is sit here on the train and stare straight ahead and think about Rodney and Faith and Kendy and what they want to do to me.

I've gone past feeling furious. Now I'm just tired. I feel my age, Olive would say.

Yesterday, after I heard Rodney drive off to God knows where, I listened until I heard the water downstairs stop running, which meant that Faith was finished her Sunday afternoon hair-washing, and I made myself go downstairs to talk to her again.

I tapped at the closed bathroom door. "Can I come in?"

There was no answer, but then I heard her hand on the knob, and she pulled the door open, about halfway. She went back to rolling her hair onto her curlers. I bit my tongue to keep from saying anything about how she should just go get a perm and be done with it. I figured it was my saying that sort of innocent thing that might have got her fed up enough to want to leave. Even though I would be just trying to help. Even though I would be telling her things for her own good.

I pushed the door open wider, stood there like some salesman on an unfriendly doorstep. Faith kept her eyes on her reflection, her fingers winding up strands of hair, sticking the picks in so tight she must be scraping up skin.

"I don't want you to go, Faith," I said.

"I know."

"So what will it take to make you stay?"

"I got this new job, Gladys. That's the end of it."

"I'll miss you."

Faith sighed. I could see she was uncomfortable with me this way—humble. I resolved to keep it up no matter what it cost me.

"I'm sorry," she said. "I really am. But I've made up my mind."

"I don't want to sell my house."

"If you can't run it without me and Rodney, I don't see any way around selling."

"Rodney doesn't want to go. I know he doesn't. Don't make him go. Please." The "please" was a good touch.

"I'm not *making* him go. I told him he could go with me or not. He decided to go with me."

"It's Kendy who's behind all this, isn't it?" I kept my eyes on her face.

"Kendy? I don't know what you mean." The hair she was winding onto the roller slid off one end, and she had to pull it out and start again.

I took a breath. What did I have to lose? "I know about his affair with her."

"Affair?" She turned to stare at me.

Now that I'd jumped in I knew I'd better start to swim. "I know she's behind all this. She came to see me. She threatened me. This is all part of some sick revenge thing, because I wasn't nice enough to her at the lodge all those years ago. She's used Rodney. To get back at me. That's all it's about. To get back at me."

Faith just stood there, looking at me for a long time, holding a roller in her hand. Finally she set the roller down and propped her hands on the sides of the sink, looking down into the drain. How much of what I'd said was news to her? I tried to imagine what was going on her mind, but I had no idea. Predictable old Faith, and I had no idea at all.

It took her forever, but at last she straightened, picked up the roller, and turned to me and said, "In the first place, somebody like Kendy would have too much class to have an affair with Rodney.

And in the second place, I don't care. I just don't care." She laughed, crazily.

It gave me the creeps, hearing her. I knew there was no point trying to reason with her any more. Because if she really didn't care about what I'd just told her she did have to be a little crazy.

She turned back to the mirror and began winding the roller into her hair at the back. She'd scooped up too big a clump, but she didn't redo it. I stood there for a few more minutes, trying to think of what else I could say, but I was stumped. So I just headed back upstairs. I could hear her give the bathroom door a kick, and it banged closed.

The train jerks ahead again. For a moment I have no idea where I am. The clatter of the cars is somehow confused in my head with Faith kicking the bathroom door shut. I start to stand up, then make myself be calm, sink back down. I'm on the Skytrain, of course, heading out toward New Westminster and Surrey. It's because I have no destination that it confused me. It's because I have no place to go.

A lot of people have gotten on at the last stop. A freckly-skinned man in a shiny suit sits beside me. He has that sour smell of unwashed underwear.

Charlie used to smell that way sometimes. He smelled that way the night he came back from Kendy's cabin.

I don't know why I didn't tell him then that I'd seen him. Maybe I wanted to hang onto that knowledge until I understood it better. Maybe I wanted the power it gave me, the power of knowing more than he thought I did.

So I never said anything, not until the day he told me he was shacking up with Glenda. I just stood there, forcing my face not to show anything.

Then I said, "I thought the only way you could get a woman was to knock her unconscious. Did you need my sleeping pills for Glenda, too?"

His face went red. He swallowed and looked away, his big announcement all spoiled, and then he slithered out of the room and out of my life.

I was rid of him. And even though it wasn't easy—it wasn't, oh, yippee, I've been dumped—at least I didn't have to turn from loving someone to hating him overnight, the way some women have to.

What's always bothered me the most is that I wasn't the one to do the leaving. I'm ashamed of that. I even had to lie to Kendy and that other one and pretend I was the one to choose. Because I should have left. How could I have stayed with him after what he did?

Rape. I might as well use the word Kendy used. The right word.

The businessman sitting across from me gets up and shuffles to the door, getting ready for the next stop, and a young woman with short bleached hair and a nose ring sits down in his place. The nose ring looks like the tags punched through the buttonhole of my new cardigan, and I reach up and rub my fingers on the acrylic thread.

She doesn't look one bit like Kendy, but, slowly, I start to imagine it is her. It doesn't feel particularly crazy to do this. Besides, what if it is crazy? I think about Faith laughing wildly and saying, "I just don't care," and maybe that's me, too, I just don't care. Maybe that's all crazy is, not caring.

So I look at this girl, and I imagine she is Kendy, and I imagine what I would say to her, now that she has gotten her revenge, now that she has so utterly beaten me.

What occurs to me is a bit of a surprise. I could tell her I'm sorry. I don't think I've ever said those words to anybody and really meant them, so why they come to my mind now, now when I've more reason than ever before to hate that woman, is a mystery. It's because she's defeated me, I suppose. Apologizing isn't as hard if you have no pride left. And probably thinking of saying "I'm sorry" is just some sort of childish bargain—as if they're the magic words that'll undo what's happening with Rodney and Faith. I don't have to mean the words. I just have to say them.

So just for the fun of it, I do say them. Out loud. To the nose-ring girl sitting across from me who isn't Kendy.

"I'm sorry," I say.

She gives me a funny look, then glances quickly away, the way people do to discourage a weirdo.

But saying the words has felt okay. Imagine that. I *am* sorry for what happened to Kendy all those years ago. I'm sorry for my part in it. And I'm sorry I didn't boot Charlie's sorry ass into the god-damned lake the next day. There.

I still hate Kendy's guts, though. That's reassuring. My brain hasn't gone completely to mush. I'm not Glenda, with her senti-mental let-bygones-be-bygones crap. Kendy owes *me* some apolo-gies, too, but I'm not going to hear any "I'm sorry" from *her,* I'm damned sure of that.

The transit supervisor is making his way down the car again. I lower my head, hope he doesn't remember me and my expired tick-et. But no such luck.

He stops in front of me and says, "Your stop is next, ma'am. Surrey Central."

"Okay."

The train slows, and I have no choice but to get to my feet and stand by the door and then let myself get shuffled out onto the platform. The train whooshes away.

My new shoes are pinching more than ever, but I hobble downstairs and buy a new ticket from the dispenser and then climb the stairs on the other side to wait for the train back to Vancouver. The platform is crowded. Above our heads a small bird bangs itself repeatedly against the glassy roof. A starling, probably, too stupid to see it can fly easily out either open end.

I feel more tired than I've felt in a long time. The platform smells faintly of urine, and it's hot and airless. I set the box holding my runners down in front of me and take off my cardigan.

"So. Gladys. It *was* you, wasn't it?"

The voice is right in my ear, a terrifying whisper, and a hand is on my arm, pushing me, pulling me, I'm not sure. I whirl around, ready to beat away whoever is here to hurt me, who has come for revenge. There are so many faces. Which is the one that spoke?

I step back, and I stumble over the shoebox. As I half turn to right myself, I can hear the exclamations around me. "Oh!" "Watch out!" "Careful!" And then a hand reaches out, and in that split second before I can decide whether it is there to help me or to push me, in that split second when I must decide whether to reach for it or not, I do nothing.

I stumble back farther, my ankle going over on my stupid new shoes with their clumsy heels, the cardigan I'm holding tangling my hands, and then I am tottering, reeling, and the voices around me are screaming now, saying, "No!" "Grab her!" "Help!"

And I fall. Not onto the platform, which I should have felt under me by now, but a longer fall, filled with a rush of air and a glitter of sun very high above me, the bird still fluttering there, and the horrified open-mouthed faces, and I can see the one who spoke to me, and I know who it is, oh, I know who it is.

Elke
Early August, 2000

Dear Dr. Bugosi:
I'm enclosing suggested revisions to your article
"Olfactory Influences on Aggressive Mood Disorders." . . .
Dr. E. Schneider

"It's someone called Faith."

Andrew sounds annoyed. He wouldn't have answered the phone if he'd thought it wasn't for him. He's preparing a case for trial next week, and he always gets irritable and tense if he thinks he might lose. I've told him that Faith is someone I met in the Yukon years ago, but he's forgotten. It's just as well. I'm relieved he is preoccupied, that I do not have to tell him anything more.

"Just a minute."

I come in from the garden, where I've been pulling weeds and spreading mulch, and wash my hands at the kitchen sink.

Faith: I've seen her several times in the last month and have grown quite fond of her. She's been a nice change from the academic friends I usually lunch with. She has interesting opinions and a sly sense of humour relying on sharp observation rather than the verbal wit I am used to. When I am saddened to think of the education she wanted so much and that was denied her, I tell myself I am being patronizing. Just as I tell myself that the way Kendy and I are interfering in her life is *not* patronizing but helpful. Faith has assured me vehemently she is grateful for our intervention, but I am still uneasy about it. Faith is gambling her life on Kendy and me, and I wonder if we might be a rigged game.

Kendy joins us for lunch sometimes, mostly to discuss the job she is engineering for Faith at her new Victoria office, but she is too busy setting up the store to come very often. When Kendy is with us we are a little more nervous, but also a little more alert and lively, as though someone has turned brighter a light we hadn't known was dim.

I dry my hands on the kitchen towel and go into the living room, where Andrew is still holding the receiver with one hand but frowning at the clipboard he's clasping in the other.

He's been losing weight, I realize, seeing him in the old tank top and shorts he likes to wear in the summer. His arms and thighs are downright spindly. I hope it's not something his antidepressants are causing. Perhaps it's simply because he's getting old, something I try not to see or think about. His face remains relatively unlined, and his dark and deep-set eyes can still summon the interrogative glitter that makes his cross-examinations fearsome. Once, after he won a particularly challenging case by unnerving a prosecution witness into contradictions, the head of his firm began calling him Can-opener Campion. I have been the recipient, too, of that cutting, judicial stare that implies more knowledge than it possesses, and it is not a look I can cajole into compromise. Still, I would far rather see him like this than the way I have seen him too often, listless and indifferent.

"Thanks," I say, taking the phone.

He nods, still frowning at the clipboard, and runs his hand through his grey hair, which is surprisingly thick for a man nearly sixty.

"If we have to," he mutters, in the way he has sometimes of speaking to his papers instead of me.

He wanders off to his study. I change my grip on the receiver, prepare myself for Faith. I am not eager to talk to her today, I must admit. I imagine she will want to continue our last conversation, when she was tearful because Gladys had told her Rodney and Kendy had had an affair.

"I told her I didn't care," Faith said, sniffling, "but it's not true. Of course I care."

"Well, it's utter nonsense," I said firmly. "Gladys thinks Kendy is involved in anything bad that happens, so she's made some wild guess as to how. She likely doesn't believe it herself. She just wants to upset you, to cause trouble."

I wish I had been as sure as I sounded. The truth is that, after my first laugh of incredulity, deep down I thought it could, just possibly, be true. The Kendy I had known was a carefree girl with a blithe and pragmatic sexual amorality; she is no longer carefree, but I have no idea about her sexual amorality. What would she stoop to? So to speak. Besides, people's sexual lives are sometimes as dismaying and inexplicable to themselves as to others. As far as I know, Kendy has never met Rodney, but "as far as I know" is not a great distance. Kendy obviously tells me the full truth about things only when she has to.

When, for example, I upbraided her for not telling me Charlie had raped her, she shrugged and said she hadn't wanted to upset me. I didn't say it had upset me far more to learn of it in Gladys Pratt's living room. For the next few nights I dreamt the rape was happening to me, and I would wake up shuddering and covered in sweat, thinking that this was Kendy's nightmare, except that for her it had also been real, and that she had been like the soldier stepping in the way of a bullet aimed at me. What was I to her then except a foolish girl whose protection had come at too high a price? What am I to her now except exactly what she had predicted, a reminder of the bad old days? Lately I have had almost as many misgivings about my interference in Kendy's life as I've had about my interference in Faith's.

I clear my throat, take a long breath. "Hi, Faith."

She is crying, deep gulping sobs, unable to form words. Oh, God, I think, my heart sinking. It must be true; they *did* have an affair. Faith has found some proof.

"She's dead."

"What?"

"Gladys. She's dead."

"What ... what do you mean, she's dead?" My mind cannot seem to understand.

"Dead!" Faith has raised her voice. "Dead!"

"How? What happened?"

"She fell. At the Skytrain stop. In front of a train."

A spike of vertigo pounds through me. "She fell ... in front of a train." My voice is barely a whisper.

Me, creeping up behind her on the platform, wanting to push her onto the tracks.

Faith blows her nose, the phone clattering as she bangs it on something.

"But ... how could it happen? Was she sick? Did she faint? Was she alone?"

"A whole bunch of people saw it. The police said she might have stumbled over a package she'd just set on the ground, a shoebox, maybe. But someone else told them she seemed to have gotten a sudden fright, that maybe there was somebody, somebody who spoke to her, or even grabbed her or pushed her or something."

Pushed her. I almost start laughing hysterically. Yes, it is my fault, mine, I implanted some evil intention into the subway air, some deadly doppelgänger biding her time.

"When did it happen?" My voice has only the tiniest tremble.

"A few hours ago."

"Does Rodney know?"

"Yes. He's still at the police station, I think."

"Is there anything I can do? Do you want me to come over?"

"Oh, Elke. Yes. Please. Come over."

⚙

I'm driving too fast, I know it and can't stop it, as though I am rushing to avert some tragedy rather than to meet the daughter-in-law of a deceased woman I disliked.

Gladys. Deceased.

They are words which, when linked, I might have expected would make me gleeful, but I suppose I should have known better. It is not that easy to take pleasure in the death of one's enemies.

A car honks at me, and I realize I have cut into the left lane too abruptly; the driver I cut off has every right to be annoyed. I give a small wave of what I'm sure appears not to be apology but just further rudeness. I must slow down, calm down.

I pull into the parking lot of a drugstore and turn the car off. There is a pinging sound in my right ear that could be either from the cooling motor or from my tinnitus.

I make myself take deep breaths, try to empty my mind. But of course it fills immediately with the story of Gladys and me, of Gladys and Kendy and me, of those four months that have kept such a disproportionate claim on my memory. And then there are the last two months. How much space will they claim? How will I understand this in five years, in ten years?

I left messages for Kendy everywhere I could think to do so before I left the house. I couldn't tell an answering machine what happened; all I could say was that it was urgent she call me. If she does, I hope Andrew will remember to tell her where I've gone. I have no idea what she will feel. I just hope she won't change her mind about hiring Faith. Although perhaps Faith will now no longer need to get away.

It isn't until I turn the car back onto Kingsway that I feel a nudge of suspicion about Kendy.

Could she have somehow been involved in Gladys's death? Could she have been the person on the platform who spoke to her? Could she have been the person who might have—

No, of course not. Of *course* not. Besides, she was already enjoying a better revenge by having Faith and Rodney move. What would be the point in killing Gladys now? Hadn't she said everyone got to have death and we needed something more original?

No, that was me. *I* said we needed something more original.

I hear myself making some whimpery little noise. If Kendy is guilty of something, then so am I. I am the one who began this business. This childish vendetta.

I turn on the radio, push at the buttons until I find someone talking, a voice other than my own.

When I get to Gladys's house Faith is sitting on the front steps petting a black and white cat on her lap. The cat watches me with slitty-eyed disinterest as I come up the walk.

"I didn't know you had a cat," I say. It sounds stupid but I suppose makes as much sense as anything.

"It belongs to the neighbours," Faith says, standing up, jarring the cat free too bluntly. It barely is able to land on its feet. "Gladys wouldn't allow any pets in the house."

I nod, and we stand there silently, in apparent respect, as though Faith has said some equivalent of "the woman was a saint."

"Come in," Faith says at last. I start up the steps, but she says, "No, come around the back. To our entrance. This is to the upstairs. To her part."

I follow her around the side of the house, which is overgrown with holly and ornamental cherry trees but pleasantly cool and moist-smelling. The lack of sunlight has killed most of the grass, which exists only in small weedy clumps, and I can't help thinking how I would plant some ivy or periwinkle or other shade-seeking ground cover here.

Faith is barefoot, I realize, wincing as I see her step on a hard twig. She seems not to notice. In the stiff squareness of her shoulders I recognize the tension which, when I see it in my clients, I always have the urge to press gently down.

We go in through the back door, and then down the stairs into the basement suite. It is roomy and expensively furnished and decorated, but, still, it is a basement suite, with its windows at ground level and a faint mustiness in the air. I can't imagine anyone choosing to live here for thirty years. I glance up at the ceiling, can almost hear the creak of Gladys's footsteps.

Faith gets us coffee, and we sit across from each other on matching brown leather loveseats. The stereo in the corner is playing softly, and I am surprised, in a way I decide immediately is snobbish, to hear Bach. Perhaps she has put it on just for me. Perhaps that thought is even more snobbish. When she passes me a bowl of something curly and pale yellow and says, "Have some," I decline, and only when she takes a piece herself do I realize they are not pork rinds but dried twists of pineapple. I feel even more ashamed, wonder if I would even have thought of pork rinds if I had been in the house of other acquaintances.

"Well, Faith," I say, "This was so unexpected."

She nods, runs her finger around the rim of her cup. She is

pale, but her face does not show the redness of recent crying, so in the hour since she called me she must have calmed herself. Pulled herself together, as my mother used to say, an expression I have found, from a clinical perspective, interesting. Faith is wearing a giant, grey sweatshirt and black leggings, more attractive than her business clothes, into which she seemed to have been inserted against her will.

"When the policeman came and told me I actually laughed," she says. "I thought it was Gladys playing some joke. Some desperate joke."

Desperate. Could we have driven Gladys, tough, cold-blooded Gladys, to desperation?

I can feel, probably for the first time, a little sympathy for the woman seep into my own cold heart.

"Do you think," I ask carefully, "that she might have been suicidal?"

Unexpectedly I envision the last scenes of *Anna Karenina:* the woman looking in misery and revulsion at the people around her on the train platform, muttering not to herself but to the power that made her suffer, flinging herself finally under the wheels of the second carriage. Could Gladys, *Gladys*—

It is a relief when Faith answers me with a laugh, even though it is an odd clatter of a sound. "Suicidal? Gladys?"

"No, it doesn't seem like her, does it? She wasn't one to ... give up." I start to add something about how it is hard to imagine her capable not so much of suicide as of the depth of suffering and self-awareness that must precede it; but I make myself swallow back the words, which would surely only sound pompous and cruel.

"She never in her life backed away from a fight," Faith says. "She wouldn't have let me and Rodney win so easily over this house business."

"I suppose you're right."

And they *have* won, I realize. This is no longer Gladys's house. Unless Gladys left a disinheriting will which could surely be challenged, it belongs now to Faith and Rodney. A little prickle goes down my spine. I am aghast to find myself looking at Faith and thinking, could she and Rodney— Could Faith—

I wrench my gaze away, but then I am looking at the stairs, and that feels worse, because now I am thinking how they are the only way out.

Good grief. Pull yourself together, Elke. I take a deep breath, the way I learned to do in yoga class. Breath is the drawstring to pull oneself together.

"... platform was."

"Pardon?" I make myself look back at Faith, make myself see the person I saw when I arrived.

"I said, the police have no idea who the other person on the train platform was."

"But they're still looking, I assume."

She nods. "They're taking statements. But nobody's come forward. Surely someone would have come forward."

"Unless ..." Unless the person pushed her, obviously. My not saying it makes it seem worse. I take a sip of coffee. It is so strong my tongue curls up in fright. "How are you feeling about her death, Faith? I imagine you might have rather confused and conflicting emotions." I have clicked on my therapist button. I suppose it is another way of pulling myself together.

"I wish ... I wish I could have been both, well, assertive *and* kind to her. That's what I've been thinking about. About how when I tried that it didn't work. If I was kind, I was weak, she thought. And if I was assertive, well, then I wasn't behaving like I was supposed to."

"That's quite perceptive."

"But I *do* understand why she was the way she was. I don't think in her whole life anybody really loved her."

"That's, again, quite perceptive." I sound so much like a condescending psychiatrist that I deserve the slight frown Faith gives me as though she must correct my perception that she has been fishing for compliments. "I mean," I add, "it's good that you're able to see the reasons for her behaviour. There's this saying, 'To understand all is to forgive all.'"

Why did I say that? Faith looks at me dubiously. Perhaps it was

Kendy I was thinking of. Besides, from my professional experience, the saying is sentimentally optimistic: understanding all often means forgiving nothing.

"I don't know about that," Faith says. "I just mean I know she didn't have much love in her life when she was young. I was luckier. My mom loved me. She was a wonderful mother. And Rodney ... well, I guess he loves me, too. Not all the time, maybe. At least I thought he did. I mean, I think he does."

The silence that follows her words means, I am sure, that we are both thinking of Kendy. It is probably a mistake for me to articulate that, but I do. "I'm sure there was nothing between Kendy and him, Faith."

"But just the fact that I had doubts says something, doesn't it? It shows I don't completely trust him."

"And Kendy? Do you trust her?"

Faith looks down, picks at her fingernails. It takes her a moment to answer. "*You* do, don't you?"

It is an effective parry.

"Yes," I say.

Faith nods, rubs at the back of her fingers so hard it pulls the skin white over her knuckles.

"How is Rodney handling his mother's death?"

Faith seems relieved to angle us away from Kendy. "He seemed so, well, dazed. He just sat there staring at the wall." She pauses, pulling her legs up to her chest and tugging her sweatshirt over them. "But just before he left for the police station he said, 'You know what I've been remembering, Faith? I've been remembering what she said when Dad died: *Good riddance to bad rubbish.*'"

"Was he ... suggesting he felt that way about her?"

"No, I don't think so. Not *really*. He didn't hate her. It was probably just this ... this angry thought. Because of the house business."

"Of course. The house business." I add quickly, "He's still in shock, too, you have to remember. People say things they don't mean."

The phone rings. When Faith answers it, she mouths "Kendy"

at me. Andrew must have remembered.

"Yes, Elke's here," Faith says, but she doesn't hand me the phone. "I can tell you why she called. Gladys is dead." She listens. "Yes. Dead. She fell in front of a subway train."

I wish I had been the one to tell Kendy. I can only guess at what she is saying, at the tone in which she's saying it.

"That's all I know," Faith says, and then she listens, wrapping the long phone cord around her fingers. "Okay," she says. "We'll be here. Come to the back door."

She hangs up, says to me, "She was in her car, somewhere close, so it shouldn't be long."

I want to ask how Kendy sounded, if she was shocked, but of course I can't. "I hope it's okay that I called her."

"No," Faith says. "It's good that you did."

"You haven't ... told her what Gladys said about her and Rodney?"

She looks at me as though I were mad. "Of course not."

We sit and wait for Kendy.

Faith wants to talk more about Gladys, and I can hardly discourage her; I nod, murmur gentle encouragements, sometimes retrieve a phrase for an elaborative question. But a part of me seems to take a seat across the room and watch me, as though I need to be watched, as though I will make mistakes.

Perhaps I am shamed by the apparently forgiving things Faith says about Gladys, and that is what makes me uncomfortable. Perhaps I am thinking unkindly it is only being dead that makes Gladys sympathetic. Perhaps I am wondering if Faith has always felt this way. I try to recall our earlier conversations, but the voices I hear are those of Kendy and myself railing against Gladys, dredging up the pettiest of our ancient grievances, and Faith sighing and acknowledging but not really adding to the froth of our anger although she had a lifetime worth of reasons. We dismissed her silences as those of someone long and habitually oppressed, but what was she really thinking? That we not only didn't understand her but that we didn't understand Gladys?

Knowing difficult people is supposed to teach us compassion.

Maybe I just didn't know Gladys long enough. The thought makes me shudder.

"I remember," Faith says to me now, "my mom telling me about one day at the retirement centre where they would meet to play cards. There was this woman who had some kind of dementia, and she would get these spells and stop in the middle of a game and stare off into space and say odd things. Everyone was tolerant of it or just thought it was funny, but it made Gladys so mad. As though the woman was doing it on purpose. This one day they were playing and she looked off over Mom's shoulder and asked, 'Is that a cake going by?' Mom just smiled and said, 'No, dear,' and they kept playing, but Gladys was fuming. After, she told Mom, 'You *encourage* her. You let her get away with that stuff.' That's how Gladys was. Always sure people were trying to get away with something."

I think of how she ran the lodge, always imagining she was being taken advantage of.

"It's hard to ever please people like that," I say.

Faith nods, and we sit in silence. A movement at the window, the sound of branches being disturbed, makes me look over, and I get a glimpse of a woman's leg moving past.

"Was that a cake going by?" I ask.

Faith stares at me, and then laughs so wildly I wish I hadn't said anything. The doorbell sounds upstairs, and Faith leaps up, swallowing a spasm of laughter into a hiccup.

She leaves me sitting with Bach, straining to hear what she and Kendy are saying upstairs. But their voices are only murmurs. I want to get up and open a window, because although it is pleasantly cool down here the air is also stale and too heavy with the chemical smell of a citron air freshener recently plugged into an outlet.

They come downstairs, Kendy first. She looks slim and glamorous in a white belted suit jacket and flared skirt several inches above the knee. She catches my eye, and grimaces, an expression that conveys apprehension or warning or incredulity or perhaps all of these.

"Sit down." Faith brings Kendy a coffee, which Kendy takes a sip of and then widens her eyes, as though the caffeine has gone straight to her eyeballs.

"Wow," she says.

"I made it stronger today," Faith says. "When I heard."

"I still can't believe it," Kendy says. "That she's gone. Just like that."

"I know you both hated her," Faith says. "But still. She was … she was a big part of my life. You know? She was a big part of my *life*." And she sinks down into the loveseat beside Kendy and starts to cry, small mewing sounds. Kendy gives me a glance and then puts her arm around Faith, patting her shoulder.

"It'll be okay," Kendy says.

Faith picks up a tissue, blows her nose. "It's so soon after we had that fight, about us leaving. The last things we said to each other were so, so *mean*. My last memory of her is of her mad at me."

Gladys mad was probably a permanent condition, but I know what Faith means. A part of me feels it, too, a wish to have settled things. I have listened to far too many people berate themselves after a death for unresolved quarrels, for things left unsaid, for the absence of conciliation.

"It'll get easier," I say.

"Give yourself time," Kendy says.

It'll be okay. It'll get easier. Give yourself time. Such banalities are all we can offer.

"You know you've still got the job in Victoria," Kendy says. "Whenever you're ready. And if you change your mind, I'll understand."

I give Kendy a relieved smile. Everything will turn out okay, I tell myself. Gladys's death was just a horrible coincidence. In a year's time perhaps Kendy and I will have virtually forgotten about her; in a year's time perhaps Faith will think, even if guiltily, that this was the beginning of finding a life of her own.

There is a sound upstairs, a door opening, footsteps on the stairs, and Faith sits up, tensely, as though she has been caught in something illicit.

The man must be Rodney. He's tall, with even features, and while I can see far too much of Charlie in his face he has shuffled in Gladys's genes in the places it does the most good. He could be described as handsome, despite his thinning hair and a surly look; the two deep lines pinched in at the top of his nose as though by a clamp seem to have pulled his brows into a permanent downward slant. I can tell from the way he's squinting through his glasses that they must, like mine, be bifocals and that he's not used to them.

He stops abruptly, stares at us, lowering his head a little to look through the top part of his lenses. Is there recognition on his face as he sees Kendy? The hostile look he gives us both equally is, ironically, reassuring. I glance at Faith, am dismayed to see her eyes flick nervously between the two of them.

"These are my friends, Rodney," Faith says, with only a slight quaver. "Elke and Kendy."

"Kendy." He frowns. "You the one my mother knew?"

Kendy smiles. "She knew both of us, actually." She quickly turns her expression more lachrymose. "I'm sorry about your loss."

"Yeah," he says. He goes into the kitchen, and we hear him opening a cupboard door, pouring something into a glass. We sit still, rigid, not sure what to do. Faith is pleating the cloth of her sweatshirt in her fingers, then smoothing it out on her thighs, pleating it again.

"We should go," I say.

"Stay just another minute," Faith says. "Please."

Rodney comes back into the room. He stands looking down at us, making no move to a chair.

"How ... was it?" Faith asks.

"I had to identify her body," Rodney says. "How do you *think* it was?"

"And there was ... no doubt? It was her?"

"It was her."

"What about that person on the platform?" Faith asks. "Do the police know anything more?"

Rodney takes a gulp from his drink, which might be a gin and tonic. "If they do they didn't tell me."

I get to my feet. "I really should go. If you'd like to talk more, Faith, just call." I have sounded too formal, and now I make it worse by adding, "or if you do, Rodney ..." I turn to him. "I'm a psychologist," I explain.

His look implies I could be an amoeba for all he cares, but he nods and says, "Yeah, sure."

Kendy gets up, too. She offers Rodney her hand, and I feel like slapping it away as I see the look of apprehension on Faith's face. *Damn* Gladys. How well she has kept this last bit of her poison, however diluted by improbability, working on us. I give Faith a hug; she trembles a little.

As we start up the stairs, I can hear Rodney asking Faith about the will. I stop, and Kendy bumps into me. "Elke," she hisses.

"Sorry."

At the landing at the top of the stairs, we hesitate, looking up into the kitchen in Gladys's part of the house. The faint smell of cloves drifts down to us. I wonder if Kendy has the same urge as I do, to go into the kitchen, to look for something, maybe Gladys, and if that is why we jostle each other reaching quickly for the outside door.

We take deep breaths of the fresh air. There is a sense of stifled hysteria about us. I run into a spider's web that must have been spun while we were inside, and Kendy says something I can't quite hear as I flail at it and wipe it from my face. I am aware of walking past the basement windows, aware that Faith and Rodney are probably watching our feet going by.

We head up the front walk to our cars, Kendy beside me now. When we reach the sidewalk she says in a low voice, glancing back at the house as though she doesn't want it overhearing, "Let's go for a walk."

"All right."

We head for the beach. For some reason we set a brisk pace, like walkers out for exercise, and we don't speak. The sun is in the west now, but still hot, and there is no cooling breeze coming up from the water. The streets are full of people, most of them young and tanned and noisy, wearing minimal clothing. Kendy and I must seem overdressed as we cross Point Grey Road onto Kitsilano Beach. Kendy slips off her sandals, but I don't want to take off my runners and socks; I smile as she grimaces at the hot sand.

"Maybe this isn't such a good idea," I say. "Maybe we should go to a restaurant."

"No, no," she says. "This is good." She heads, in mincing, fast steps, for a log shaded by trees at the edge of the sand, and we sit down with our backs against it. I'm wearing slacks and a polo shirt of Andrew's, but Kendy's outfit is expensive, and I wish we had a towel to sit on. She doesn't seem to care, leans back and raises her face to the mottled light. I breathe in the ocean air, which today smells faintly medicinal, of liniment. I imagine it cleansing, perking my blood with energy and oxygen, though I remember, too, it is oxygen that burns us up, oxidizes us, makes us rust.

"So," I say. "Gladys is dead."

"Hard to believe."

"Poor Faith," I say. "She feels awful."

"Yeah. Can't say the same about myself, of course."

"How *do* you feel?"

It takes her a minute before she answers. "I think I feel ... cheated."

I nod.

"What about you?" she asks. "The old Warthog who stole four months of your life and money and self-respect is dead. How do *you* feel?"

I think about it, turning my face up to the leaf-strewn light. Mostly, there is still just surprise at the suddenness. Someone I know has died. Perhaps the initial response is the same no matter who it is. But I make myself think about it more carefully. It is Gladys who is dead, Gladys, the cruel old Warthog of that dreadful summer.

It takes me so long to answer that Kendy sighs impatiently and begins picking up handfuls of sand and straining them through her fingers.

Finally I say, "Well, maybe there's a little bit of guilt—"

"Guilt!" Kendy snorts.

"—because of how miserable we made her life right at the end—"

"Good!"

I am ignoring her interjections. "—but mostly I guess there's a sense of ... incompleteness. As though I didn't record the last half-hour of a movie or something. Okay, that's a trivial analogy. But my hatred of Gladys—it seems to have, I don't know, dissipated. She's dead. There's no one to hate. It seems simple. I don't feel any sadness, either, which is a relief, because that surely would be suspect."

Kendy is quiet. We watch a Frisbee skid onto the sand in front of us, a laughing child retrieve it.

"I'm sure it *is* too simple," I say, feeling from Kendy's silence a need to elaborate. "Things usually turn out to be more complicated."

"What I'm feeling isn't complicated. I still hate her. I wanted to punish her. I wanted revenge. And she's escaped. I'll have to sort that out, I suppose."

"I could recommend someone for you to talk to. If you feel the need. You could talk to *me,* of course—the professional me, I mean—but I think I'm too involved."

She gives me her wry smile, her lips pulling down a little at the corners. "You invite Rodney to come see you, but you wouldn't see me?"

"God, I did invite him, didn't I? I was babbling. He'd never come, though. Surely."

"And you invited Faith. You'd talk to her, too."

It takes me a moment to understand that Kendy might actually be hurt, even jealous, the way she might have been jealous of Alice all those years ago. It annoys me that I seem to feel pleased, flattered, in exactly the same childish way I did then.

"Apparently I did," I admit. "But I shouldn't have. Talk about a conflict of interest. Every time Faith might say something kind and forgiving I might urge her to admit how she wanted to strangle the woman."

That gets me a smile, at least, even if it does look a bit noncommittal. Kendy leans forward and picks up a small, white piece of driftwood near her feet. She turns it over, blows the sand off, and replaces it, the darker underside now facing up.

"Remember?" she asks.

And instantly I do. "It's your gift to the wood. To expose its underside to the air."

"Charlotte said it was bullshit."

"Did she? Well, she was angry at all of us. In her mind I suppose we were all to blame for Basement Bobby's death." Too late I remember Kendy's involvement with him. I wonder if Charlotte knew.

Kendy touches the piece of wood with her toe. "Maybe it was Bobby's ghost on the platform with her. Whispering, 'Jump, Gladys, jump.'"

"Or maybe it was Here Boy. It wasn't a shoebox she tripped over, it was Here Boy."

"I think they'd have done something sooner. This is a long time to wait for revenge."

"I dunno," I say. "Look at us."

"True. Though we were inconvenienced by not being dead."

I smile. "Do you think we could have, well, actually contributed to her death?"

Kendy looks at me, sits up straighter. I can hear the bark of the log rasp against her suit jacket. "What do you mean? Like, made her commit *suicide?*"

"No.... But, well, there's the timing of it. I see Gladys, have an urge to push her in front of a train. Then we get Faith on our side, get her to tell Gladys she and Rodney are moving out, and, poof, a few days later Gladys falls on a train track. My evil fantasy down to the last detail."

"Only if she was pushed."

"Yeah," I say. "Only if she was pushed."

"You didn't do it, I suppose?"

I stare at Kendy. She has asked the question so casually, almost certainly as a joke, but still she has made it a question; there was that slight raised inflection at the end, the requirement of an answer.

"Jesus, Kendy. Of course not." I am aghast, but I cannot deny that the shiver that ran up my back also contained something unwholesomely thrilling: someone thinks me capable of murder! I make myself laugh. "What about you? You succumb to a moment's temptation?"

Her laugh sounds as forced as mine did. "'Fraid not," she says.

But the question lies between us now, the fact that we both asked making us ashamed and sombre.

⊗

It isn't until we're leaving that I tell her what Gladys said about her and Rodney. Immediately I wish I hadn't, wish I could quickly push some human version of my computer's Command-Z, which magically undoes, unsays.

"She told Faith *what*?"

"I thought it would amuse you." Did I? Is that why I had been watching her face so closely?

"Faith must have laughed and told her to go to hell."

"I guess so, essentially. But it, well, it upset her."

"Upset her? Surely she couldn't imagine I'd do something like that."

Why hadn't I kept my mouth shut? Now I had only made Kendy annoyed at Faith, not at Gladys. "No, but for one panicky moment, well, one would think, my God, could it be true—"

"One would, would one?" Her words are layered with scorn.

"There's always the remote possibility," I blunder on. "Like my being a ... a serial killer, or a transvestite, or the mother of quintuplets. It's not impossible, that's all I mean."

"What you *mean* is that you think I could be the sort of nasty bitch who'd sleep with the husband of a friend. Maybe you think I've been fucking yours, too."

"Oh, Kendy." I can hardly say even that, her words have so sucked the breath from me.

"Well, there's that 'remote possibility,' right?"

"There's a remote possibility for nearly everything." I struggle to regain my calm, professional voice, even though I suspect it might be part of what annoys Kendy. "I've found that, especially when it comes to people's sexuality—"

"This isn't about my sexuality. Or the fact that I'd have to be deranged to sleep with a Pratt. It's about what you think I could do to my friends."

"Don't be angry with me. Please."

"I'm not angry. I'm disappointed."

Disappointed. Worse than angry.

I can almost hear Gladys laughing at how well her weedy accusations have grown.

Elke

Late August, 2000

Dear Dr. Bugosi:
I assure you that my editorial changes were suggestions only,
and it was never my intention to alter in any way the sub-
stance of your article. . . .

Dr. E. Schneider

"So how did you come up with my name?"

I make my voice casual, smile at the constable sitting opposite me in the uncomfortable wooden chair that was vacant only because I'd moved its usual occupant, my big spider plant, outside to spray it.

Andrew is sitting at a right angle to us, frowning, steepling his hands at intervals under his chin. He is making me more nervous than the officer is.

"Mrs. Pratt gave it to us."

"Mrs. ... Pratt." My heart takes a leap. Gladys must have filed some kind of complaint against me— "Oh. You mean Faith. When I think of Mrs. Pratt I think of Gladys."

Andrew leans forward, but doesn't say anything. I wish he would leave. I have heard it makes the police suspicious when someone they are interviewing wants a lawyer present, even if it is her own husband.

"Yes. Faith. The daughter-in-law."

"I'm not—I mean, I'm not sure why she'd give you my name."

"We just asked her if she had any idea who it might have been on the platform who spoke to Mrs. Pratt. That's all. She gave us a few names, yours among them."

Before I reach for my coffee cup I make sure my hand is steady. "Well, it wasn't me. As I told you, I worked for Mrs. Pratt—

Gladys—one summer long ago in the Yukon, and then I ran into her and Faith—the daughter-in-law—a few months ago downtown, but I saw Mrs. Pratt only once after that. I've had lunch with Faith a few times, but not with Gladys. She was, well, she'd been my boss and it wasn't very comfortable being around her."

Andrew positively scowls at me. I pretend not to notice. I know he wishes I hadn't volunteered that last sentence. He has often said it is when people say too much rather than too little that they incriminate themselves.

"I see." The officer flips back a few pages in his notebook. "The daughter-in-law also gave us the name of another woman who met her in the Yukon. A Mrs. Kennedy? You know her?"

My heart is banging so loudly he must hear it. The telltale heart. He seems not to have spoken to Kendy yet. "Oh, yes. Mrs. Kennedy and I were both waitresses there in the sixties."

I am dismayed to hear myself echo his "Mrs. Kennedy." Faith must have provided him with the "Mrs." Kendy, if she must have a label, uses "Ms." Now she will have to correct him. But I was no more assertive for myself, meekly answering to "Mrs. Campion" when I should have said that I use "Schneider." I suppose it was Faith who gave him Andrew's surname, though I am surprised she remembered it. I usually sidestep both "Mrs." and "Ms." by using "Dr." though I know it is pretentious, a defensive instinct from academia, reaching for my Ph.D. the way the policeman in front of me might reach for his gun when threatened.

Surely the officer couldn't care less what women our age call ourselves. I am fretting over trivialities.

The constable flips forward to the page he was writing on. I sense from his posture that he is near the end of his questions. "So the last time you saw Mrs. Pratt was ...?"

"In early July sometime."

"Did you notice anything unusual? Did she say anything unusual?"

I have to fight back laughter. *Unusual!* I want to exclaim. *You should have been there!*

"Well, I can't really say. I mean, this was the first time I'd talked to her in thirty-five years. She seemed ... healthy. Her mind was clear."

"I see." He looks down at his pad, taps his pencil on it.

"May I ask why you need this information?" I make my voice sound puzzled, concerned. "Do you think she might have ... that it could have been ... deliberate?"

The constable gives me a terse smile. "We don't know at this point. That's why we want to talk to the person who spoke to her. Have you any idea who it might have been?"

"No, none at all. But weren't there lots of witnesses? Why do you need to talk to this particular one?"

Andrew is frowning again. I am amazed he has been able to keep his mouth shut. He must know both that his interference would annoy the constable and that it is important not to annoy him.

"It's just procedure," the officer says. "Cases like this, we just want statements from as many people as possible before we close the file." He gets to his feet. "Well. Thank you very much for your time, Mrs. Campion."

Andrew gets to his feet as well, and they shake hands. "Glad we could be of help," Andrew says.

I am not irked that he has now appropriated the situation, because what he does is turn me again into the wife of a respected lawyer. I am, surely, completely trustworthy.

But when the door has closed behind the officer, Andrew's urbane smile disappears, and his eyes snap with irritation. "What the hell was—"

I hold up my hand. "Wait. I have to make a call." Even if Kendy is still angry with me—no, *disappointed*—we have to talk.

The phone rings just before I touch it. I snatch the receiver up, ready to say, no matter who it is, that I can't talk now, that I must make an urgent call.

It's Kendy. "Thank God I got you," she exclaims. "Would you believe a *cop* was just here—"

"I was reaching for the phone to tell you the same thing. I was hoping I could warn you. What was Faith *thinking*, to give them our names?"

"I called her a minute ago to ask her exactly that. She was all upset, afraid the cops are suspicious of her or Rodney. She gave them our names as character references more than anything else, I think."

"Character references!" I exclaim. "Good Lord. I wish she would have forewarned us."

"What did you tell them?"

"Just how, no, it wasn't me on the platform. How we all met at the lodge in the sixties. That I recognized them on the street, we got together with Faith for lunch a few times, we went to the house once and saw Gladys. What did you say?"

"About the same. But, Jesus, Elke. If they're investigating it means they must think there was, you know, foul play."

Foul play. The term sounds so melodramatic and archaic and oxymoronic.

"The cop said it was just procedure. Just taking statements so they could close the case. But I did say that Gladys wasn't very comfortable to be around, and Andrew is here with me, and I could tell from his frown I probably shouldn't have volunteered that." I have mentioned Andrew to let her know that this call is not private. Andrew is in the kitchen, rattling something in the refrigerator, but I know he is listening.

We seem to have blundered into an awkward silence, thinking about what we can and cannot say. Finally Kendy says, "Look. I have to go to Victoria for a few days. One of my suppliers is letting me use his condo there while he's away. A great place. Why don't you come up for a day? We can talk, have fun, get drunk, you know. Whadya say?"

I am more than a little surprised. After the things Kendy said to me the other day on the beach I thought she would never want to see me again.

I think about her invitation for only a second. "Okay."

When I hang up it is with reluctance, knowing I will now have to talk to Andrew.

He comes into the room holding a glass of iced tea and sits

down across from me. He is wearing a polo shirt and navy suit jacket and slacks because he was getting ready to go to the office, but one of the many reasons he is annoyed with me is surely that he has had to talk unexpectedly to a policeman without having on shoes or socks.

"What the hell is going on, Elke? Who are these Pratts?"He takes a drink from his tea. The ice cubes rattle.

"I've told you about the Pratts," I say. "The same thing I told the constable. They owned that awful lodge in the Yukon where I worked the summer before I started university. I ran into Mrs. Pratt again. And Kendy, the other waitress. Kendy and I have had lunch a few times."

He sharpens his eyes at me. "Can-opener" Campion. My story seems suddenly made of the flimsiest tin.

"And this other Mrs. Pratt?" he demands. "The one who gave your name to the police?" He sits down, pulls on the socks and shoes waiting beside the chair.

"Faith. Gladys's daughter-in-law. She was up at the lodge, too. Her mother was the chambermaid there."

Andrew grunts. "What else should I know?"

And I start to say, *nothing, nothing else,* anxious to divert us onto something neutral, to ask if he's bought the cat food, when I realize that I no longer need to tiptoe around him.

I haven't had to for some time. Maybe a whole year. I have let habit hobble my brain. Andrew's okay now. I don't need to be afraid for him. He is strong now, often even overbearing, to the point where sometimes I miss his more fragile self with his sad reliance on me to interpose myself between him and unpleasantness; but surely a little imperiousness is not an unfair price for his health, his confidence, his life.

So I tell him what else he should know. I tell him how brutal the Pratts really were. I tell him about Charlie coming to the cabin and how Kendy intervened and what she did and what happened after I left. I tell him how I wanted to push Gladys onto the train tracks. When he keeps interrupting me with picky lawyerly questions I tell him, a little thrilled with my daring, to shut up and listen. I tell him of meeting Kendy and how we confronted Gladys, how Kendy gave Faith a job in Victoria, how she and Rodney were planning to get the house sold and move to the island.

"So that's it," I conclude. "Rather feeble as a revenge plot. Not exactly luring the woman we hate into the vaults for a glass of amontillado and then walling her up alive. We just offer her daughter-in-law a better job. How evil. Though I think it did have the desired effect. Gladys was probably going to lose Faith as her doormat, and also lose the house she was using to control Rodney and Faith."

Andrew sits for a while staring at his hands. I watch him nervously, wishing I hadn't told him to shut up and listen. What if that had been too much, what if he can't handle it—

He looks up. "Am I allowed to talk now?"

"Yes, yes, of course. I'm done."

"First of all, do you have an alibi?"

"Alibi?" I laugh, mostly in relief that he is still talking like a lawyer. "Whatever for?"

"For when Gladys died." His eyes scowl at me. "Look. In all probability, this is the end of it. They take enough statements to make it look good and then they'll close the case. But what if they've reason to be suspicious? If this Faith gave your name to the police, she could be trying to make you look questionable. She could have told them about your little murder fantasy—"

"I never told Faith about that. I only told Kendy."

"Well, whoever," Andrew says, as though Faith and Kendy are both essentially the same, and both untrustworthy.

"Okay. Alibi. God, I don't know. I was probably home, working. Alone. Maybe I sent some e-mails—they'd have a date and time on them. Would that help?"

"I doubt it. Too easy to fake. Might make an interesting precedent, though." He drums his fingers thoughtfully on his thigh, and it annoys me, as though he is almost hoping he will have a chance to test this defence in court. "Anyway. I don't have time to deal with this now." He gets up, looks briskly at his watch. "I'm late." He finishes his iced tea in one quick swallow. "Just be careful. And don't ... embarrass us." He smiles, but I have the feeling the smile is an afterthought, an adroit corrective.

"Embarrass us."

"You know. And stay away from those people."

Stay away from those people. It is the exact thing my father said to me about Alice, because her family was Ukrainian. *Stay away from those people.*

I don't tell Andrew I have just made arrangements to visit one of "those people" and that I don't intend to cancel.

"Yes, Petruchio," I say instead.

He gives me a puzzled look. "Oh. Right." He hesitates, and I catch my breath, think that whatever else he decides to say will be important. "You flatter me," he says.

It could have been worse.

When he is gone I pour myself a large glass of wine and collapse onto the sofa. The cat jumps into my lap. I ask him how he would, on a scale from one to ten, rate my recent performance. He meows, twice.

"I was better than *that*," I say.

In fact, when I review my answers to the constable's questions I can't see much I would change. His visit was just routine, anyway; he said so. He does not think I pushed Gladys in front of the train. He does not think Kendy did. Or Rodney or Faith. We are just some paperwork he has to complete. Surely. Andrew's talk of alibis and suspects is merely his lawyerly instinct; even he said this is in all probability the end of it. I take a big gulp of wine to swallow down my doubts.

As for telling Andrew about Kendy's and my little plot ... At the very least, I have set a precedent. Like the e-mail defence. I have been reassured he can handle such things. And I suppose he has learned that I might not be as predictable as I was. He has ceded to me, after all, the power to embarrass us. I can feel my mouth pull and prickle with irritation as I remember his words, but I reach up and rub the sensation away.

Thinking of e-mail makes me go to the study to check mine. I am both relieved and apprehensive to see one from David in

Portugal. I click it open.

Hi, Mom—

just a quickie to ask if you could get another couple of thousand to me ASAP. Maybe three. I'm counting on it. I've met these French guys and we're going to go hiking through Spain. So, look, could you get that money into my account by the weekend? Appreciate it—

love, David

I sit there for a long time, looking at David's message. Something in me goes very dark. My fingers are shaking as I push "Reply" and start to type.

David—

I've had enough of your irresponsible bullshit. You are not getting one more penny. It's time you woke up and realized I am not here to cater to you and your holidays forever. Get a job. Go to university. Grow up.

I stare at what I have written. My fingers on the keys are still shaking. There is a ticking in my ears that seems to grow louder and louder with each heartbeat.

It is not David, or not just David, that I am so angry with. It is all the people in my life at whom I have had to smile when they treated me badly. It is my father, *damn* him for his selfishness, for cutting me out of his life because I wanted to be more than his servant. It is my colleagues who used me, put me on every committee they thought was beneath them and then called me uncreative, and I told myself I was *hurt, hurt* was the easier word, when I was outraged—I wanted to slash their tires, I wanted to pour acid into their filing cabinets. It is Andrew, who has taken me for granted and expected meekness from me when he was strong and strength from me when he was weak and is now going back to being domineering and inconsiderate and I will not stand for it. And the Pratts, of course, Charlie that rapist bastard, and Gladys, vicious Gladys, but now they are both dead.

Breathe in, breathe out.

I look up at *The Wanderer Among the Mists.*

Slowly my lungs stop feeling as though they are being squeezed in a fist. The noise in my ears fades.

Perhaps what is under the mists is the past. Perhaps the wanderer is not observing as much as remembering.

I wondered, not long ago, if my preoccupation with Gladys was because I was bored, looking for some diversion. But perhaps I was simply allowing myself to hate, indulging that forbidden emotion against an easy target. The best scapegoat is, after all, one who is not exactly innocent.

I suppose, in a grim kind of way, I can even tell myself that I owe the Pratts something, rather like what I owe my father: they made me excessively diligent at university, because I knew if I wasn't I would always be at the mercy of bullies like them. Though that is like thinking it is good to suffer because it teaches one fortitude.

I look back at the message I have written David. Then I click "Delete." I won't send him the money. But I won't send him the message, either. I don't want him to be, when he is my age, remembering this nastiness, damning me for being selfish, for thwarting his life, the way I've just done with my own father. I will think about it for a day, will write something more neutral.

There is another message in my in-box, from Ted at the journal. He says he is attaching three more manuscripts and would I get to them ASAP? I click "Reply" and type:

Ted—

I've been doing more than my share of the reading.
Please ask one of the other editors. I'm busy now.
Elke

I go back and remove the "Please" before "Ask" and then, before I lose my nerve, I press "Send." It's done. What can he do? Fire me?

I sit on my hands. The cat has come in and sits looking up at me.

"Whee," I say.

⚭

We are sitting on the edge of the pool, dangling our feet in the water. The condo is more impressive than I could have imagined. There are only half a dozen units, all staggered and screened from each other, and all with a dazzling view across Cordova Bay. Mount Douglas Park borders us on one side, and the breeze pulls in the pleasing and gently sour scent of pine on a hot day. Behind us, weedless and sculpted flower beds of phlox and alyssum are rumbly with bees. We are the only people at the pool.

Kendy rummages in the cloth bag she brought down with her and finds a bobby pin, which she affixes carefully to the stub of the joint we have been smoking. The fact that she has had to improvise a roach clip reassures me she indeed has the joint only because, as she claimed, she confiscated it a few days ago from a young employee at her Burnaby shop.

She takes a long pull, hands the cigarette to me. Andrew would scream. Tough. I inhale deeply, holding in the taste, the sensation, which are exactly as I remember them from thirty-five years ago. I close my eyes and I am at Kluane Lake, sitting under the pine trees with Kendy, looking up at the night sky, which has never since been so filled with stars.

"Whoa," Kendy says.

I realize the cigarette has burned down to the clip, and ash is drifting onto my thighs. Kendy takes the bobby pin, releases the stub and flicks it into the pool. It doesn't sink. She slides the bobby pin into her hair, leans back, and rests herself on her elbows, raising her face to the afternoon sun.

A ginger cat steps out of the shrubbery and sits watching something in the air to my right. I look but of course see nothing. A cat can see things at a pitch too high for human eyes. I think of telling Kendy Faith's story of the old woman with dementia who saw a cake going by, but it seems like too much effort.

We both know we should go in, or at least reapply our sunscreen oils to ward off what David as a child called the ultra-violent light; but it is so pleasant to sit here in our bathing suits with our feet in the warm water. Kendy is wearing a white bikini, and I feel frumpy and old in my one-piece grown crispy with too much sun and chlorine.

We have not referred to the last time we saw each other, though there was that awkward laughter and averting of eyes when I arrived, and our conversation seems politer than usual. The things we said to each other on the beach still linger between us, but the marijuana has made them fuzzy and less important. Besides, now we have something else to think about.

"Are you *sure* Faith didn't say what she was bringing?" I ask.

Kendy sighs. She picked up the message from her service an hour ago. "She said, 'I know who was on the platform. I'm bringing you the proof. See you soon.' That's it."

"God, the suspense."

"I know. She has my cell-phone number. She's used it before. And she needn't have called at all, just shown up here as we'd planned." She glances at her watch. "If she'd told me which ferry she was on I could have met it. Now she'll have to take a cab."

"As I say, she wants to keep us in suspense."

"It's annoying."

"Ah, there are mysteries to young Faith we might little comprehend." I watch my feet make small circles in the water. "Did you wonder if, well, if just maybe she could have pushed Gladys?" I slide my gaze toward Kendy without moving my head.

Kendy sits up, pulls one leg to her chest. "No," she says. She doesn't elaborate. I resist the urge to say something again about remote possibilities, to skate out again onto the thin ice of how little we all might really know each other. After a moment Kendy says, "What about Rodney? Maybe he did it."

She is staring lazily across the pool as though her mention of Rodney will not make me uncomfortable. Perhaps she is testing me to see if I am still imagining they had an affair.

No, of course she isn't. She has simply moved past the

indignation and sulking about who owes whom an apology. And I will have to swallow my pride and hurt and do the same. Hurt: I think about that word, nudge it to see if it is a euphemism for anger. A little, I decide. Not enough to want to pour acid into her filing cabinets.

"He might be capable of it," I say genially. "And he had a pretty strong motive. Plus, with Faith finally standing up for herself he might have been desperate."

Kendy nods. "And we know how Gladys could provoke people." She pulls her other leg out of the water and tucks it under her in a half-lotus. "If he did kill her I'd like to give him a medal."

I laugh, but it saddens me to still hear such hatred in her voice. Everything I think of saying seems like something she would frown at and say, "Thank you, Dr. Christ." We sit looking at the sun chipping sparks off the water.

"You know," Kendy says, "the day after she died I had this memory of a movie I saw once. I can't remember anything except the first few minutes. A limo pulls up at a graveyard. A well-dressed man gets out carrying a cassette player. He walks slowly over to a grave, sets the player beside it, turns it on, it plays loud tango music, and he steps up onto the slab and dances. The camera is fixed on his feet. After a few minutes he stops, turns the cassette off, and walks back to the car. The driver asks, 'All done, sir?' and he says, 'Yes,' and gets into the car and they drive away."

"Is that how you feel?" I ask tentatively. "You'd like to dance on Gladys's grave?"

"And on Charlie's. Maybe it would be cathartic."

"Maybe." I tell her about the e-mail I wrote to David but didn't send.

"'Irresponsible bullshit.' How wonderful. I'd have sent it."

"I was tempted. But he was just, I don't know, the visible target." Maybe the way Gladys was for me, too, I don't add, because it would trivialize Kendy's anger. "It would just have escalated everything."

"Well, I'm glad we escalated Gladys. I wish I could have personally escalated her a bit more."

"She's dead. We win."

"No, we don't. I still feel cheated. There wasn't any, I don't know, any cause and effect."

"Maybe Faith will bring us some."

"Oh, right. Faith." Kendy stretches her arms up over her head, squints out at the pool where the joint is still floating and the breeze is cuffing slim ripples from the water. "Let's go up. I should check to see if she's left another message. And when she comes she'll have to buzz up."

"'I know who was on the platform.' What a tease."

We go up to the condo, which is on three levels, each level with at least two bedrooms and baths and sitting rooms. We change into shorts and T-shirts and then meet on the top level, which has curved floor-to-ceiling windows to take advantage of the view over the bay. On one wall I notice a small painting of a seascape, in pale shades of grey and blue and white. A Lily Briscoe.

Kendy goes into the kitchen and starts to make us cucumber sandwiches because, she says, it seems like the kind of stylish thing one should eat in a place like this. I pick up the fallen blossoms of the potted bougainvillea by one of the south-facing windows. When I crumple them in my hand they sound like crepe paper. I toss them off the deck and they land pinkly on a huge oak tree whose branches reach to this level. I look at the way the oak's big limbs near the base fork in the same way as the smaller twigs do, as the veins in the leaves do: repeating patterns on various scales. Fractal geometry. It feels like the kind of stylish observation one should make in a place like this.

Kendy comes back with the sandwiches and we sit on the wide, velvety sofa and put our feet up on the coffee table and eat. We talk about where we have travelled and why. Not surprisingly, Kendy has been almost everywhere. I tell her how the children took the time and energy I would have used for travelling and how then they simply flew away themselves.

"I know one isn't supposed to expect gratitude for imposing life on someone, but one does." I am surprised at the resentment I hear in my words.

"At least you *had* kids," Kendy says. "I never seem to have made the connection between sex and procreation."

"Yeah, well. The road not taken. I wasn't completely wrong to think, there goes the career, when I found myself pregnant with David."

"At least when you got pregnant it wasn't because you were raped."

I look at her, feeling sick.

But in some dark crevice of my brain, in some neuron where a filament of what is known has already touched the filament of what is feared, I am not surprised.

"At least you didn't have to have a back-alley abortion."

"Oh, Kendy."

She holds her hand up, as though I am going to come walking into her. "Hey. It could have been a lot worse. I could have *not* been able to get the abortion. I don't often think about it. But it was, you know, part of this hating-Gladys thing."

"I'm so sorry." I try to swallow, but my throat has clenched shut.

"Funny how I knew right away I was pregnant. I almost went crazy. I was going to go back to university after the abortion, but by then the term was half over, and I just drifted into different things."

"You should have told Gladys," I say. I don't bother to add, and *me.* "Gladys should have known the worst of it."

"I suppose. Maybe I just didn't want to hear her say I deserved it."

"Surely even Gladys wouldn't have said that."

But perhaps that is exactly what Gladys Pratt would have said. I can imagine her brittle laugh, her fingernail-on-blackboard voice raking across Kendy: *Serves you right, you tramp.*

But it is pointless now to wonder what she would have said. In any case, it was never contrition from Gladys that Kendy wanted. What she wanted was revenge.

"At the end of that summer," Kendy says, "you said our time there might be ... you had a German word, it meant 'key experience'—"

"*Schlüsselerlebnis.*"

"—and I laughed and said something about life having such glorious adventures in store for us we'd barely remember even being there. Well."

We are silent. My mouth feels dry, tight, incapable of forming words. There seems suddenly to be too much light in the room.

When I get up to go to the bathroom I put my hand on Kendy's shoulder, and she gives me a quick smile, but I can sense a rebuff in it, a warning against pity. She is right, of course, that things could have been much worse, but when I think of what she had to go through, how probably none of it would have happened if it hadn't been for what she did to save me, I feel the helpless tears well up.

In the bathroom I wash my face with cold water, press a wet washcloth against my eyes. The mirrors above the sink are a triptych: there are too many views of my face. One is too many.

When I come out Kendy is tidying the kitchen. I join her, and we say the kinds of things women say to each other in unfamiliar kitchens: where does the butter go, is there a separate knife drawer, aren't the granite countertops nice?

We go back into the living room, but, as though we must avoid the chairs we were in before, as though they retain some imprint of our earlier conversation, we walk through onto the deck and sit in the thickly cushioned patio chairs under a huge, blue umbrella. Kendy puts on a pair of sunglasses lying on a side table. She probably doesn't intend it, but the glasses hide her eyes from me, like something tactical. We drink wine, more quickly than we should, and talk about men, making silly jokes. Then I tell her about Andrew's struggle with depression and how hard it was for us. She tells me that a depressed husband would have been preferable to *her* first husband, who confessed on their second wedding anniversary that he'd had five passionate affairs since they'd been married.

"Five!" I exclaim.

"Five! Five *passionate* ones!"

We laugh, giddily, survivors.

"Did you want revenge?"

"Oh, absolutely. I got it, too. On my second husband. The sweetest man alive. I slept with his brother."

"Oh, dear."

"The victim becomes the victimizer." She pauses. "It's why I said those stupid things to you that day on the beach. You hit a sore spot. I *was* the sort of woman who could sleep with her best friend's husband. I'm sorry."

I'm sorry. How easily those words have undone the mischief Gladys made between us. *I'm sorry:* perhaps there is, after all, a human version of Command-Z.

"Well," I say. "I'm reassured to discover you aren't perfect. I thought you were, you know, that summer. I thought you were absolutely perfect."

"Oh, I was, then."

She picks up an orange from the fruit bowl on the side table and starts to peel it. "Did you know," she says, "that sometimes when you plant an orange pip a grapefruit or a lemon will grow from it?"

"Really?"

"It's true. Makes you wonder what strange creatures we might be carrying around inside." There is a beat of silence, barely noticeable, before she continues. "When you're planted, what would you like to have grow from you?"

"Oh, grass, I guess."

"Grass." Kendy makes a face. "I'd like something more ambulatory. Something with no brains but lots of teeth." She pulls off a section of orange and pops it into her mouth, bites down, hard, with lots of teeth.

When the intercom buzzes, we jump.

"Faith!" we exclaim, together. Our eyes and mouths go comically round. Kendy tosses off the sunglasses, goes to answer. I follow her into the living room. A voice crackles on the phone.

"She's *here*," Kendy whispers at me, splaying her fingers dramatically on her chest.

She opens the door, and I can hear Faith coming up the outside stairs, can hear her say, "My God! What a place!"

"Great, isn't it? When you start work over here, you'll meet the guy who owns it. He's one of those weirdos who's both rich *and* nice."

For a moment I feel envious of Faith, starting a new life in a new city, meeting weirdos. I would not have her courage.

Then I hear the murmur of another voice, a man's. The taxi driver? I stare at the doorway, resist going over beside Kendy to look down the stairs. Surely Faith hasn't brought *Rodney*?

"Come on," Faith says. "They won't bite."

Kendy's profile tells me nothing about what she is seeing. Then Faith steps clumsily across the threshold carrying a suitcase the size of a steamer trunk, as though she were staying for two weeks instead of just two days. She sets it down, panting, and waves at me across the room. Her face is flushed, excited. Her hair sits on her head in tense little curls.

Kendy has stepped aside and is looking with an uncertain smile at the man on the landing behind Faith. Faith takes his arm, pulls him inside.

He is old, stooped, his face so scored with the wrinkles that come from an outdoor life that his skin looks weathered as tree bark; but when he takes off his hat I am surprised to see a headful of thick, black hair. He is dressed in a grey suit that looks old and is too big for him. Under his pant cuffs I can see cowboy boots with the heels worn in such an uneven way they should be in an ad for orthotics.

It is the boots, I suppose, that tell me, by the time my eyes have travelled back up to his face, who he is.

"Why, it's Upstairs Bobby," I say.

"Elke!" Faith exclaims. "How on earth did you know?"

I am almost as surprised as Faith that I should recognize him. Even thirty-five years ago he was only a man with a big grin who would sit at the Pratts' table. I suppose he must have stayed in my memory only because he was pointed out to me as Basement Bobby's father.

I am embarrassed now, to have them think my life has not found enough new faces to crowd out one so peripheral to me.

"Lucky guess," I tell Faith.

Kendy seems unable to stop simply staring at the man, so I invite him in, gesturing in the direction of the wide, white sofa and expensive chairs. Faith still has his arm and she shuffles him over to a big leather recliner. She sits near him in a thin-legged Queen Anne chair upholstered in white brocade.

"Of course Upstairs Bobby isn't his *real* name," Faith is explaining, as though we need to be told that. Perhaps we do. "His real name's Robert Wainwright."

"Hello, Robert," I say. "I'm Elke. And that's Kendy." I nod toward the door, where Kendy has just banged her knee on Faith's gigantic suitcase.

"Hello," he says, in a low and raspy voice, nodding awkwardly first at me, then at Kendy. He turns his hat around and around in his hands until Faith takes it from him and sets it under her chair. "Just call me Bob," he adds.

"Hello, Bob," says Kendy. She gives Faith a look that seems not just puzzled but annoyed. Faith is too excited to notice. Her face is shiny with perspiration. She's wearing a dark blue suit jacket and matching slacks that look too warm for this weather.

"I'll get us some lemonade," Kendy says, turning toward the kitchen.

"No, no," Bob protests. "I'm not staying." He pushes himself forward on his chair. From the way he keeps glancing at his hat I can tell he wishes he had not relinquished it.

"That's okay. It's already made." Kendy goes into the kitchen, leaving the three of us sitting in the living room smiling nervously at one another. I see now that Bob's lush hair is probably a toupee.

"So," I say to Faith, "how did you and Bob meet up again?"

"*Well*," Faith says. She is bursting to tell us, and she glances toward the kitchen as though she must wait for us all to be assembled before she can begin. She has kicked off her loafers, and her toes are clenching and unclenching in the thick carpet.

Kendy comes out with the iced drinks in tall and delicately fluted glasses on a tray and distributes them to us. For one unnerving moment I see her again as that perfect waitress she was thirty-five years ago.

"Faith was starting to tell us how she and Bob met again," I say when Kendy sits down.

Faith smiles, eagerly. "He just came by the house," she says, gesturing at Bob as though perhaps we aren't sure whom she means. "Didn't call first or anything!"

"There was only one Rodney Pratt in the book. I figured it had to be him."

"Lucky I was home!"

Bob nods solemnly. "I'd have just gone on back to Prince Rupert." He starts to take a package of cigarettes from his shirt pocket, hesitates, decides against it.

"He was looking for Rodney," Faith says. "But he was just as glad to talk to me."

"Little Faith," Bob says. "Married to Rodney." He seems both to shake his head and to continue nodding.

"He didn't *have* to drop by, that's the thing," Faith says. "The police didn't know."

Police. I think of Faith's promise to bring us proof of who was on the train platform the day Gladys died, and I feel a chill in my neck. I stare at Bob in sudden apprehension. Faith hasn't brought him along simply because they ran into each other again. This isn't a social call, some clumsy reunion.

"I came to tell Rodney, you see," Bob says. He clears his throat, shuttles his jaw quickly back and forth, back and forth. But he doesn't go on, just glances at Faith, who is gazing raptly at him as though she has no idea what he could say next.

"Tell him *what*?" Kendy finally asks.

"It was me," he says.

"What do you mean, it was you?" Kendy taps a fingernail, click click click, on the chrome end table.

"On the train platform."

The whole building seems to be holding its breath.

"And?" Kendy demands. "Then what? You pushed Gladys off the train platform?"

"*No*, no!" Faith exclaims, reaching a hand into the air between Kendy and Bob, as if to keep them from leaping up and attacking each other. "He was the one who *spoke* to her!"

Bob nods. "It was me." He clears his throat again but doesn't go on.

Click click click, goes Kendy's fingernail on the end table.

"Faith, maybe *you* should tell us what happened," I say.

"Okay," Faith says. She licks her lips, takes a deep breath. "He told me that he recognized Gladys on the platform, and that he went up to her and touched her arm and said something to her, just hello, something like that—"

"And I scared her!" Bob bursts out. "I scared her! I was glad to see her, after all these years, and I went up to her and touched her arm and I didn't mean to scare her but I did, it was all my fault, she jerked away and stumbled back and I reached out to her and ... and there was a moment, I think, when she could have grabbed my hand but she didn't, she didn't recognize me, I was just this guy who'd scared her."

We sit in silence, the three of us, staring. Bob seems to shrink down, the leather of his chair making a soft crumpling sound.

Finally Kendy stands up, and Bob lifts his hands slightly, as if he should cover his head in preparation for a blow. I can smell his sweat, can see it darkening his shirt collar. Even I am nervous about what Kendy will say.

"So it was an accident," Kendy says. "Just an accident."

"Yeah," Faith says. "Just an accident."

"Why didn't you tell the police what happened?" Kendy demands, frowning at Bob.

"I was just ... shocked. I panicked, I guess. I ran away. I went back to the motel and checked out and drove back to Prince Rupert."

"Well, you sure left a mess," Kendy snaps. "Didn't you think about how it would look? People see someone apparently accost Gladys and the next minute she's lying dead on the tracks."

Bob winces at the word "dead."

"The police thought she might have been murdered, for God's

sake." Kendy is relentless. "They interrogated all of us. It wasn't fun."

"I made a mistake," Bob mumbles. The small muscles at the side of his mouth and eyes pull in a way I know can presage tears. I am surprised, for some reason.

And, as perhaps I have over the years been programmed to do when I see such vulnerability, I want to ask questions—what are you feeling; why?—and I have a wish to know more about this man, this stranger. What has his life been like? How did he deal with his son's suicide? Has he married, had other children? But I am unlikely to have my curiosity satisfied. He is not here because he wants to become my client, or my friend.

So I resist my intrusive questions and say, instead, perhaps for Kendy's benefit as much as for his, "But you did come forward now. That's the important thing."

Faith nods, looking uneasily at Kendy. "That's right. He didn't have to, you see. But he thought he owed it to Rodney."

"I owed it to Rodney," Bob says. He has blinked back any tears, though the effort seems to have left his right eye in an odd squint.

"Well," Kendy says, sighing. "Better late than never."

"It can't have been easy," I say. "And to come all this way to tell Kendy and me, too—well, we're very grateful."

Something in my words must have signalled a dismissal, because he quickly drinks down what is left of his lemonade and gets to his feet. Despite his stoop he is almost as tall as Kendy. He is looking so determinedly at his hat that Faith gives in, retrieves it from under her chair, hands it to him.

"I just came down here because ... for Faith. She wanted me to tell you. In person."

"And he'd never been to Victoria," Faith says. "I thought he'd like to see Victoria."

Bob looks down, like someone chastised. "It's true. I never been to Victoria." He starts purposefully for the door, as though Victoria is a boat about to leave without him.

"Oh—" Kendy flicks me an interrogative look which I can

only send back unanswered. "Shall I call you a cab?"

"No, no. I drove."

"Are you sure?" Kendy gives an awkward little laugh. "What am I saying? Of course you're sure. You'd remember driving a car here."

Kendy's attempt at civility only seems to make Bob more uneasy. "A truck," he says cautiously. "I drive a truck." He is at the door now. "Faith." He nods at her.

"Bob." Faith goes to the door. She seems drained now of the energy she came with. "Thanks for coming."

He shifts from foot to foot, making his boots creak. "I'm so sorry," he says.

Faith nods. "At least now we know. We all know."

"I was glad to see her," Bob says. "That's the thing. I was glad to see her."

And he is gone. Kendy and I just stand there watching Faith slowly close the door behind him.

It has all happened so fast. I have the urge to call him back, say, "Wait!" But of course that is foolish. What more can we say to each other? He has done what he came for and is glad to be gone.

When Faith turns we all seem reluctant to look at each other. We keep our eyes low, on the wall, the carpet. Perhaps the others see it, too: Gladys, the hand reaching out to her, her pulling away, startled, frightened, expecting a mugger or purse snatcher, stumbling over her shoebox, Bob standing horrified on the platform watching, watching her fall.

"I think," Faith says at last, then pauses, chewing at her lip, "Mom told me once she thought Gladys was in love with Bob. I know she liked him. And there weren't many people she did like. I think she may have tried to find him after Charlie left her."

"Charlie left *her*?" Kendy says. "I thought she left *him*."

"No. *He* left *her*."

"Ha!" Kendy says.

"Her life was just so, so *sad*," Faith says. "You know? To the last minute. She'd be pushing people away, suspicious, expecting the worst of everybody."

I want for Kendy to say something like, *It will be hard to keep hating someone who died because she was afraid to reach out to her heart's desire.* But she doesn't. She isn't Woolf's Lily Briscoe who at the end suddenly sees what must be done and completes her painting with the final, perfect line. Well, Gladys wasn't Anna Karenina at the train tracks, either, I think, and the comparisons make me smile a little. Death or redemption: there are many other endings.

Faith goes to the window, gazes out at the sea flecked with twilight. After a while Kendy and I join her.

Three middle-aged women, looking out at the water. The sun has almost set, but it catches on the wings of a seagull rising on a thermal. It seems unusually graceful, floating very slowly past us. Like a cake going by, I think. Except that all three of us see it.